The Pit

The Pit

J. L. GRIBBLE

Chapter 1

Forget what you've heard about not sweating the small stuff. The only small stuff in this life is the stuff that happens to someone else; some other guy you either don't know well or at all, and you do not particularly care all that much about. That's the stuff that makes up someone else's life. That's the small stuff, if there truly is any small stuff in this life, the fact of which at this time I am not at all certain. When it's your stuff in your life, it's all big stuff and well worth sweating over, because it is really all you have got. That is to say, all that small stuff in the end adds up to being the big stuff that is ultimately you. I am not suggesting that you become obsessed with the minuscule details of your life like keeping a running tally of the number of hairs lost with each shampooing and comparing that to any new growth you might discover on your scalp. It is simply a matter of prioritizing the events, decisions and dilemmas that make up your life, and then expending your supply of sweat on these situations proportionally in any manner that your version of common sense dictates.

The very notion that our lives can actually experience small stuff is a manifestation of our limited ability as human beings to fully comprehend the absolute meaning of the daily events of our lives. Let's say, for the sake of illustrating my point, that some average guy employed at a meat processing plant has his right arm amputated by the sausage grinder. As a result, he spends the next several years, justifiably so, feeling he has been cheated by life. Having only one arm the strength in the appendage develops considerably by virtue of having to do the work of two. Let us further embellish this situation by agreeing that this poor disabled creation of our collective imaginations is of the opinion that the loss of his arm was the biggest event of his life and the additional work required of his remaining arm was a burden of relative insignificance.

Now put this theoretical, unfortunate individual out in the woods on a camping excursion with his family. Suddenly, as he and his young child are hiking along a mountainside path, the child slips and begins to fall into a treacherous ravine, clinging precariously to an outcropping of shrubbery protruding from the side of a sheer cliff wall. You know the scene, it happens in Bugs Bunny cartoons all the time. This dilemma creates a situation requiring our one armed man to lie upon the ground and reach for his son, pulling the boy to safety. Let us further contribute the strength in his arm, which saves the life of his child, to the seemingly meaningless, traumatic accident, which tore his other arm from its rightful place. Any man that claims to be a good father would gladly hew off his own arm with a dull instrument if he were assured this would insure the survival of one of his children at some point in the future. The man in this scenario, like the rest of us, had a limited ability to interpret the true significance of what appeared to him to have been a cruel travesty of justice thrust upon him by fate. In reality, it was preparation for him to execute the most significant achievement of his life, saving that which he held precious above all else in life; the life of his son.

If I've got you a little confused so far don't feel like the Lone Ranger. I'm leaning that direction myself. It might be more advantageous to tell you the story that was relayed to me that clarified my understanding of the idea I am striving to illustrate.

As was his habit, my brother, for no apparent reason, posed a hypothetical open ended question that had absolutely nothing to do with the current conversation or task at hand. "So tell me," he began, "What do you know about the construction of the Great Pyramids of Egypt?" I gave a run down of pretty much everything I could remember from watching TV and my brother continued his line of inquiry. "So, do you think if a man were to dismantle one of those pyramids and lay the thousands of stone blocks that went into its construction out on the desert floor, would it be possible to pick out the most important one, the one most critical to the integrity of the over all structure?" I was pretty sure that no one I knew would be able to do that, and for that matter I didn't know anyone that I would have guessed would have been able to put a pyramid back together. I conceded that it would be next to impossible to tell which was the most important. My brother continued, "If that be the case, what about when the pyramid is assembled, could that most valuable, absolutely critical to the exclusion of all others, stone be identified?" I ventured a guess or two, corner stones, the one in the center; I was winging it without a clear objective.

After exhausting my attempts at solving this riddle, my brother weighed in with the heart of the matter. "You see, the only stone that can be removed from the pyramid without resulting in a partial or complete collapse is the one on the top. But once the top stone is removed, the pyramid ceases to be a pyramid. Life is like a pyramid, each moment of which adds another block to the structure. The years, months, days, hours, minutes, and seconds that make up our lives are of an incalculable value. Never minimize or dismiss a one. Be thankful and appreciative of each because the elimination of just one would have the overall effect of making you someone other than yourself."

It is from this perspective that I propose there are no small events in life. There are however, many which are incomprehensible to us at the time of their occurrence, and many will remain a mystery throughout this life. The mere fact that you or I have limited, or no understanding of an event in no way detracts from the impact that particular event will have on our lives. It's like your pituitary gland, some people know where it is in the body and what its function is, but most don't. Just because you have limited or no knowledge of this lobe in no way diminishes its impact and value. If you don't believe me just have someone remove yours and see what happens.

A more appropriate orientation I would offer for achieving and maintaining a healthy prospective on your place and role in this life would be to seriously consider the old adage, "Live each moment as if it were your last!" Because somewhere, sometime, in that unforeseen future that beckons all of us, one of those details of life which the current trend in self improvement and actualization would quantify as small stuff not worthy of sweating, will be the last, and quite possibly the most important experience of your entire life.

Let's say, for the sake of continuing this argument, God is a busy guy out there creating universes, exploding old burned out stars, mixing up dark matter, and generally keeping the universe in good order, tidy and running smoothly. It doesn't much matter why He does it, could be just to give folks here on earth something to wonder about while starring into the evening heavens, provided of course that you find yourself in an existence graced with the leisure time to indulge in such a past time. Let's also assume that some sort of existence awaits us after this life here on earth ends, and God has set it up in such a way that we spend eternity reenacting the last moment of our earthly lives in the ether world awaiting us. It could happen. If you take a close look at a lot of the things that go on in this life everyday and you believe in God, you will have to admit the guy must be a practical joker at heart.

How would you like to burst a blood vessel in your brain and expire screaming because someone attending to your frail needs in the twilight years had the audacity to warm your oatmeal before serving it to you? I read a story once about someone like that. A rich, miserly, infirm, old woman she was, millions in the bank. Refused to part with a few farthings to have a hot meal each morning. Had her daughter cook a big pot of oatmeal on Sunday and she would eat that humble gruel cold the rest of the week. The old woman blew a gasket and keeled over dead, bellowing at her daughter for re-heating it. Didn't want to waste money on electricity to warm the damn stuff back up.

Or, worse yet, how would you like to bite it telling yourself the situation you were experiencing is nothing more than, "small stuff not worth sweating"? It could happen. I read a book one time and this guy was talking about how people these days complain about being bored. His advise was to rephrase the assessment as, "I am boring," and from that angle determine what can be done to improve the situation. I like that. My advise (if I were the type to give it) for the don't sweat the small stuff crowd is the next time it seems like small stuff ask yourself, "Am I small stuff?" Then take a closer look at all those so-called small events. Each one is a viable seed of human experience, planted in your soul awaiting just the right conditions under which to germinate and reveal to you the secrets stored within.

Personally, I wouldn't care to enter those Pearly Gates and have as my last memory of my earthly existence being that I didn't sweat it. Back when I was a younger man and spent a considerable amount of time lifting weights and admiring myself in the mirror, if someone asked my advice about lifting weights I would let them in on my philosophy. Not like giving advice or anything like that was something I would ever consider doing. But, the polite thing to do if someone asks is to give an honest answer to the best of your ability. Advice. I don't give the stuff and I damn sure don't have much of an appetite for it either. Like turnips and okra. They both turn my gizzard and I wouldn't dream of ramming either one down the throat of my worst enemy, that is if I had any, enemies that is, not turnips. I looked at weight lifting like sex; if you don't work up a good sweat and feel a little sore the next day, chances are you didn't get it right or get much out of it. You could make a case for looking at life in the same way.

Speaking of those Pearly Gates, did I explain to you my theory on how we get to heaven? Near as I can figure God knows and sees all. No secrets from the Big Guy, right? Well then, He must know the reason I do a lot of those things that I do and have done, because there have been countless times when I haven't a clue about what my motivation was. Remember when you were a kid and did something stupid and a grown up would demand to know why you did it and all you could say was, "I don't know?" I wasn't lying back then, and I'm not lying now! That being the case, He knows that everything I have ever done has been what I thought, with my limited ability, to do so at the time was the best thing I could manage to do at that particular point in my life in that situation. It may not have been the right thing, but it was the best I could come up with given the demands of the circumstances and the finite personal resources I had to work with. Five minutes later it may look to me to be the stupidest move I had ever made, but at the time it was the right thing for me to do. In his twisted mind, Hitler must have thought he was doing the right thing too, I would guess. No one could make those kinds of decisions and put that much effort into an agenda if they weren't 110% convinced they were on the righteous path, God on there side and all that.

Don't get me wrong here. I'm all for pitching the majority of mankind into the fiery bowels of the earth, dig a big hole down to the Devil's hotel and march them buck-ass naked, smothered in molasses off a plank into those eternal, torturous flames. Given a close enough inspection, everyone I've ever known had enough sinful deeds and thoughts in the closet to make a strong case for making them fodder for the Damnation Cremation. But, before the devil gets his pitchfork into them and the free fall into the bellows of Hell begins why not have someone read the verdict, preferably over a worldwide public address system equipped with language conversion software, to the rest of us as a warning about the kinda stuff that pisses God off. You can't have a fair ballgame if some players don't know the rules until the game is half over, or if some don't hear that there are any rules until they're dead. If you take a gander at things from a historical, global perspective we are all pretty much guilty of the same universal failing; we're all human.

If a fella was to take an objective look at all the religions of the world, he could make a pretty strong case for having divine authorization, or condemnation, for just about anything he thought people ought, or ought not, to be authorized by God to do.

Most religions preach that you should not kill anyone unless some politician, general, or religious figurehead says it's all right. Read the Old Testament. Every time you turn around God was firing the Jews up and turning them loose on someone to smite them off the face of the earth. Would have been a tidier operation to send in some carnivorous beasts of the wild, at least they would have cleaned up the carnage and reduced the possibility of the spread of pestilence in the aftermath.

And most religions really frown on you killing yourself. As of late however, there have been significant modifications to these guidelines, over and above the gradual ones that ebb and flow with the cultural dynasties that have sought to rule the known world, in God's name of course. If you look at the situation in the Middle East and the conflict between the Jews and Arabs you can see an example of subjective interpretation of religious doctrine to suit the political agenda of the day. There are Palestinian terrorist groups that advocate the utilization of suicide bombers. In the process of recruiting potential bombers, the leaders of these organizations tell these mostly disillusioned, young, impressionable, idealistic boys that a martyr feels no pain when giving his life facilitating the deaths of the enemy Jews. They are also assured by this twisted interpretation of the sacred Koran that a vivacious, compliant virgin awaits their arrival in the next life. Nice work, if you can get it. Be a shame if you got there and found out that if you accidentally blew your penis off in the process here on earth it would not spontaneously regenerate in the hereafter. The exact number escapes me at the moment, but these bombers are also assured that upon detonation they are immediately awarded something like fifty-seven passes to the afterlife for immediate family members. I can only assume there must be an express line at the Pearly Gates just like at the airport for first class passengers. Wait! It gets better! And I'm not even making anything up yet. The argument has been further refined to draw a distinction between what sorts of Jews can be blown up and still secure a seat in Heaven in the lap of the virgin awaiting your arrival. Those dispatched by exploding devices must be True 'Enemies of Islam'; thus establishing a difference between the civilian and military populations, but in Israel everyone is in the reserve, so I guess it doesn't make much difference. Mind you, I am using Islam as a convenient example. History abounds with religious absurdities of this nature across the spectrum of denominations.

In general, the way I read the rules as they stand right now, a guy gets a one-way ticket to the eternal barbecue as the main course for the crime of being stupid. If you're stupid and make a bunch of bad choices in life, pay for it in Hell. I don't remember being presented with that choice anywhere in school, "Do you want to be smart or stupid?" I hate to be the one to say it, but if I end up being worthy of a ticket to the good place after this life, who the hell isn't? The same goes for the one way trip in the opposite direction. I'm reserving the right to check out the residents of both afterlife resorts before signing any long-term lease.

Chapter 2

Everything in your life is worth sweating over. I don't, and neither should you, give a damn what anyone else thinks about it. The important question is how much of your sweat is the present challenge worth to you? The art of living this life is in the knowing of the difference between the proper amount of sweat and the point at which one is over doing it. W.C. Fields, one of the world's great philosophers, once said, "If at first you don't succeed, try again. If that doesn't work quit! There's no point in being a damn fool about it!" A bit radical and absolutely ahead of his time, there is a deep vein of truth in his advice. A sagely man who earned the right to give the rest of us a few pointers on the finer nuances of living a good and just life. His message was there's a difference between being tenacious and stubbornly bull headed. Tenacity implies creativity and some semblance of progress, while bull headedness is indicative of mindless, repetitive utilization of inept, impotent interventions.

Come to think of it, I can't think of anything I have ever acquired or achieved in this life which I considered to be of any merit or value that did not entail a copious contribution of perspiration. Not that I have acquired much of material worth or achieved anything worthy of documentation in the annals of history, although there are a few episodes that might well have made the headlines of the National Enquirer. I'm just an average guy doing regular guy stuff every day: go to work, take out the trash, try and not drink or smoke to extremes, or swear the way I did in high school. By all assessments I'm a regular, well-rounded, family man.

But anyway, by perspiration I mean something more than, and in addition to, the organic byproduct of mere physical exertion. The sweat I am referring to is the catalyst of all human alchemy, achievement, and creativity. It is that mystic potion which allows the indomitable, human spirit to rise above the limitations imposed upon it by the general rules and regulations governing this realm in which we all live. And in too many unfortunate situations the even more restrictive, oppressive norms and stifling expectations imposed by the strata of society in which we are born into or out of. Indeed, this is the only polis which is capable of breaching the bastion of self imposed defeat; that fortress of faithless self doubt which disassociates us from our dreams and forces us to disavow the lofty aspirations residing deep within our hearts. This mythical sweat is that inner voice calling and encouraging you to persevere when all those about you are celebrating your imminent demise and failure. Without this sweat, dreams wither and die.

If you have ever read John Steinbeck's book *The Red Pony*, you'll recall one of the main characters Grandpa, the old Indian fighter who spent all his time endlessly retelling tales of what he called the "Westering." This Westering encompassed all facets of the western migration of a wagon train of settlers Grandpa had led across the plains and over the mountains, battling everything man and nature could muster to encumber their exodus. The westering was not something you could explain, it was something that you were, a shared dream, something a man shared with the ground beneath his feet, the air in his lungs, and the heavens above. When they reached the Pacific Ocean, their ultimate goal, Grandpa, a young man then, assumed that having accomplished such a great deed would yield dividends of self-satisfaction for the duration of his life. What he found was that once the journey was over, in many respects, so was his life. Without anything to sweat over, he resigned himself to reliving those glorious events on the wagon train heading west. Initially, he mistakenly assumed that the destination was more important than the journey. In the end, he understood that life was about doing battle with obstacles, overcoming hardships, crossing mountains, and conquering raging rivers. Without a challenge to overcome, without anything in life to sweat over, he found that in virtually all facets the living part of his life was over as well. All he had left to live for was reminiscing about the glory of his one great excursion when he was the westering and the westering was in him.

As a school counselor talking to students about their futures I always look for that smoldering ember of passion; something in the soul that is unique to the young person before me, that special whisper beckoning, that something they have a love and calling for. The westering. I try to nurture that glow into a flame that will warm the soul of that student and provide a beacon into the future. In far too many cases at best that glow will have been neglected and left untended over the years. And, more often than not, pissed upon by some well meaning adult trying to shape a young persons life into the one they failed to live when they were young. If you consider this to be a baseless claim, plan to attend a few kids' athletic exhibitions at your local school or park. Listen closely to the remarks made by so called grownups and coaches in the presence of young children. Look at the faces of longing for their progeny to hit the homeruns they were never able to, passing on the obscene, American obsession with sticks, clubs, balls, and nets.

Somehow we, as a nation, have been duped into the belief that having our children thoroughly immersed in competitive sports will prepare them for successful futures and inoculate them from the perils to be negotiated while growing up. Time and again I talk with kids that are convinced if they do well in sports the doors of college and the coffers of the NBA & NFL will swing open and deposit their cash of wealth and opportunity at the feet of their signature Nikes. Now kids don't come up with those kinds of fairy tales on their own. Only a grownup could cook up such a preposterous fabrication, and only corporate America combined with media exploitation could figure out how to market that fantasy and capitalize on it, turning athletes like Michael Jordan into a vehicle by which millions of dollars of consumer trinkets are sold.

Or better yet, take a drive in the heartland of rural America and take notice of the accomplishments notarized with monuments and memorabilia outside and inside of schools. With our voices we proclaim the sanctity and value of an education, with our actions we extol the virtues of the athlete. Think back and try to remember the last time you ever saw a school take time out of the instructional day to conduct a pep rally to fire up a bunch of seniors preparing to take the SAT. Silly, right? Maybe one school in the nation, one time during the year, if that. Odds are that on any given day of the school year you could find a school in your state that was sacrificing instructional time in the name of athletics. If you're bored reading this, grab a phone book and start calling schools to see when the next such event is scheduled.

I was working with a kid who had world class potential as a runner; several prestigious colleges were courting him. The kid got a swollen head, compliments of well meaning adults, and figured he didn't need an education. I talked to the track coach at one of the schools he was considering and the coach advised him to skip track season his senior year and hit the books instead. The kid and his parents ignored the advice and he played all year. At the end of his senior year of high school all of his offers for college scholarships had dried up. I ran into this kid several years later in a small town outside of Spokane. It was ten in the morning at a McDonalds on a weekday. The kid was sloppy, blurry-eyed drunk.

Granted there are those that turn athletic abilities into careers, you see it on TV all the time, right? Just the other day I saw Godzilla get killed by the Tokyo Smog Monster on TV too, but I'll be damned if he didn't come back and save Japan from those things that looked like flying, microwaved, peanut butter and jelly sandwiches just a week later. My point is that adults should help the children in their charge to discover what it is in this life they truly love. Adults should not coerce the children who look to them for guidance into performing vicariously in rituals construed to have redemptive powers for the personal failings and feelings of inadequacy on the part of the adults. I'm convinced that deep in the hearts of many adults there dwells Henry David Thoreau's "Life of Quiet Desperation." Somewhere along the road to the future they lost sight and grasp of the essence of their individuality. Out of this desperation, without premeditative malice, come the tentacles of manipulation driven by a subconscious desire for their children to accomplish that which they did not. But it doesn't work that way. The only way a river regains its rightful path to the sea is when men cease to dictate how it should flow.

My brother Bill, that's who this book is about, had a saying that epitomizes the point I am striving to flesh out. He told me once, "A man spends the major portion of his life discovering who he truly is. The rest of life is a test to see how successful you are at living your life in harmony with what you have discovered about yourself. Any man that pretends to be something he is not is essentially a nonentity, because when a man turns his back on his true nature and aspires to be that which he is not, he is neither himself nor that which he pretends to be." He went on to stress that there was no travesty in the pretending so long as you are aware of the fact you are putting on a performance tailored to a particular setting. He warned me however, the majority of men play the game too often, too long, and with much too much seriousness eventually arrive at a point in life where they believe the charade themselves. According to Bill, the real danger is that a man can not be sure what his individual threshold of endurance is; at what precise point he will no longer be pretending, that point at which he transmuted into that which he pretended to be. Like becoming an addict. How many drinks or how long does it take to become an alcoholic? It's different for each of us. The best advice is to partake sparingly and conservatively.

This was a fairly abstract point to be making to a kid my age when he talked to me about it. But that was my brother for you. He never made distinctions about when the appropriate age was to discuss such matters. When you could engage him in intelligent conversation, as far as he was concerned, you were old enough. At the time I thought he was stressing the virtues of not being a phony. As the lesson matured along the way of life with me, I began to realize that it was more than that. He was illustrating how easy it is for a man to loose sight of who he is, to become so engrossed in social contortions that it becomes increasingly more difficult and eventually impossible to return to a normal state. Be your own man was the way he put it.

I like to tell kids who are obsessing about sports the Brian Bosworth story. This guy signs a multi-million dollar contract with the Seattle Seahawks with a clause that he gets cashed out if he gets hurt. A shrewd businessman, complements of the business education he actually got his own homework for while attending college, the Boz knew how uncertain a career in professional athletics was, especially for a guy using steroids; the stuff drives up the synovial fluid that lubricates the joints and can cause major malfunctions. He entered the world of professional sports knowing the fact from fiction. He knew that the majority of people that make it don't stay for long and most of them end up busted up, broke and unemployable because all they did in school was fondle their balls. The Boz's shoulders blew out during his first season, and he blew out of Seattle with a duffel bag full of cash. When his athletic career came to an end, his life didn't. He knew he was performing as a football player. He knew there was more to life than his abilities on the gridiron. Mohammad Ali, arguably the greatest boxer of all times, indicated during an interview that he would never advise a young person to enter boxing as a career. He said it should only be utilized as a temporary means to get someplace better in life.

For me, that ember of passion about what to do with life was fanned into a firestorm by a bellowing, bovine of a behemoth guidance counselor I had in high school. She would have dressed out at over two hundred pounds easily. I never looked down upon her because of her obesity, but I think she may have misinterpreted a situation that inadvertently led her to think I did. Or, it could have been that she had it in for me because I was skinny. I never did figure it out and she wasn't the type to sit down and talk about her problems, at least not to me.

I had been summoned to the counseling center. I was walking leisurely down one end of the long hallway and she was at the other. As she approached me, I took note of how one of her immense thighs was continuously in contact with the wall, alternating with a slow methodical stride, which carried her gargantuan frame towards me. I fought off the panic which was demanding that I turn and take immediate flight, but I'm sure it must have been written all over my face. Have you ever seen one of those movies when someone is trapped in a tunnel with a speeding train heading for them, no room on either side to escape from the imminent obliteration bearing down? That's how I felt! But, it was like watching the locomotive barreling down on me in slow motion. I decided to make a sprint for the office door of my destination, estimating I could swing the door open and take sanctuary before the hatch was sealed by the approaching tsunami of human flesh. My timing was good, but my neglect of details was once again my downfall. I bolted down the hall, running headlong towards the approaching storm. A twinge of self-doubt struck, "What if she suddenly picked up speed and we collided? Would I ricochet off into oblivion or be absorbed into this seething sea of cellulite, never to be heard from again?" As I reached my foxhole and scrambled to safety, I neglected to hold the doorknob securely in my sweating palm. The door flew open with considerable force and collided with the poor woman who, like a battle ship, needed a lot of room and time to change course. I remember how surprised I was that the only noise I heard when the door crashed into her was a loud thump, like the sound you hear when the side of an above ground swimming pool is whacked, or when a ripe melon is thumped. The door rebounded, slamming shut, only to be flung open shortly thereafter, nearly torn from the hinges by the enraged guidance counselor. She cornered me in that little office screaming with such volume and intensity that I swore the curtains were caught in the wind eddy her bellowing generated. Fearing for my personal safety, I remarked something to the effect that she was lucky nature had endowed her with such unique, physical attributes, making it next to impossible for a door flung open with any human generated force to hit her in the head, hoping this might help in some small way to defuse the situation. It was hard to figure out just what she was trying to say as she screamed in my face. One thing was for certain, the veins on her temples were bulging, looking just life those skinny balloons street clowns blow up and twist into poodles that look more like giraffes and other indistinguishable, animal shapes. And, it was pretty clear that she must have eaten a pound of chocolate and a few cloves of garlic for lunch. It didn't seem to make any difference what I said, she was like one of those forest fires that reaches a point where it creates its own wind, sucking in the surrounding fuel and oxygen to feed an exponentially growing firestorm. Foam was forming at the corners of her mouth, frothing up like the head on a warm beer. This scud would be sucked back in when she took a breath, only to reappear in ever increasing volumes when the bawling recommenced. There was a slice of sunlight separating her and I. It indicated that this frothing brine was being atomized by her flagellating lips, contaminating the air around me. I was attempting to synchronize my breathing so as to minimize inhalation of this frontal, germ warfare assault. This controlled breathing was also assisting in my Herculean effort not to say anything more that would further aggravate this human geyser of wrath. I could picture the headlines, "High School Counselor Drops Dead of Heart Attack, Inadvertently Crushing Troubled Youth!" Just then, I noticed that several students had congregated at the door, listening to the torrent of verbal abuse to which I was being subjected. Embolden by an audience to play to, I changed my mind about provoking her. I let her spew forth yet another barrage of demeaning remarks, then I said, "Thanks for all your help, I feel so much better now. And just think, only a few minutes ago I was gonna kill myself." Pointing to the kids at the door I remarked on my way out, "Here are some more poor, confused souls whom I'm sure, could greatly benefit from your screaming and insults."

I tried to avoid her the rest of my time in high school, but was forced to listen to her address my senior class of three hundred students just before graduation. We were seated in the auditorium and she was on stage with a microphone, talking about what the valedictorian would be doing. I didn't know what the hell one was, so I had to ask. Her reply was, and I quote from thirty years ago, "I always knew you were an idiot, but you proved it to all of us here today with that stupid question!" That was my invitation to liven things up. I discovered rather late in my high school experience that the only time I really enjoyed the education I was being subjected to was when I was engaged in conversation or debate, preferably combative but always respectful, with an authority figure. During the first ten years of my schooling they had convinced me that this counselor was correct, I was stupid. When I discovered that my teachers were all practically as dimwitted as I, some even more so, well let's just say, "Payback is a bitch." I jumped to my feet proclaiming, "Yes, I freely admit I am an idiot, but I'm your idiot! Your school educated me!" Then, addressing the crowd, I asked, "OK! How many other idiots are there out there? Come on, don't by shy! Stand up and be counted!

Who else doesn't know what a valedictorian is?" The counselor on stage was trying to restore order to no avail. I had the moral high ground and a full head of steam, and when the situation called for it I could turn up the volume and compete with any public address system. As I encouraged students to raise their hands, to my delight, well over half of the kids in the auditorium held hands high indicating they to had no clue as to what a valedictorian was. I turned to the stage and smiled, relinquishing my control of the floor back to the counselor. That poor lady held the crumpled text of her address in her hand and wore a countenance of defeat. My last words to here were, "See, we're all idiots!" From that day forth, the muse within me was fired up and convinced that I had a calling to become an educator and make school a better place for children. Thirty years later I'm still working at it.

She gave me the will, commitment and determination to acquire a formal post secondary education. All I wanted to do with my life after high school was get a college degree and come back to my old school and flaunt it. But many times determination is not enough. Sometimes you need to add a little self-confidence and inspiration.

My inspiration came from an experience, which I hope all students have early and often in school, and hopefully, do not end up spending twelve years in public education before it happens, like I did. I had a teacher who treated me with respect and compassion and actually indicated to me in front of the entire class that I was intelligent, a first for me.

Mr. C brought an amusing philosophy to the profession of teaching that might well be the salvation of our educational system; he taught out of a loving dedication to the vocation and, more importantly, a loving dedication to children. As a reward his peers scorned him for his unorthodox techniques and students rumored that he was a homosexual pedophile. If you are a high school teacher and not elderly or completely obsessed with sports and you're too nice to kids you, by default, must have some perverse, ulterior motive for choosing education as a profession.

His occupation was that of a businessman, and he had no monetary need for the pittance of a salary offered up to a professional educator.

He drove a brand new Cadillac and Corvette each year. I became friends with this man because he was the first educator I have encountered that didn't give me the impression that I was little more than an inconvenience to them. I felt our friendship allowed me to question his materialistic orientation and how it conflicted with the lofty platitudes he espoused. I asked him one time, point blank, if he ever felt a twinge of guilt about having amassed a considerable fortune and indulging in such extravagant, creature comforts. He replied, without any indication that he was defending his life style, "Well, I do have a lot of money, and I work hard for it. I have an accountant that keeps track of what I earn and what I spend. I have given him the authority to donate a dollar to charity for every dollar I spend on myself. I drew up a list of what I consider worthy charities that my accountant can choose from. So if I spend a thousand dollars when I go to Vegas next month, the trip actually costs me two. So, even if I loose gambling I come home feeling like a winner, because I know I just donated a thousand to a worthy cause." I came away from the conversation convinced that this guy was indeed a winner.

It was the first day back at school of my senior year and I had Mr. C for a psychology class. My brother Scott, two years my elder, had borrowed the new pair of shoes I had planned to wear to school, hitchhiked to the ocean, got drunk, and failed to return with my shoes. Always the opportunist, I choose to attend school shoeless, thus making a philosophical statement. What I was really doing was being a premeditative pain in the ass. I knew that someone would call me on it. That would be my cue to debate my virtuous dedication to obtaining an education even if getting to school to do so meant walking bare foot through a swamp filled with broken glass, razor blades, and man hating, snapping turtles. I would thus place school authorities in the position of defending and defining the true goal of public education. Were they serious about educating all students as they propertied, or were they more interested in maintaining standards of socially acceptable attire, like wearing shoes?

My bare feet caught Mr. C's eyes and he questioned why it was I had no shoes on? As this was our first encounter, I expected an accusatory inquisition, not the curious inquiry he initiated. I gave him my story about being a poor soul willing to walk naked across the Sahara Desert to attend school. Rather than questioning my sincerity, he asked, "Do you have a stereo at home?" I indicated that not only did I, I further elaborated about the technical and sound quality of my system. His next question dealt with the expansiveness of my audio library. Here again, I went on detailing a considerable collection of tapes and vinyl. Then he got to his point, "If you can afford a fancy stereo and all those tapes and records, how is it you can't afford another pair of shoes?" I had anticipated his line of inquiry and had played along solely for an opportunity to relate the following tale to the audience in the classroom, "All the records and tapes I got from those mail order clubs. You see, being a minor and entering into such a contractual agreement is not legally binding, so I get the stuff on the introductory offer, twelve titles for about two bucks, then never buy any more at the rip off regular club price. Then you wait a couple of months, join the club again using your dog's name, and get another twelve records. Now the stereo was a different matter. I got a mail order catalog for electronic stuff. They had a great stereo in it, but you had to fill out an application with credit information before they would ship anything. I filled it out saying I was a doctor and made a lot of money, just to see what would happen. About a month later I just happened to be home during the middle of the week, suspended from school for something. The delivery guy pulls up in the driveway saying he has something to deliver to a Dr. Rabble. I tell the guy the doctor is out for the day. He tried to get me to sign for the stuff but I refused. He decides, 'What the hell!' and unloads a couple of hundred pounds of top-notch stereo gear. When they send the bills in the mail I throw'em in the trash."

Mr. C thought for a moment and said, "It's pretty clear from this conversation that you're smarter than I am, so let's drop the subject and get on with things." It was the beginning of a beautiful friendship and the first time that any educator gave any indication, in public or private, that they could discern any trace of intelligence in my being. Up to that point it had been twelve years of overt and covert messages from public education that I was too slow, stupid, or lazy to amount to anything.

This, which incidentally, brings to mind the year I was placed in special education in grade school. The principal, whom we had affectionately nick named "gorilla" in recognition of copious outcroppings of wiry pubic hair sprouting from every exposed inch of his epidermis, entered our classroom to make an announcement. He indicated that I, along with two other students, would be transferred to "Mr. Dicknam's class." We had a name for his class to. It was for the "retards." I never knew I was one until that very moment. I spent a year in the retard class and had one hell of a good time. Had I known early on that being mentally deficient could generate educational placements of this nature I would have manifested my malfeasance much sooner. But alas, for all his faults and overwhelming body odor, Mr. Dickman worked his magic on me in the short span of a year and I was back in the mainstream of public education.

I was skipping Mr. C's class one-day that it had snowed, a rare event in the geographical location in which I resided. The snow seductively whispered to me and I helplessly heeded the call. I was outside his classroom engaged in a snowball battle in full view of the more conformist members of the class from which I was inexcusably absent. The whole scene was choreographed for the benefit of those poor, compliant captives sitting in those uncomfortable, stiff-backed chairs. I let fly with an erratic projectile, it veered off course and shattered the window behind Mr. C, showering him with shards of glass and snow. I took off running, assuming that with thirty some witness to inform on me I was now a marked man for whom retribution for my transgressions of school protocol would descend the moment I submitted to formal attendance. I figured that if I was screwed I might as well enjoy the rest of the day and come back tomorrow and face the music. And just why was it that I kept coming back? If school was the abhorrition to me that I asserted it was, why not leave never to return? Be done with it. But alias, a young man is a captive to his heart and many a fair damsel showered me with favors for which I will be eternally indebted. Had it not been for their extraordinary kindness I would surely have long ago burned out like a comet passing too close to the sun.

When I returned to Mr. C's class the next day, I was expecting the general consequences for my behavior: suspension from school, paying for the window, a pummeling with a dead cat, something of that nature. The students informed me that Mr. C had reported he had not seen the perpetrator of the vandalism, which was technically correct. The entire class had seen me do it, and friends assured me that Mr. C was well aware that I had been seen outside the window frolicking in the snow. The circumstantial evidence would seem indicative of my guilt in the crime. He had made it clear to the class at the time that he had no interest in playing detective and conducting interrogations of students in the class to determine the identity of the perpetrator. I didn't bring the subject up again, but I did feel a debt of gratitude to this teacher and acted a bit more humbly and respectfully toward my classmates.

Had I encountered the punishment I anticipated, it would have been just another incident added to a long list with no detectable impact on my long-term behavior. While the response by my teacher and classmates may have not been entirely honest, their collective decision had more change force on me than any punishment the vice-principal could legally have merited out to, for, or on me.

As the course of that school year played out Mr. C systematically put me in charge of leading discussions during his psychology class. At first I thought it was a scam on my part. I could bullshit with a class full of my peers about any topic I was interested in for an hour and not have to listen to some windbag adult, or have to pretend I was doing schoolwork. As the situation began to evolve, Mr. C began to funnel books in my direction, indicating he was too busy to read them and wanted me to take a look and let him know what I thought about them. The sneaky bastard tricked me into reading more books in his one class than I had read in my entire, high school career. As I am now sure was his plan, the material in these books began to creep into the classroom discussions. I also noticed that for the first time in my life I had begun to extrude a bit of perspiration in an educational endeavor, preparing and presenting the Bohemian lessons for which I had somehow become responsible. It was demanding and a bit intimidating, but most of all it was exhilarating. I can still see Mr. C sitting at his desk reading a book while I was running his damn class, our psychology textbooks stacked neatly in a pile behind his desk. He had handed them out to us the first day of class just long enough for us to put our names in the front, and then they were collected and returned to their respective place in his classroom. I would shoot him a nervous glance from time to time, looking to see if I were quoting accurately from the authors he had steered me to, or if I had drifted into a restricted topic of discussion. It's been awhile, but as I reminisce, I can visualize the look on his face. He wasn't reading at all! He was listening more intently than I was to myself. The smile on his face was one of satisfaction, satisfaction with the expertise with which he had facilitated a self contained, educational environment in his classroom. Everyone entered the class in an orderly, timely fashion, sat down in our circle, and waited to see what topic of discussion I was going to present to the group. All students were actively involved in the discussions, and we monitored ourselves ensuring that everyone abided by a few basic tenants of respectful conversation. Not to brag or anything like that, but I was a consummate mystero of the spoken word during that phase of my life. I played the crowd like a piano tuned to high "C." I could bring them to the precipice of disclosing the most catastrophic intimate details of their collective unconsciousness, and then rescue them from the brink of self destruction with the sincere reassurance that we all shared the same demons and saints in our souls. That oratorical spring dried up some time ago and may have recently erupted in another form of expression. You can be the judge of that.

For years I took credit for having made that psychology class a success, but in the process of putting this down on paper I realize that it was Mr. C who deserves the credit. Most teachers would sacrifice their first born to have a class of seniors that came to class everyday, each one contributing on a daily basis to the activity taking place. It's the only time I have seen it happen in all the educational settings I have witnessed. On average Mr. C spoke less than one hundred words to us at the beginning of the class. The rest of the time we students were locked in moral and philosophical battles over discussing and defining the human condition. Any student in the class could have opted out of the discussions, sat at a desk outside the circle and engaged in more traditional schoolwork. No one ever did though. There was some kind of glue there that held us together as a group. I could sense that even when the topic was uncomfortable for some of the class members they felt a moral obligation to maintain a presence in the circle.

I have since become an educator and must admit that I have never been able to emulate Mr. C's magic in my own classrooms, nor have I seen the spirit of that experience replicated in a single one of the hundred something college courses I have taken. I have, as a result, come to believe that there isn't any formula one can uniformly apply to instruction and produce successful results. Teachers must authentically bring whom they are to the classroom setting and from this foundation incorporate components of successful instruction, compatible with and complementary to, the individual traits making them who they are. If you think this sounds easy, spend some time in your local school volunteering, but not just for a day. Stick it out until the novelty wears off for you and the kids. You will soon realize that what a good teacher brings to school is a well stocked toolbox and their own personal magic, with a boundless supply of love and respect for children. Without these key ingredients, the show never really gets on the road.

If you added up all the classes I have taken in college, I would have sufficient frequent flyer miles to hitch a ride on the next space shuttle mission. The educational experiences that I sweated over, like the preparations for leading Mr. C's class, are the only ones that made an appreciable, lasting impact. Those learning experiences have been scarce in the life I have lived so far and even more rare in the formal education, which I have ingested at this juncture.

I would like to be a teacher like Mr. C someday, but the verdict is still out on that one and I can honestly say the chances are slim and decreasing as time rolls on. I think his magic was that he let it happen; he didn't try to control it or make it happen. He was like a good riverboat pilot, he didn't talk all that much, never ran the class aground, and never considered having his passengers pack the boat overland.

Mr. C. gave me inspiration, he showed how powerful of a tool an education was by the way he fostered authentic learning in his classroom. He gave me inspiration and confidence that I could achieve that coveted college degree. But there was still something missing.

Chapter 3

$\mathcal{J}$ was lucky enough in my youth to have my brother Bill, whom this story is really about, to counterbalance my overall negative public school experience, as well as many other negative influences in my youth. Bill was a rabid advocate of education, convinced that it was an invincible shield of protection from being exploited by the capitalist system. He was the prime mover in my eventual acquisition of a formal education, with its accompanying credentials of certification verifying that I had done, and was capable of doing, more than clinging to the operational end of a goon spoon. He accomplished this by stressing two major points. The first point was that an education is a worthwhile and valuable commodity in this life. The second, and most important to me, was that as a person I was a worthwhile and valuable commodity in this life, capable and worthy of a formal education. Without the latter the former point is unachievable. What my brother gave me was the heart, self esteem if you like, to see myself as valuable enough to be worthy of a college education.

He was also an advocate of intelligent tenacity in the pursuit of ones goals in life, believing that if you wanted something bad enough you would expend the amount of sweat required for the acquisition. At the time, I thought it was all about sweating to get something or someplace. I came to understand later in life, after having pumped out enough sweat to raise the level of the Dead Sea by a foot or two, that the process of sweating itself was valuable and, arguably, the most valuable of all life experiences. Especially valuable when you are sharing the experience with someone you love and respect. Kind of like lifting weights at the age of forty-five in comparison to when I was twenty-five; the experience is the same but the results are radically different. Back then I was getting bigger and stronger each day, now days I'm trying to keep things from freezing up or falling apart. During my early years of lifting I thought it was all about hitting goals, lifting more weight, getting bigger. With age has come a trace of wisdom and I now see goals as climaxes in this thing we call life. When the average fellow becomes sexually active, the climax is construed to be everything, the only thing. With some time and experience, a thoughtful individual begins to realize that the process towards that ultimate goal can be much more exhilarating that the point of arrival. The example can be generalized to the entire spectrum of life experiences. When you quit sweating during sex or lifting weights, I'm afraid you are just going through the motions.

Bill told me a story once about a visit he had with the principal of the school his son Steve attended. Bill indicated that his son struggled with school in general and math in particular, and requested that he be allowed to change his math class from Algebra to a more general course.

The principal responded by saying, "Steven is quite capable of passing the class, he does have the potential of being a good math student."

To this Bill inquired, "You look like you're in pretty good shape, how fast can you run a mile, four minutes?"

The principal laughed and said, "No, I don't think I'm that fast."

"Well, with the proper training, time and motivation, do you think you are capable of running a four minute mile?"

Detecting the direction of the conversation the principal tried unsuccessfully to refocus the topic of conversation, "This meeting is about . . ."

Bill interrupted, "You brought up the subject of potential. I'm asking you what your potential is on the track."

"I really don't see what this has to do with Steven's math problems."

"It has everything to do with them. He has the potential to pass the class, just like you have the potential to run a four-minute mile. But my guess is that neither of you will ever put the time and effort into successfully achieving those individual goals. I want my son in a math class that will provide him with the basic, computational skills he will need to manage his financial affairs and those required by a typical employer."

The conversation was over at that point and Steve was transferred into consumer math. Bill knew that Steve's primary motivation was to complete high school and he didn't have the inspiration to apply himself with the intensity that would be required to master Algebra.

Einstein said something to the effect that invention is 5% inspiration and 95% perspiration. The Greatest, Muhammad Ali, pitched in with the remarkable conviction that every fight he ever won he accomplished his victory in the gym, training with such focus and determination that when it came time to step in the ring and face his opponent all he was doing was putting the finishing touches on a task that, as far as he was concerned, was already completed. According to the Greatest, the man was knocked out long before the first bell rang or the first punch was landed. That's why Ali was uncannily accurate in his predictions about when he would knock an opponent out.

These two men understood that the perspiration of which I speak is a coveted magic. A magic, if applied in the proper quantities with the appropriate conjuring and evocations to one of the boundless, ovulating opportunities which living presents, can achieve what the alchemists of old were unable to do. This magic turns the lead of mere existence into the gold of an extraordinary, self-realized, fulfilling life; a life lived in a way that means something to you, something more than mere existence and survival. The lead in this life is constituted of all the ignored, minimized, unrealized dreams and aspirations laying dormant or discarded, awaiting to be nurtured, coaxed, or if need be, forced into existence by a human spirit with the will to forge them in the fires of faith into an amalgamation of reality. The lead in this life is all those things you didn't sweat. The gold of which I speak is a bounty, which could not be contained by all the bank accounts in Switzerland. It matters not what moniker you desire to attach to that place which resides within you that makes you an individual, distinct and separate from all that have passed this way, all that dwell in this day, and all that shall come after your passing. The vault residing within the human heart, spirit, soul, or whatever you choose to call it, can only house such wealth. The only gold worth coveting in this life is that which will glitter in the gallery of your reminiscing recollections when you see and feel the last breath of life escape from your lips, dissipating into the enigmatic void with your fleeing, liberated spirit. This treasure is truly the only priceless one. You are the only one that can secure your individual treasure, and you are ironically, the only one that can stand in the way of your acquiring it. Once acquired you and your gold will become one indivisible entity, which not even the hands of death possess the power to dispossess of you.

It's funny how people are. If you watch a small child master a new task, opening a cupboard door or making a new sound, it's clear that there is a considerable amount of intrinsic joy and self-satisfaction in the learning of any new task. This same little kid will devote an inordinate amount of time and effort, sweat if you like, to the learning and execution of the newly acquired skill; sweat that is a byproduct of a labor of love.

As we grow older and are indoctrinated by the lie that learning is for the most part an unpleasant task, thanks in no small part to the public school system, we tend to shun learning. Here again, visit your local school. Start out in Kindergarten then work your way up to the high school. Look to see how engaged and motivated students are. You will see two things taking place, instruction will shift from active, hands-on activities to formal lecturing, and as this takes place you will also see progressively more students off task, disengaged and disruptive. Maybe they're trying to tell us something.

I've never read any of the best selling books about not sweating the small stuff, but I can tell your right now if I did I would hate them just as much as I do right now, maybe even more. When is someone going to write a book titled, "Get Off Your Sorry Ass and Do Something with Your Life Today!" I could write that book, but I'm busy sweating my ass off digging a swimming pool, which is what this book is about. I'm getting to that, but for now let's get back to the small stuff debate. I'm here to tell you that it's up to you. Do you want to look back and say, "I really had a small stuff life!" or do you want to remember having had a big stuff one? As individuals, we arbitrarily assign big or small value to the life experiences we encounter. For instance, what is the absolute big or small value of getting off of work a half an hour early? For one person it may be a small thing because it happens every day of the week. To another it may be a big deal because he is working on a home project he would like to have finished before his wife gets home. Events do not come into our lives with a preordained, intrinsic value. Things happen and we assign arbitrary, big or small value after the fact. I hate to employ the worn out analogy of putting a puzzle together, but I will. Some pieces fall into place right away, while others get pushed off to the side until the bigger picture comes into focus. Then there at those that seem to keep floating back into your hand demanding their rightful place in the greater scheme of things be determined. There is a distinct possibility that the first segment of the puzzle you handle may be the last to be positioned properly. You may also find that a few pieces are missing and spend the rest of your life tearing the house apart looking for them. At the beginning all the pieces have no value or utility, it is only when you begin to sort them out and see where they fit that you assign what each individual segment means to you. My point is this, if it's up to you to determine the value of events which make up your life, why not put as many as you can in the big event category? The day will come when all you will have left are memories of the life you have lived. The decisions you make today will determine the caliber of recollections you can access when you are near your life's end.

When it comes down to it, you are the only one that has first hand experienced your life. Others can have shared experiences and feelings, but no one can see and experience this world exactly as you have. Cut your finger and I can empathize and revisit the sensation lingering from all the times when I have cut mine, but I cannot actually feel the same pain as you. I can never be absolutely sure that we experience and receive pain in the exact same way. If you have ever read accounts of prisoners of war that were subjected to unimaginable torture and inhumane living conditions you will realize that people do not process the stimulus of pain in exactly the same manner. If that were the case, a uniform threshold of endurance would be evident and the process of forcibly extracting information could be standardized. What happens is that each individual perceives and processes stimuli in an individual specific manner which is not replicated in any other being. Close, sure. Identical, absolutely not.

If this were the case for pain, it would have to be reciprocated in the realm of pleasure, which would mean that everyone would relish raw oysters with hot sauce as I do. The majority of people I know don't. I can cry with joy and share the happiness when a friend is blessed with the birth of a new child as I relive the ecstasy of the arrival of my own children. However, the true essence of this miraculous appearance of a new life on earth has a secret, individual specific meaning to all those involved to whatever extent. The blessing of a new child is similar to the mother and father of the child, but not the same in every respect.

The whole concept of love is another great example. Have you ever loved two people in exactly the same way? Ever heard the saying "I love you just as much, but not in the same way?" Given an exacting examination, I am convinced that no two loves have ever been, nor ever will be, identical in all aspects. I could go on in some depth and detail about love—one of the few subject in which I can be considered an expert and authority by virtue of having done considerable field work—but for the purposes of the present investigation it is sufficient that you know I could have written *The Book of Love*, or at least done the illustrations.

The limitations of human ability to communicate in both the expressive and receptive domains, the frailty and briefness of this life, all condemn us to the ultimate isolation which becomes manifest in that quirk of humanity we refer to as individuality. We can strive to get closer and closer to conveying to others who and what we are, just as we struggle to know the hearts and souls of those we love. At best this is a process on a continuum, because in reality we don't ever even really know the whole story about ourselves, evidenced by the fact that if you pay attention you will learn a little something new from yourself about yourself each day.

Our lives are like kaleidoscopes; every thought, emotion, experience, a different colored lens added to the end producing a variant hue and dimension to the individuals that we are. The you of this moment may be radically changed for life by an event, which may have an insignificant, altering impact on the life of another. Imagine you are at the funeral of a loved one, lingering graveside as the gravedigger tosses the first shovel full of dirt on the casket. You both experience the same event but come away with entirely different residual feelings and recollections. The image may be burned into your soul from that day forth; bringing back a torrent of vivid emotions any time you encounter a digging tool spooning sod. The gravedigger may well forget the details of the situation while drinking a beer on the way home after work, associating the shovel and the accompanying movement of earth with the ever-present ache in his overworked, underpaid back. Two people experiencing the exact same situation in life, each coming away with an entirely different impression as a consequence of the postscript added, complements of interpretation through one's individual kaleidoscope. The event was neither big, nor small in any objective sense, it derived meaning only to the extent it was ascribed by those who experienced it. So if this logic has any validity, every event that you experience in life is individually unique because the way in which you interpret and ascribe meaning to it will ultimately be yours alone. In the end, you decide the value of the events of your life. And in the process of doing so ascribe the ultimate value to your entire life.

Life is a give and take kind of thing. You do things to it and it does things to you. Luckily, there are things you can do today to ensure that their will be a smile of no regrets on your face when that inevitable moment of the end of this life comes calling to collect what's left of you here on this earth. Quite simply, you can begin to compile a scrapbook of memories right now (making sure they are of the quality that will bring you joy and pride when reminiscing back upon the life you have lived.) If you lead a life of thrilling adventure and yet have no appreciation for that which you have accomplished, you will join the ranks of those disappointed with life and find its many fruits withered on the vine and bitter to the palette. Or you may live a humble, unglamorous life, toiling at a menial job, spending your leisure time feeding ducks at the park, choosing to be content with your lot, reveling in the peaceful serenity found in the effortless manner with which the ducks skate on the surface of the water, cherishing the evolution and strengthening of the bonds of trust developing between man and foul. So the true value of a human life is how it is perceived by the person living it, not by the events encountered in this material world, and most certainly not by the blundering evaluations of those around us eager to pass judgement for the sole purpose of avoiding self-reflection.

This is not to say that money and material possessions, the gold you can see, touch, and use for barter are of no value. Quite the contrary. If you can, think back in your childhood to the time you first received some sort of monetary reward for your labor or an accomplishment. Compare the pride and exhilaration you felt back then in relationship of your deed and its reward to the money in your pocket right now. Is it even possible to determine exactly what you did for the dollar in your pocket this moment? It's the same stuff; the difference being the path that lead to securing it and, most importantly, the individual value you assigned to that which you accomplished in the process of acquiring that dollar. The majority of the value of a dollar is subjectively ascribed. What's left of its value resides in its innate utility. A dollar has a lot in common with a shovel. A dollar sitting in a bank account has potential much in the same way as does a shovel leaning against the wall in a garage. It is not until the instrument is taken in hand and actually applied to a situation requiring the services of its specific abilities that it takes on any true value. A man admiring his winter woodpile runs the risk of letting his family freeze to death should he forget that the wood has no utility until such time that it is placed in the hearth and coaxed to give up its stored heat energy, thus warming the shelter in which he resides. If you or someone you know has ever had the fortune, or misfortune, of falling heir to an unearned fortune, then in all probability you have had first hand experience with this axiom. An earned dollar has a completely different value than one acquired vicariously, the result of the labor of another.

Consider the immediate reflections of two different individuals given from the summit of a formidable mountaintop. Let's say that one of these individuals spent two years training and preparing for the logistics and rigors of a climbing expedition to conquer the peak in question, working ten hours a day and religiously hiking five hours each evening with a one hundred pound backpack. Suppose that our other mountaineer arrives at the summit via a private helicopter, got out, and took a few pictures, smoked a twenty-dollar cigar, then returned to a civilized lunch to boast of his exploits. Both individuals would have stood at the same vantage point on this earth and viewed the same panoramic scene. Their respective interpretations and impressions of that which was witnessed would, (I am convinced) be radically different, complements of the efforts, (sweat if you like) required in the process of surmounting the obstacles impeding the ultimate conquest of the summit. The observations perceived by the climber—who had worked hard for years to give birth to the dream of standing on the precipice of the mountain—would be a collage of the indomitable human spirit's ability to refuse to be defeated or dissuaded from its aspirations, no matter how high or rugged the mountains which blocked the path. The sweat we expend in this process of life inevitably establishes the arbitrary values we as individuals assign during those brief moments when we pause to reflect on where we have been, are, intend to go, and who at the end of this journey it is we want to be.

Have you ever known someone who was a natural at something like drawing and could, with a minimal amount of effort, produce a better sketch in an hour than you could in a week? Such a person does not consider this ability to be much of a talent or gift as it comes to them as naturally and effortlessly as drinking beer does to someone like me. If there's not sweat involved, we tend to not value the accomplishment.

In reality, there are very few individuals who achieve greatness simply based on natural talent. The trick is to know where your talents lie and cultivate a love and appreciation of them. I once had the opportunity to speak with an accomplished pianist at a concert. I had been lavisously indulging in libations and somehow managed to weasel my way into conversation proximity. I made some remark about her being born with a musical gift and this young woman bristled. She proceeded to inform me that we are all born with a gift, the gift of life, which bestows upon us unlimited potential. She assured me she had no keyboard experience inutero, and, that during the last eighteen years, she had forgone practicing at the piano less than twenty days, playing on average more than eight hours a day. After being put in my place, I felt an extended bladder bantering and excused myself from her presence taking with me a valuable lesson on how the world really works. Innate talent can make a person good at something, but without hard work and dedication, you can never become great at what you are good at.

Chapter 4

My father passed away when I was about four years old. Such being the case, as I grew older my natural instincts drove me to find a substitute to fill that missing part of my life with something or somebody. That was (and still is), my brother Bill. I don't really know if I looked at him in the same fashion as other boys do their fathers, but for me it was this simple: if Bill did it, it was a man thing to do, if he didn't, then a man just wouldn't do it. As far as I knew, my job was to grow up and be a man, so I figured that it was a process of imitation. At the current age of forty-seven, I still find myself projecting my brother into situations I encounter and asking myself how he would handle them. I have given up on trying to be just like him or any other individual I have met and admire. I have learned over the years that the lessons about life he imparted to me were meant to inspire and illuminate my journey, not create a brazen image I should try to emulate.

Early on my brother began to fill that void in my life created by the passing of my father. More precisely, he ensured that the void never had a chance to become chronically entrenched. Often times something can be missing in your life and you can't really tell what it is, but you can feel it there; an empty self-consuming void deep inside, feeding on itself, demanding reconciliation of an insatiable appetite. More often than not, a simple solution is to placate the hunger with self-destructive activities such as over indulgence in creature comforts. In my day it was sex, drugs and rock & roll. By the time that empty space grows influential enough to become manifest in your consciousness it could very well have adopted cancerous, celestial, black holeish qualities, which succeed in consuming your spirit and those of the loved ones endeavoring to assist in your salvation. That's why that whole 'say no to drugs' is such a joke. If you don't have something just as powerful to 'say yes' to, drugs will inevitably come back into the picture. As I grew up, Bill seemed to naturally assume the majority of the critical duties and roles of a father so I never got the chance suffer the primary adversities of a boy growing up without one.

I never got the sense that Bill took on this responsibility at any obligatory level. He had a wife and four kids of his own to fend for at the time. It was more of a natural assumption of an unsolicited opportunity presented to him in life; an opportunity to make the world in which he lived a bit more of a humane place. He was a deeply religious being in all of his thoughts, convictions, and actions, but he wasn't aware of it at the time. Claiming to be an atheist he had an intense aversion to any organized religion, demanding adherence to a blind dogma, propagating any sort of holier-than-thou attitude. His disdain for organized religion stemmed from a voracious appetite for historical literature from which he derived the conclusion that religion throughout history had been bastardized as political tools to dupe believers into subjugating and obliterating those deemed to be unbelievers and infidels. I have not spoken to him about religion and his convictions for some time so I can't really say if he has discovered that he's been a clandestine, closet Christian most of his life. Although, his wife recently informed me that not only had Bill been baptized and begun to attend church on a regular basis, but he also was entertaining the preacher at their abode periodically.

In his every fiber, Bill felt compelled to do all within his power to improve the lot in life of his fellow man, paying scant attention to his own. He derived the greatest satisfaction in life by doing for others, tallying his wealth in accordance to the worldly possessions and creature comforts he could afford to live without. He prioritized serving his family but always seemed to find time and resources to assist those friends and acquaintances on the fringes of a wide spread, extended family. While never clarifying to me what it was that drove this dedication, it was evident he derived spiritual sustenance from this commitment, attributing to our mother the inspiration and moral imperative he felt to walk the path of loving and serving his family and fellow man. No adherent to any formal religious doctrine he did one hell of a job personifying the ideal of loving thy neighbor and not in some esoteric sense. He actively searched out those in need and offered his services to friend, family, and stranger alike.

I can remember him talking about the indigent travelers he encountered from time to time riding the rails while he was working as a railroad engineer. In his official capacity he was mandated to eject them from the train or inform the railroad security (more affectionately know as rail dicks.) He would make sure any rail hobos he discovered had adequate provisions; often providing a pack of cigarettes, his lunch, or a couple of bucks. Before sealing the door to conceal the travelers from the rail dicks, he would find out where they were heading and let them know the closest stop the train would be making. When the train pulled into the station of destination, Bill would stroll to the car housing the transients, unbolt the door, and then return to his duties.

On the subject of the rails, while just a youngster I was exploring with a friend of mine along the railroad tracks near my home when a train happened along. Rails are nestled in a bed of crushed, throwing sized rocks and a train presents a multitude of slow moving targets just begging a young boy to show off his pitching arm. We armed ourselves and commenced a boulder bombardment of the passing freight. Later that week, Bill was visiting and indicated that someone he worked with had been on board that very same train and had made a positive identification of me as the perpetrator of the attack. I was twelve so Bill was maybe thirty-five. I thought I was dead. Rather than the verbal, (or possibly physical) thrashing I thought was imminent, Bill instructed me in the manly art of waging guerrilla warfare against a moving train. A summary of his instructions was to let the projectiles fly with abandonment but run for cover when you see the caboose approach as it is typically manned. And, if the caboose happened to be your target, assail it from appropriate cover. It was one of those rare child-adult conversations in which, you as a young person, could actually believe the adult not only had, at one time in ancient history been a youth, but this one had retained some recollection and understanding of the experience. Bill was able to make that connection with all kids because he had not forgotten what it was like to be one. He seemed to derive considerable entertainment from these periodic bombardments by rebel youth on the trains he was piloting. When some coworker would sound the alarm over the train's communications, Bill would get on the line and in a sarcastic feminine voice would shriek, "Help! The boys are throwing rocks at us again! I'm gonna tell my mommy!" Then he would begin crying and wailing, broadcasting his lament to all onboard. When his coworkers would interject that the train was sustaining damage Bill would wail all the more. He was amazed that grown men would become so agitated by kids throwing rocks, as if they had never done so in their youth.

I believe that in his soul he knew that having had a father to guide and love him had been crucial to the evolution of the man he was. I also believe he felt honored by an opportunity to return to this life some of that which it had favorably bestowed upon him while a youth.

I spent a lot of time as a youth at my brother's home. His door was always open to me, as was his unconditional love. My mother had remarried shortly after my father died. I can remember her telling me one time that marrying her second husband was the only selfish thing she had ever done in her life. I never spoke to anyone nor witnessed an event that could rebuke that assertion. The man she felt would be her knight in shining armor turned out in the long run to be an alcoholic sonofabitch. His idea of a weekend with the family was to drink a fifth of whiskey and a case of beer. I can still see him sitting in the kitchen at five a.m. reading the paper in his bathrobe, indulging in a continental breakfast of beer, cigarettes, and ninety-proof spirits. You could tell how long he had been up by the magnitude of the tremors rolling across the newspaper from the convulsive shaking, and twitching of his hands. Once his nervous system was sufficiently saturated with alcohol, the trembling subsided and the hands that clutched the paper ceased to tremble like condemned flies thrashing in a spider web.

This man had no idea how to be a decent, compassionate, human being, but I think he came as close to it as he could in his interactions with me. You could no more fault the guy for his inability to initiate an act of human kindness than you could condemn a skunk for stinking. He was a miserable piece of work incapable of even a pretext of human decency; he had no grasp of the concept. For some unknown reason he liked me. I was offended and insulted by his attention and in retrospect, I may have considered his attention to me more of an affront to decency than my mother and brother Scott did the emotional abuse for which they were the primary targets. In many respects, emotional assaults are more detrimental than those of a physical nature. When you get a beating you know when it begins and ends. When abuse is psychological, there are no definitive milestones, it is administered on a continuum and often never ceases.

My brother Scott's birthday was the day after Christmas. I recall my stepfather coming home drunk. As he entered the house he threw a brown paper bag at my brother and blurted out, "Here's your Goddamn birthday present." As a young child I felt astonishment and confusion. I can remember pondering the dynamics of this sort of behavior, "Would I be that way as an adult? Was it OK for an adult to treat a child so? Was there something I didn't know that made him treat my brother is such a manner?" The conjecture soon faded and was transformed into unadulterated hate, even though the present was a coveted Etch-A-Sketch. I hated him more for the way he treated my mother and brother than I would have if he had beat me. The message he gave my brother was that his birthday was anything but a joyous event to celebrate. His words and actions imparted to my brother that his birthday was a irritating burden that had to be endured, one my step father would have preferred to ignore.

Then there was that pleasant memory of how he introduced my mother to his parents shortly after mom had a mastectomy, calling her his "tit-less wonder." He was a pitiful excuse for a human being and made it his goal in life to make the world a more miserable place to live for all of those he was able to enshroud in his drunken, dark cloud of self-pity. Poor bastard couldn't understand why I despised him. All I can say is that he did the entire world a favor, except for my mother, when he committed suicide.

As the word of his suicide worked its way through the grapevine at my high school the message reached Mr. C. Out of concern he inquired how the act had affected me. I told him in all sincerity that it was my heartfelt belief that the world would be a better place without old Kermit around. He didn't even have the decency to kill himself outside of the house. Alone, at home, with my sixty-year-old mother, this creature put a poorly placed, small caliber bullet in his head, leaving her to witness the convolutions of his death throes. Her only inheritance was the pain he left behind, years of hoarded misery amassed from a life wasted; pain he was unable to deal with and reconcile, he passed on that terrible burden to my mother. I couldn't then and still can't fathom how he could have done such a thing to the only person in the world who gave a shit about him. Intentional or not, his last act on this earth was to inflict the maximum amount of pain and suffering on the only human being that would grieve his death, my mother. Only she could have found something to love in such a detestable creature. Thinking back on the situation I can now see that he had died inside long before he killed himself. My mother had been his life support system for several years. He was like a parasitic fungus, which clung to her and derived it sustenance from her life force. I have given up trying to understand the dynamics of the relationship between the two of them.

I felt guilty when it happened, but not out of any concern for him or in second-guessing that I could have prevented the suicide. The guilt I felt was from spending so much time at Bill's and leaving my mother to deal with my degenerate stepfather. I felt that I could have minimized the impact of the event on my mother had I been there. When I expressed this guilt to Bill he retorted, "Bullshit! You did the right thing by staying away from a situation you knew would cause conflict and upset our mother. She loved the man for whatever reasons. They were married and deserved to have the opportunity to try and make it a successful one. It was her marriage, not ours, and we owed it to her to respect the sanctity of those vows. Our mother needs us now more than she ever did when Kermit was alive." This was long before the 'it's not your fault' obsession in American child rearing theory. This was a mentoring, compassionate hand reaching across the chasm which separates the young from the old in an effort to assist the younger in coming to terms with one of those situations in life with the potential to cause irreparable damage to an impressionable, young mind.

At the time I didn't completely understand what he meant, but his delivery was reassuring that I was not lacking in the virtues of being a good son. Thirty years later at the funeral of my best friend I came to understand what Bill meant about honoring the marriage of someone you love and respect. This friend of mine had remarried after the untimely death of his first wife. His second wife had honored him in every aspect of their wedding vows for twenty-five years. His grown children did not approve of his new wife, as is often the case when a widowed parent remarries. No one came out and said it, but his kids were not about to consider anyone a worthy replacement for their mother. They were just as adamant in their collective conviction that no one was good enough for their father. The children had few kind words when speaking about his wife during his demise and after his death. I found myself coming to the defense of this woman when judgment was being passed harshly upon her, and I wondered at the time what was motivating this uncharacteristic behavior on my part. I myself cared little for the woman. At an angry moment during a discussion with my departed friend's son I blurted out, "If you criticize the woman to whom your father was married, you are dishonoring his marriage and him at the same time. I'll not stand for another word of disrespect about his wife." Those were my brother Bill's words reverberating across the ravines of time, springing forth from seeds planted long ago and bearing fruit in a time of need. Funny how that works.

I leaned hard on my brother in that situation. When I saw my mom after the suicide, she was in the spare bedroom at Bill's house. I had just arrived home from school. As I entered the bedroom I saw my sister in law, Glad, sitting on the bed holding my mother's hand and stroking her silver-gray hair, tending to her with the attention and devotion of a devout disciple of some earthly saint. When my eyes met Glad's hers pleaded with me to do something to take away the suffering that was consuming the soul of my mother. Forty years a farmer's wife, two husbands in the grave, eight children, and one buried as an infant, had all taken a toll on the old girl. I couldn't help but notice how frail my mother looked in her nightgown; her back and spirit bent; but as of yet, unbroken from close to a half century of service to her family.

Her words on seeing me were, "Here's something strong I can hold on to." The child like warble in her voice was that of innocence swept away by the waves of pain radiating from some unexplainable, inescapable source. She had passed the point of understanding her suffering; all she knew was the pain in her heart and the longing for it to subside. Justice demanded cessation of her agony, experience assured the hurt would eventually retreat but never completely dissipate. I don't think I've ever cried that way before or since. Rather than starting out with a few preliminary tears escaping prior to full-blown weeping these tears exploded in a torrential deluge like two, rain-swollen streams cascading down my face. As I hugged her I strove to maintain the muscle tone of my body, fighting the urge to relax and give in to the embrace that had sheltered and nurtured me my entire life. It was really the first time my mother had ever needed anything from me other than my love, and I would have rather been impaled on a skewer and slow roasted on a bed of smoldering coals than disappoint her by being anything less than the pinnacle of strength and stability she needed me to be at that instant. The hate for the man who had done this to my mother spawned the bile I tasted, giving me the strength to stand tall for my mother in her time of need. I'm sorry to say it wasn't the power of love that sustained me. My tears were the only outward indication I gave of my grief, they flowed of their own volition and managed to comfort both of us.

I never put much stock in prayers, I figured that God made this world and us, and that was his gift and the end of his responsibility. Ours is to do some good with both of them. There was one thing I did pray for as a child. During a class party while I was in elementary school several student's mothers brought treats for the occasion. During this event I noticed that my mother was considerably older that the mothers of my friends. Later that day when I returned home Mom spoke to me about the party and good naturedly teased me about being embarrassed at having a gray haired, old mother who wasn't as pretty and young as those of the other kids. I was ashamed at having felt that way, and even more regretful that she had been able to see into my heart and discover my feelings. I felt I had dishonored my mother.

Shortly after my realization of her advanced age, I deduced that she would ultimately die much sooner than the Mother's of my friends, sooner than me. I use to pray that God would take some of the time allotted me on this earth and give it to my mother. It wasn't a little kid's egocentric desire to have his mommy forever. It was a simple determination on my part that she had earned and deserved it. Now that I think back that's what it felt like when I embraced my mother on that day. I felt her gaining strength while we embraced. I don't know that God ever answered that prayer, or any others for that matter, but he gave me a mother, family and friends that fulfilled just about every need a boy could have while growing up, so I can't complain. Maybe we have it all mixed up. Maybe God spends all his time praying that the people he put here on earth will appreciate the gifts he has given us and quit asking for more.

As funeral arraignments were being made for Kermit Bill talked to Scott and I in private saying, "I think you boys should talk to mother about getting hair cuts for the funeral. Let her know that you think Kermit would have liked it that way." Scott and I were both the hippie types with more hair between us than a Mongolian Yak in the middle of winter. Bill could see the chagrin in our eyes and went on, "I'd cut my right arm off if I thought it would help mom get through this any easier. We all have to do whatever we can. She's been through more pain and heartache than we'll ever know. Anything we can do to comfort her, we have a family obligation to do." It was the closest Bill ever came to telling me that I had to do anything. I was convinced he was dead serious about hacking off his arm in order to appease the demons tormenting our mother and most likely he would have done the same to Scott and me if that was what the situation required.

When I talked to mom about it her reply was, "He's gone now and there's no need for you boys to be subjected to anymore of his overbearing belligerence." She had begun the process of closure on this tragic chapter of her life. At the time a hair cut would have been synonymous to a visit to the local spade and neuter clinic, both my brother and I assumed our romances were contingent on the length of our hair.

If I had despised Kermit while he was alive, what I felt for him after his death was a raging hatred. What made it worse was there was no opportunity to vent my venom against him, siphon it off so it didn't back up and poison my system. For years he visited me in my dreams; an aberration haunting otherwise pleasant frolics of nighttime fantasy. It was an unsettling experience and I began to experience some self doubt about my feelings as they related to his memory.

Several years ago my wife gave me a book by a fellow named Nathan Mcain, titled, *What's Goin' On*. In this book of essays the author told a story about a friend of his who had killed someone, gone to prison, and there was subsequently killed himself. At the funeral of this friend Mcain met the mother of the man his friend had murdered some years ago. To his surprise, Mcain found that the woman had forgiven his friend for the senseless brutal murder of her son. When Mcain tried to explain to her how much her forgiveness would have meant to his friend she replied, "I didn't do it for him. I did it for myself."

Some time after reading that book I did the same thing. I let go of the hate, indignation and all the unresolved issues relating to that episode of my life. I didn't need to have all the hanging questions answered anymore. I let the past go its way and freed my spirit so that I might continue my journey. I don't have any love for the man, nor any hate.

During the funeral, all I could think about was how life might have been had my father not died when I was young. Even though I was only four years old when he died, I can still remember my father lying on the couch in our old farmhouse. His body didn't seem to fit, he was too big for it. I remember jumping up and down on him while he lay there. I don't recall him giving any indication if the attention was enjoyable or not. He was dying of cancer and I can only speculate as to why he endured what must have been less than a pleasant pummeling from my small feet upon the abdomen in which grew the cancer consuming his life force and incrementally dispossessing him of his ability to provide for his family. He must have felt that any interaction with his infant son during the little time he had left was worth any amount of discomfort.

All of my kids enjoy doing what we had dubbed *The Atomic Doggie*. I lay on my back on the floor with a pillow on my stomach and the kids take turns jumping on my mid section. I'm hoping that my abdominal muscles hold out until they get old enough to loose interest in the *Doggie*. I can tell by the look in my twenty-year-olds eyes that sometimes he would like one more shot at the *Atomic Doggie*, but he's too cool now to play with his old man.

I like to think my dad cherished those few moments. With children of my own today I can't imagine the desperation a husband and father would have facing such a situation. He was leaving behind a wife of thirty years and a marriage that had been dedicated to raising seven children, caring for elderly parents, tending to a brother with Downs Syndrome, and farming one hundred and sixty acres. He was leaving behind a massive financial burden with no reasonable expectation that his wife could manage it. He was also leaving my brother and I, two little kids not yet in school, with a mother in her forties who had no skills marketable in the workplace. I can't fathom a heavenly afterlife that would be worth enduring torment of that magnitude as an admission requirement. Maybe I'll change my mind, if I have one after I die, but not in this lifetime. I was never angry that my dad died, but I've always felt there was something missing in my life. I still do.

I have a few snapshot images of my father in my mind that are bonafided recollections and others that have been embellished and personified by the stories I have heard from family and friends. I remember talking with my mother about these remembrances and mentioning that I could not recall any instance of hearing my father speak. Laughing, she assured me that he was a quiet man whom she often had to prod to get a word out of.

I have rich, rewarding life and can easily count my regrets on the toes of the paw of a sloth. I do lament not knowing the sound of my father's voice. Even though I was fairly young when my dad died, I feel blessed by the recollections and stories I have managed to retain about him. I think my favorite story about him is the one when one morning a milk cow offended him in some manner and he punched the uncooperative creature between the eyes and knocked it to it's knees. Judging by the family folklore and pictures I have seen, he was big and strong enough to do it.

Another is an experience I had at a funeral of a distant relative. I was talking to an elderly relative about some topic which escapes me at this time, but that's no impediment to the crux of the recollection. We were at our family cemetery, I was in a squatting position, and conversing with the gentleman I mentioned. I had a cigarette dangling from the corner of my mouth and I struck a match on the rough hued top of a head stone as I spoke. I let the match burn out in my hand without igniting my cigarette as I was in the middle of making a critical point in the conversation. The fella to whom I was speaking, his name and face I can no longer recall, was starring as if he were witnessing a legion of our ancestors rising from the graves behind me. Then he said, "Talking with you just now I saw your father in you. Your dad and I had a conversation sittin' 'round like this a long time ago. He was hunkered down like you, and I was sittin' on the grass about the same as right now. He was a tellin' a story, don't remember what the hell about, but anyhow, he was gonna light a cigarette he had a hangin' in his mouth while he was talking, and I'll be damned if he didn't light up a match and let her go out while he talked, like you did just now." It may have been coincidence but I felt that the spirit of the father I never knew at that instant had touched me. I was caught in the confluence of two, tumultuous, life forces: the injustice I felt at being deprived of the chance to have spoken to my father and know the sound of his voice, and the pride I felt that someone with the authority to know could see something of my father in me.

Before the passing of Bill's wife Glady, she made me promise that if I had any inclination to buy her flowers, she wanted them when she was alive and not at her funeral or on her grave. She was insistent that the only thing she wanted on her grave was a shot of whiskey when I came to pay my regards. I always take a fifth out to the family bone yard and provide libations to those departed souls whom I know would appreciate the gesture. During a recent visit, I happened to encounter my cousin Joe, who supervises the maintenance of the cemetery. I told him I would not be able to take part in the coming annual field day at the graveyard but I would be willing to make a donation. Joe replied, "Donations are always welcome!" and he reached for the jug in my left hand rather than the twenty in my right. I clarified that I intended to make a monetary donation and went on to explain to him the libation tradition.

We made the rounds and offerings together, reminiscing about the ancestors who preceded us. While reflecting over the grave of my father, I repeated the story of never having heard his voice. Joe laughed and told me that he could remember many occasions of visiting my mom and dad and the only words he heard my dad say were hello and goodbye. It wasn't that he was antisocial he was simply a man of few words who, if he did have something to say to you, would not walk away from a conversation until he was assured his point had been made.

As a small child I remember playing with two items that belonged to my dad, his boxing gloves and a belt. The old, worn out, boxing gloves made great slippers for a little kid. I spent hours trying to keep them on my feet as I skated around the floor. At the time they meant nothing to me that I could have explained then or even now, but for some reason they held a strange allure. The belt was of an unusual design, it had two tongues, one that was inserted underneath the belt buckle and the other fastened to the buckle. Here, again, not the sort of toy you would expect to captivate the attention of a preschooler for any prolonged period of time, but for some reason it did. I fondled that strap of leather until it was as soft and pliable as a shamie. I can still remember rolling that belt up and unrolling it over and over.

Typically I'm frugal when spending money on myself, but when I stumbled upon a replica of my father's belt in a sporting goods outlet store, I bought it without checking the price. About the only time I can remember ever making a purchase without first ascertaining how much booze a similar amount of money would secure. I have no recollection as to the fate of the original belt or those boxing gloves and I guess it doesn't really matter. The memories are more important than the material items. I have transferred all that his belt represented to the belt I am wearing right now, and I take considerable comfort from this link to my past, a reminder of who and what I am, and from whence I hail. I have worn that belt every day for the past ten years, except for several days spent in jail during that time. Each time I put it on or take it off I say a few words in my heart to my father. Interestingly, my daughter who just turned five has developed a fascination about that belt. When she sees me putting it on she runs to me pleading to help buckle it.

But this story is about my brother Bill and the lessons I learned helping him on every crazy project he ever dreamed up and one such project in particular. There was one lesson which, if I had paid closer attention to, would have saved me considerable inconvenience and expense. It pertains to that little hiatus I spent in jail. My brother Scott rented a beach house for a little Fourth of July get together. About a dozen people showed up for the weekend. I had every intention of keeping a low profile and out of trouble. My wife and daughter were in attendance. I was in possession of a forty-caliber Glock handgun, and three hundred bucks worth of high-octane, illegal, fire works. I had the handgun in a hip holster and a Washington State Concealed Weapons Permit, albeit expired. We set up camp on the beach and put on one hell of a fireworks show. From our command post we had established a no mans land swath on the beach about fifty yards wide in which no one would dare set foot for fear of being incinerated by the burning projectiles or the continuous rain of embers. As we touched off the last skyrockets I stepped away from our fire and fired off thirteen rounds from my Glock due west into the ocean, then sat down to await the fireworks display from town. About ten minutes later our camp was encircled by the Rockaway Beach Police Force, all four of them. The Chief approached and said, "We had a report of someone wearing a cowboy hat and leather jacket firing a pistol."

Including me, there were three people at our fire matching that description. I answered saying, "Been shooting of some fireworks but no guns." The Chief was being reasonable, but one of his deputies thought he was Dirty Harry. He got into a heated exchange with someone else at our campfire. It looked like things might get out of hand so I confessed to having the handgun.

My wife, the only sober adult around the fire, sighed and whispered in my ear, "Thank you."

On the way to jail I talked with the Chief and made the point that I couldn't remember a Fourth where someone had not discharged a firearm. I also elaborated that in the town where I lived I could sit on the front porch, drink beer and fire my pistol with impunity and without a complaint. The Chief lamented that Rockaway had once been like that, but civilization had encroached changing the landscape physically and culturally. My wife maxed out our credit cards to make my bail and to this day has never mentioned the incident in any rub-your-nose in it manner.

The district attorney recommended a month in jail, three years probation, no booze, no guns for the rest of my life, and a grant to the police a right to search my home or person without probable cause. A lawyer got me off with four days in jail and eighteen months probation. Incidentally, that trip to the beach was our belated honeymoon. My wife had waited without complaint for seven years and what did she get? Whatever she got it sure as hell wasn't what she expected, kinda like marrying me.

That same summer back east somewhere, acting on an anonymous tip, the cops nailed a juvenile gang banger with a criminal record. He got popped for carrying a concealed weapon. The ACLU took the case to the Supreme Court and they ruled the cops were out of line and that an anonymous tip was not sufficient cause to conduct a search of an individual's person. The scumbag had not cooperated with the cops and he gets his gun back. I cooperate and now some moron with a tin badge and the brain of a hermit crab is packing my gun.

All I could think about was one of those lessons my brother had tried to impart to me as we toiled side by side in the pit. He was always reading the strangest stuff and had a head full of facts and figures. I don't remember just what they were, but what it boiled down to was that something like nine out of ten people in federal prisons at the time were there because they had confessed, or somehow or another aided the state in their prosecution. He indicated that had those individuals simply kept their mouths shut, they would never have been convicted. At the time I wasn't sure why the hell he was talking to me about matters of the law. I was just a kid. I wasn't going to have any trouble with the cops, right? Every boy eventually turns into a man and there are ample opportunities in between to engage in troubles and tribulations. My brother was planting seeds, which he knew would serve me well in the future.

Unfortunately, for me, they bloomed a bit too late. I should have taken my cue from President Ronald Reagan. During the Iran/Contra investigation when he was interviewed by a congressional committee. The guy said, "I don't recall," or "I don't remember," over one hundred times in a single day. Chances are that he really meant it. Poor old boy, I remember when he fell off his horse right after he retired from the big house on the hill. The doctors checked him out and discovered he had water on the brain. Water on the brain or not, he had sense enough to keep his mouth shut. If I had as much I'd still have my side arm and no criminal record. Come to think of it, keeping your mouth shut would in all probability be advantageous in the majority of situations having the potential to evolve into hot spots.

This situation, like all others, has two sides. As I put some time between this particular Fourth and myself I have developed an appreciation for some of the more subtle details. The Chief declined to administer a breath analysis of my blood alcohol content, against the recommendations of the booking officer at the jail. Had he done so, the prosecuting attorney would have had a much stronger case for hanging my ass out to dry, which he seemed intent on doing. The lawyer I retained informed me that the DA was none other than his brother-in-law. So this lawyer of mine writes a rather combative letter claiming my innocence and offering not to sue the county if they returned my property, drop all charges, and apologized. I specifically questioned my lawyer about this proposition, making it clear that I didn't want to "piss" anyone off and end up in a protracted court battle and eventually in jail. He assured me we were on solid legal standing. The letter pissed the DA and the Chief off and I ended up doing some jail time. All and all, I figure I got off easy and in the end, as usual, I had no one to blame for being in a mess but myself.

Chapter 5

It was one of those hot, summer days. Hot enough to turn the road tar into mud puddle size pools of bubbly, hot, black taffy, smelling like they had just laid the stuff. You could walk barefoot on the road and hear the little bubbles in the asphalt pop beneath your feet. If your feet were tough enough to walk on that black goo your calluses were too thick to feel them burst under your feet; unless you happened upon an extremely hot puddle fluid enough to push up in between your toes, causing the liquefied tar to ooze out on the dirty, but tender, top of your foot. Prior to becoming enamored with the opposite sex and being obsessed with removing all my clothing at the slightest invitation, in my younger years of innocence, I anxiously awaited the arrival of summer and took any opportunity to go barefoot and remove as many garments as the law would allow. The kids I ran with did the same. During the summer we would compare the soles of our feet (how thick our calluses were) and trade war stories about how we had received the specific cuts and scars adorning the palms. If we happened to be smoking cigarettes, I took macho delight in being able to hold a burning butt on the heel of my foot and scorch a hole in the callus, extinguishing the butt without flinching. On a dare I would even go so far as to put a cigarette out on my tongue. The trick was to roll your tongue and make sure you had a good glob of spit in the middle of it so that the cherry of the butt would actually be out before it made contact with your fleshy, taste buds. That was the theory anyway, but I have a feeling that my crew was more impressed with the performance I put on when the theory did not translate into reality. I never have been much of a dancer, but when you place a smoldering ember on one of the most sensitive parts of your body, your feet just take their cue from the alarms going off in your nervous system.

Now I can never talk about being young and smoking without recalling this story. I was a river rat as a youngster, spending my summers on the bank of the Clackamas River with my friends. On those nights when the warmth of day lingered long into the night, we would build a fire on the bank purportedly to lure fish to the bait dangling at the ends of our fishing poles. That was the official rationale. Truth be known, it was a simple situation of boys playing with fire and needing a pretense other than combating the cold of the night. We must have been low on cigarettes because a friend of mine across the fire asked if he could have a drag off mine and naturally I obliged. When the butt was returned to me, to my chagrin, I found that my jocular compatriot had, as a joke, spit into the filter. A good laugh was had at my expense, but there was a lingering tense expectation in the air as my crew awaited the retaliation I was obligated to execute.

As we sat roasting marshmallows I decided to immerse mine in the flames, as it was my inclination to eat the little morsels once they had become thoroughly cremated. As the molten substance began to sputter and spew forth fiery globules I bent my stick back in an arch and announced to the perpetrator of the befouled cigarette that I had prepared a fiery feast for him. As I let fly the blazing treat I was horrified when it landed on the side of my friend's face. If I had any intention it had been to scare him, not ignite his person. The surprise frontal assault from the air evidently caught him off guard but instinct told him that if he were in the process of being consumed by fire a prudent response was to seek out water. Unfortunately, in his disoriented state of mind (no doubt resulting from the combined influence of the homemade blueberry wine and the flaming glob of goo adhering to his cheek) he was oblivious to the fact that he was sitting not more than five feet from a river full of the stuff. Instead, he chose to sprint the one hundred yards or so to the restroom and utilize tap water to extinguish the blaze. There was no point trying to catch and convince him he was heading in the wrong direction for by the time I had risen to my feet he had already covered a good forty yards. As he ran in the dark I could see that he was attempting to remove the flaming material from his face. There were spot fires beginning to erupt on his clothing where he was wiping the napalm like marshmallow on his pants and shirt.

There was some talk around the campfire that evening about creating a special event in the Olympics where the runners and other athletes would be motivated and inspired to perform by the added incentive of attempting to extinguish flaming material applied to their bodies. Something along the lines of what the clowns did to Dumbo the elephant in the Disney story. Made the little guy dress up like a baby, put him on top of a burning building, and had him jump into a fireman's net which breaks, and then Dumbo splashes into the tub of water beneath. Might be more exciting than Ping-Pong.

Poor Paul, it was the second time I had set him on fire. The other time I was chasing him around the house with a lighter and a can of aerosol deodorant. When the deodorant was dispersed past the pilot light, one had in his hands a compact, formidable flame-thrower capable of blasting a funnel of flames several feet. He took refuge in the bedroom, buttressing the door against further torment. I waited him out, quietly, patiently, like a cat perched outside a mouse hole. After about ten minutes he opened the door just a crack and that was my cue, my window of opportunity, and I let fly with a blast of the righteous flaming Right Guard and instantaneously Paul's eyebrows and curly red hair burst into flames. Luckily for him he fell over backwards which allowed me to move the chair barricading him, giving me the opportunity to extinguish the flames. He put up quite a struggle as I gallantly executed my duty as a junior fire fighter. I ignored the revulsion inflicted on me by the smell of burning, human hair as I rose to the occasion. In a crisis situation training always pays off; I remembered seeing how it was done when a fireman visited my fifth grade class. As I beat the flames out which had spread to the back of his head I wasn't sure why I met with so much resistance. I tried to accomplish my good deed. I learned later, when Paul started to speak to me again, that in his pain and fear sponsored derangement the poor guy actually thought I had every intention of bludgeoning him to death; finish him off after setting him ablaze. I was terribly offended that he would think such a thing. I had always suspected there was something a little off about the guy.

As was the case with the flaming marshmallow I apologized for the unexpectedly intense level of physical injury, which my practical joke had inflicted. He didn't seem much concerned that I felt extremely bad he had been burnt more severely than I had planned.

Indirectly though, Paul was responsible for me learning one of the most beneficial lessons about life I have ever acquired from a friend and remembered long enough to put to good use. As kids recreating on the old Clackamas River, we were continuously dreaming up innovative ways to float down the rapids. Several of us had inner tubes on this particular day, and the consensus was, we would tie all of the tubes into a train at the top of the rapids then embark on a white water adventure. By unanimous vote, with one objection, it was decided that Paul would pilot the treacherous bucking caboose of our rapid riding contraption. After a bit of maneuvering we were in the main current of the river and then in the thick of the churning rapids. Taking my cue from the river spirits, just as the caboose tube had sunk into a whirlpool, I lashed out with my foot and kicked Paul into the boiling cauldron. We laughed and watched as he struggled to regain his position on the tube, but the harder he tried, the further his thrashing gyrations pushed his tube away. Ironically, when he exhausted his attempts at survival and quit fighting the power of the river, the current transported him along side his tube and he was back in the saddle again.

An allegory for all sorts of struggles we face here on dry land. In particular, this lesson applies to the manly art of romance, the harder you try to climb into the saddle of your desire, or back into one from whence recently ejected, the further away your efforts push the mare you are trying to mount.

Tough feet were a definite asset in my youth, but there were times when the forces and elements of Mother Nature were more formidable than the thickest of soles. Like the time my best friend and I floated down the river together on a truck inner tube. It was a modern day Huck Finn adventure. We braved perilous rapids, transversed new, uncharted lands, and came to know the cultures of strange, new peoples. We even got stuck in the vortex at the intake of the water purification plant. Without a rudder, oar, or star to navigate by, we were at the mercy of the whirlpools and suction created by extraction of the thousands of gallons of water required to quench the thirst of the surrounding human encampment. We figured we were goners, soon to have our precious bodily fluids extracted and mixed with the municipal water supply and ultimately end up in someone's toilet tank or dog's, water bowl. We gave up on the idea of abandoning ship and swimming for shore, because neither of us could swim a stroke, let alone fight the suction tugging at our helpless craft. As we were kissing our asses' goodbye, the thing apparently satiated its industrial thirst and quit sucking in the rivers bounty. Elated, we were back in the main current of the river again and on our way down stream.

We made landfall at an inviting beach with good access, put to shore, then made our way up to the highway that led home. Shortly thereafter, we experienced an interesting phenomenon. Our feet had been in the water for several hours and had become super saturated. When those waterlogged dogs hit pavement heated by the midday summer sun, suffice it to say an insignificant amount of that solar radiation was lost in the transference from the blacktop to the soles of our feets. I can vividly remember thinking of myself as one of those pagan, hot coal walkers, searching for that state of mind which would allow one to stomp barefoot on smoldering embers or broken glass without the slightest bit of discomfort or physical insult. The only problem was that it hurt so damn bad I couldn't maintain the proper concentration to put the situation into that perspective. All I could think of was that I had drown in the river and gone to Hell for my exploits, my punishment being the transformation of my feet into slabs of bacon, condemned for eternity to wander the surface of a gigantic, searing, hot griddle.

Out of desperation we began to collect trash from along side of the road and wrap in around our feet to shield them from the blistering heat. We almost came to blows when periodically one of us was lucky enough to find a coveted, intact, paper bag. They were instrumental in holding layers of roadside refuge in place as insulation from the scorching, hot pavement. Rather than fight, we agreed to share the coveted commodities; they would not become the property of the discoverer. We considered them communal possessions to be distributed on an equitable, alternating schedule.

About half way home Bill rescued us. He's the type of guy that if you pay him an unexpected visit he greets you as if you were Ulysses returning and he had been awaiting you homecoming from your long, arduous trek. My brother never spoke in cliches. When he would ask you, "How have you been?" or said, "It's great to see you," it was readily evident that he was sincerely interested and concerned about the details of how life had been treating you and that it truly brought him joy to be in your presence. Bill never said anything to be merely polite, if he said it, you could take it to the bank that the message came special delivery from his heart and gut. It's a treat to watch him in action. If you have ever watched people greet each other, they go through the formalities of, "Hello how are you fine how are you." It's a ritual, a social formality with superficial meaning at best. You can see that it means little to those involved. When my brother would ask someone how they had been, the sincerity of the inquiry transforms the individual to whom it is directed. You can see a subconscious understanding on the part of the person being greeted that Bill is completely focused and interested, conveying the message that the details of that person's life are important, big stuff. Pay close attention during your daily interactions and you will find that this is actually an extremely rare event. It's an empowering experience for the person receiving such a compliment, there's nothing phony or contrived, no telltale techniques from those how to win and influence people publications. Bill comes by it honestly and, in all likelihood, doesn't even notice how gratified people are that he is actually interested in their lives in a world where so many care so little.

I could tell right away this wasn't going to be one of those visits. He was pissed off that I had embarked on such a risky adventure. I assumed correctly that my brother had come looking for me at the request of my distraught mother whom I was sure, would be home fretting that I was on the bottom of the river by now, or in the clutches of some demented fisherman patrolling the river in search of young children to prey upon, intent on (as my sensitive step father would have said), "Reaming me a new asshole." Rather than lecture and chastise, Bill concluded that the natural consequences of our actions were sufficient reward. His only judgmental remark was to point out that our mother had enough unsolicited grief in her life to deal with and was not in need of any intentional efforts on my part to ferret out additional burdens for her to bare.

Bill was the type of guy who could go on talking about most anything, and do so to the benefit of those involved in the conversation. He never did this in a situation where he knew you already felt sufficient guilt and remorse for your actions. One of the few adults I met in my youth that did not believe you could lecture a conscience into a young person.

It took over a month to recover from the blistering of the soles of our feet, a humiliating way to end the summer. The thick calluses, which I had cultivated, gingerly peeled off, exposing baby soft skin, leaving me no choice but to wear footgear for the duration of the summer. Now, rather than walk proudly in the gravel alongside the road, head held high for all passersby to marvel at and behold, I slinked down the soft path in the field dejected, head bowed, avoiding the faces passing by in the cars, ignoring the condescending remarks of the neighborhood kids arrogantly trodding the jagged, stone path next to me.

It wasn't that there was some innate desirability in being a shoeless savage, it was more of a statement of youthful rebellion, of non-conformity. I wanted to be different just like everybody else. Like the majority of statements the whole point of them was for someone to listen or notice. I'm convinced I would have never endured the trials, tortures and tribulations of acclimating my feet to the rigors of naked podiatry had it not been for adult screeches of disapproval. Bill had somehow managed to grow old without becoming afflicted by the ultimate curse of old age, arriving at that point in life where one is indiscriminately judgmental and critical of all activities of a youthful nature.

Chapter 6

It was hot! Bill had just gotten home from work. He was an engineer for the Southern Pacific Railroad and in that capacity, by his own choice, he was on call virtually every day of the year, excluding two weeks he took his family on vacation. He never really knew when he would be working until the phone rang. This being the case, he was required to spend practically all his leisure times at home—an arrangement he in no way considered an inconvenience. He was of that traditional mold that a father's greatest good was to provide the highest, monetary level of security to his clan as possible. He did this without complaint or consternation.

It's funny how the things we think are so important today fade from our memories and it's the fairly ordinary events that blossom, sink roots, and take on importance and give birth to enlightenment over time. Years ago I was listening attentively to a conversation he was having with his wife; she was questioning why a man that professed to despise money and material possessions spent so much time working. His response was, "I saw what not having money did to my father before he died, and what it did to my mother after he was gone." At the time, I had no understanding about the financial hardships associated with the farm we lost or the father I lost. The remark did however, have the impact of certifying the importance of money in being a good provider. It's not everything, but it is a critical cornerstone in maintaining a healthy family unit. I never got the details, but I did get the message that money was a lot like water, you can only live without it for a short while, even though you can't get much use out of an abundance unless you share it with thirsty people.

Later on in life, when I too became a father, Bill and I discussed this concept and where the point of diminishing returns was. He admitted that in retrospect he could see that the greatest gift he had ever received from another individual, or had ever bestowed upon another, was the precious gift of time. He regretted that he had spent so much of his time working while his kids were growing up, wishing he had given more of his time to them. A fairly mundane statement as far as casual conversation goes. Coming from Bill this was only the second time I had heard him express a serious regret about how he had lived his life. It made a considerable impression and I have integrated the understanding into the way I live my life, squeezing out every, conceivable spare moment to spend with my family. That's why I'm writing this at three-thirty in the morning, in my little office, in the garage, with a window facing the house. As soon as I see a light go on I'm done out here and go in the house to see who's up.

Bill's typical routine when returning home was to eat, get some sleep, then commence to juggle the multitude of projects which were at various states of completion, design, or neglect. His perspective on creature comforts was summed up in a favorite saying of his, "Some people live to eat, while others eat to live." He was definitely an adherent to the latter, considering eating to be an interruption; a necessary distraction from more important things. Bill spent little time on leisure activities, and whenever he did it always revolved around his family. I have no recollections of the man ever engaged in a personal, private recreation other than reading, and even this was more of an act of replenishing sustenance as opposed to an indulgence. This was of course (to the exclusion of getting drunk, which was to our way of thinking at the time) more of a vocation as opposed to recreation.

This orientation towards the utilization of time was not a sacrifice, or an aspiration to martyrdom, it was a prioritization of a precious commodity; the gift of life, which is mysteriously bestowed upon all of us in an unknown quantity upon arrival on this earth; an unconditional gift which could, and often does, unannounced, dissipate into eternity with the same suddenness with which it arrived.

It was still hot. Bill announced to his family, "Not much of a chance that I'll get a call to work before this evening. Let's get packed up and spend the day at the river." My sister in law responded with a blitz of activity, putting together a virtual cornucopia of sustenance, assuring that the individual dietary preferences of her family were meticulously catered to. Glad was a traditional housewife from the fifties. When the man of the house made a decision she went into action providing the logistical support required in order to bring that decision smoothly into reality. She was responsible for the details pertaining to the kids getting ready to go and ensuring that appropriate and adequate provisions were packed, while Bill readied the vehicle for the trip.

I didn't really care where we were going swimming, just as long as we were going to go somewhere I could get wet. Water was in my blood, just take me to it and I felt like I was returning to my spawning grounds. Come to think of it, I did a considerable amount of spawning in my youth on the banks and in the waters of the river. "Hey Bill!" I shouted, "Have you got any of those old, truck, tire, inner tubes out in the garage?" After mastering the art of independent swimming I considered aquatic toys something to be shunned like training wheels on a bicycle. But, I did remember that when I didn't know how to swim toys made an outing to the water much more enjoyable. I was thinking about Bill's four kids, none of whom yet knew how to swim. I can honestly say I wasn't all that concerned if they had a good time during the outing or not. I was thinking that if they were bored and they complained, this might result in a premature return from the water's edge, thus cutting into my swim time. Selfish on my part granted, but what difference does it make if all concerned are content and have a good time?

"I think there might be some tubes out there that haven't been cut up yet." he replied. "There should be a pile of them in the garage under the work bench, dig around and you should be able to find a few that don't have serious damage. Find the ones that look easiest to patch up. Should be some patches on the shelf by the window, you've used those heat sealing patches before haven't you?"

The reason he had so many inner tubes was because he had found a way to recycle them. You know those bungie, tie-down cords you can buy now days? Bill invented them years ago. He would pick up old inner tubes that were beyond marketable repair at local service stations. Never offering to pay mind you! If they didn't have any to give away he would take his business elsewhere. He would cut them into inch wide sections producing versatile, long, rubber bands, which worked great to bundle up sleeping bags or other such materials.

"No problem." I responded, as I headed out the door. Do you remember doing things as a kid and having an adult "teach" you how? They talk to you about it, show you how to do it, and tell you how to do it, and then, typically, get in your way and do it for you before you've had a chance to attempt to learn or master the task. Or better yet, they hover over you like some, scavenger bird waiting for you to make one wrong move so they can pounce on you with a self-righteous indignation proclaiming that you were unable to execute the task precisely as it was instructed—as if anyone were capable of picking up a violin and playing it perfectly after hearing a lecture on how to do so. With some, twisted sense of moral duty they proceed to peel the flesh from your self-esteem with their well-meaning talons of criticism. With words they proclaim boundless faith in your abilities, while actions and neurotic supervision bespeak the expectation and even gleeful anticipation of your impending failure, operating under the twisted fallacy that by virtue of their divine instruction anyone should be able to execute the task in question with flawless precision the very first time. When Bill gave you a task to work on his every fiber conveyed his faith in your ability to succeed. Underlying this faith was an understanding that any aspiration that did not meet with complete initial success was an opportunity to learn something new. To my way of thinking, if he believed I could do a credible, competent job of the task at hand, who was I to question his assessment of the situation? The first time I ever experienced this with my brother was when I was sitting in his lap, steering a battleship of a Cadillac down the side streets of Gladstone. He was giving me a few tips, hinting that it was a good idea to steer a little closer to the centerline when approaching a car parked along the street. I didn't get the hint and just when I was about to tail end a parked pickup truck, Bill grabbed the wheel and veered the Caddie on a safer path. Rather than chastise me for my inability to pilot the vehicle appropriately, my brother told me about the time he had not paid sufficient attention to a parked car and actually collided with it in a similar situation. There was no judgement within him. He knew the lessons he had learned in life I to would need to learn.

Some, twenty years ago Bill was put in charge of a training program for new engineers on the railroad. His supervisors were at first impressed with the results he was producing, as virtually all of his charges were scoring in the top quarter of the test used to certify new engineers. When they found that he was sharing the content of the examination with his student, he was questioned about such shabby, instructional techniques. Bill's reply was, "If the material on the test is what I want them to know as a result of the class, what's the point of keeping what I want them to know a secret?" Of course his supervisors, in their infinite wisdom, decreed this to be a morally flawed perspective and removed him from his teaching position. Twenty years later, the present day, cutting edge, educational research recommends that teachers illuminate the target of instruction, and that evaluation should be a learning experience as well. Tests should not be a top-secret tool used to trick students into failing. Bill was using common sense while the educational community was utilizing PHD's and millions in research funding to come up with what a rational evaluation would dictate in any educational setting; cut out the bullshit and ensure that students are clear about what the hell it is you want them to learn.

Out in the garage I dug out three, decent looking tubes. I filled an old washtub half full of water to submerge the tubes in after filling them with air to check for leaks. I marked the location of the holes by scratching the area with a nail, and then commenced the patching process. To be honest, I loved fire as much as the water, still do. Funny how that works. I remember one time I was playing with matches in the garage at home. I was putting those wooden matches with the phosphorus, strike anywhere heads that we called cowboy sticks down the barrel of my BB gun and then shooting them about. If you picked out the matches with large quantities of the self-igniting material, the friction of that match against the barrel of the gun as the match was expelled caused ignition, sending a flaming projectile out of the muzzle of that demon Daisy. If you wanted to utilize ammunition of an inferior quality with smaller tips, one had to resort to shooting, preferably at an oblique angle, at some hard object or surface, like a cement floor. While engrossed in this pass time I failed to notice that one or more of those pyrotechnic projectiles had lodged in some flammable materials stored on a shelf where our cat was nursing a brood of kittens. The match smoldered for some time and eventually gave birth to a full-fledged fire, causing considerable damage to the structure and substantial, but not life threatening, damage to the cats. The poor kittens were left with disfiguring reminders of my carelessness. One of these cats lost an ear, eye, and the tip of its tail as a result. Ironically, I have a nephew who lost an eye in his youth to a BB gun and half of the index finger on his right hand in an auto accident. When he saw that cat he knew he had found a kindred spirit. He gave that cat a good home and life. I always though the cat would have looked great with a pirate's patch on its eye like its master. Now that I think of it I never told my nephew that his cat had, in an indirect way, suffered its injury via the same medium by which he had sustained his. I still feel guilty to this day about having been reckless and starting that fire. I was never that concerned that I could have possibly burnt down our house and a considerable portion of our neighborhood, it was spawned from the knowledge that I had inflicted pain on those undeserving, living creatures.

It's funny how fate works. About two weeks before the fire I had been out walking in an area where they were excavating to expand the freeway near my house. I investigated several unlocked, work sheds at the job site and found, to my surprise and great joy, that one of them was brimming with high explosives, another with detonators. I made a beeline home and called the only person I knew that owned a car and I could trust with my newly discovered, terrorist treasure trove. My plan was to steal the stuff and become an environmental terrorist. It seemed logical at the time; destroy things that belonged to people because they in turn were destroying things that did not belong exclusively to them, according to me. I can only guess at my rationale; they did it first so that justified my retaliation. Lucky for me, my family, and all of my neighbors, my buddy refused to help me confiscate the goodies, which would have been hid in the garage, the same one I set on fire. Lucky break for all of us, including the cat family.

The landlord was an asshole and I didn't give a damn what happened to his house. On investigation and my subsequent interrogation, he construed my humility to be appropriate atonement for my sins. My guilt was driven by my responsibility for the injuries I inflicted on those innocent little kittens. To this very day I am much more careful when playing with fire of any sort as a direct result of that unfortunate experience. That is of course to the exclusion of the time a few years later when I actually succeeded in burning the very same garage to the ground. But that was a bonafide accident and a completely different story.

As I was torching the patches on the tubes I noticed the charred trusses supporting the roof in Bill's garage, testament to yet another fire, which I was fortunate enough to have witnessed. Bill and another brother of mine, Doug, were working on an old car in the driveway. Bill had instructed Doug to pour a mixture of gasoline and motor oil, a general tonic for ailing automobiles, from an old coffee can fashioned into a make shift pitcher, down the esophagus of the carburetor of the colicky car while Bill cranked on the ignition; a gallant attempt to breath new life into a vehicle past its prime and more suited to a final resting in some junk yard. From several feet away I was intently observing, striving to glean bits of manly, car repair secrets I could use to court and capture the hearts, and hopefully, the favors of females in the doldrums of internal combustion distress. I heard the motor turn about the same time I saw flames lick out from both sides of the upraised hood of the car. I caught a glimpse of Doug swirling around like a methamphetamine ballerina with leotards full of leeches, his outstretched arm on fire, clenching in his hand the three pound coffee can full of petrol, which was spewing forth a trail of fire in a strobe like arch following the erratic gyrations of his incinerating arm. As he careened about the yard I could envision him in a grass skirt on a sunny, sandy, south pacific, island beach, one of those Polynesian fire dancers that perform with flaming swords. My only guess as to why he didn't explode into a cloud of soot and charcoal on the spot was the fact the can was bent at the opening to a narrow slit to give more pouring control, considerably reducing the surface area of the fuel available for evaporation and the resulting combustion, thus restricting the overall magnitude of the blaze. Initially, Bill seemed to derive wanton entertainment value from the incident, laughing with unbridled hysteria for that brief moment preceding the realization on Doug's part that he ran the risk of becoming a foot note in a barbecue cookbook if he continued to grip the coffee can like a Gila Monster with its jaws clamped onto the heel of some yuppie, Berkinstocked day trekker. When he finally released the canister, it tumbled gracefully through the air with a fiery, comet like tail, retaining the majority of its contents until it crashed on the floor of Bill's garage, at which time it spilled its contents, instantaneously exploding into a gigantic, hungry fireball which, quite nicely, engulfed the structure in flames. No longer able to derive any humor from the situation Bill leapt into action procuring an appropriately rated fire extinguisher from the house and set about dousing the inferno. Doug and the garage both sustained what a casual observer as myself could only evaluate as superficial cosmetic damage, which posed no long term potential for loss of utility.

As I smelled the rubber and glue on the Vulcan tire patch burn, I watched as the burning process produced similar, but never identical, small, serpentine slivers of sooty smoke, which seemed much too substantial to dissipate so quickly into the air. As I waited for the first trace of a firm, black ash residue to indicate the healing, repair process of the rubber tube's completion, I marveled at how the seed of a vivid memory such as the one I had just revisited could reside in a mundane, innate object such as a charred piece of wood. I wondered if everything on this earth at one time or another, would ultimately be impregnated with a secret, having the power to conjure a story or memory for someone. Maybe this is what the Indians meant when they claimed that even the rocks of the earth contained part of the Great Spirit. Or, it could be that's what my high school counselor meant when she said I had rocks in my head. Didn't matter much at the time, I had to get the tubes in the car and make ready for a trip to the river.

Bill was an advocate of the virtues of Cadillac cars. Not for any altruistic or social status which can be equated with this particular Detroit dinosaur. His affinity stemmed equally from two, major influences. The first was that the OPEC oil embargo had caused the price of gasoline to rise to a half a dollar, making the eight miles to the gallon that a Nimitz class auto got on the freeway a liability on the resale market. As a result, used Cadillacs soon became cheap to purchase. When queried as to why he had not purchased a new, or newer, model of car which would produce a substantial increase in fuel economy Bill would respond with convincing calculations projecting the cost of fuel, the interest paid on a car loan, and how far you would have to drive a new VW over the span of five years, as opposed to purchasing a used Cadillac every year or so for a few hundred bucks. It went like this, he would buy a Caddie for three hundred dollars, drive it for a year or so, spend one hundred or so to keep it running, then sell it for two hundred bucks and use that to buy another junker. He was out two hundred bucks for basic transportation for a year. He ended his line of reasoning with the question of how a man could justify spending that much money a month on a new car when he had kids at home to care and provide for. True to his word, he never made payments on a new vehicle until all four of his children were out of the brood nest.

Except for a car he purchased one Christmas Eve. Bill had dawned a Santa suit and was patrolling the neighborhood in a Cadillac that looked like a tail fin prototype for a Boeing 707. He was spreading some Christmas cheer, visiting the homes of his neighbors, and handing out little packages of nuts and candy to the children. To his ultimate detriment, the majority of adults who welcomed him into their homes had not read *The Night Before Christmas* in quite some time. Rather than milk and cookies, Santa Bill was treated to Bourbon, Scotch, and Rum. When Santa came to his sleigh was pointing skyward at a 30-degree angle, a mangled heap atop a brand new and totaled, Buick Rivera. The police officer that responded to the accident shook Bill and reportedly exclaimed,

"Don't you think you've had a bit too much to drink Santa?" He never got a citation, but he did take over the payment of that Buick.

He took out his first car loan when he was forty-five years old. Quite an accomplishment for a working class stiff! The second reason Bill drove a Cadillac was reliability. Bill's philosophy on cars was buy it cheap, fix it yourself, and sell when the prognosis was impending major mechanical malfunction. During the three decades Bill adhered to and advocated this perspective on cars, I would venture to estimate, he owned no less than twenty of them, becoming intimately aware of their individual characteristics in terms of reliability, reparability, and resale value.

After hearing these arguments I was sold. I remember trying to count Cadillacs whenever I was in-route on the open road. I was convinced that over a relatively short period of time I had observed a statically relevant increase in the number of Cadillacs on the highway. The word had evidently gotten out. I was a bit concerned about what the availability of these monsters would be when I came of driving age, but it seemed that something always came between me and owning a Caddie.

This brings to mind the first time I was ever involved in the process by which Bill acquired a new, new to him, car. He would secure a copy of the Little Nickel Ads, a free publication utilized by lower income individuals to buy and sell stuff. He would get the jump on other shoppers by waiting at the publishers and get a copy before they hit the street. Bill would skim through the autos for the sale section and circle in red anything priced at two hundred bucks or less. Then he would call for more details before making a trip for a test drive or visual inspection. He quickly narrowed the choice down to one vehicle. The ad said it didn't run and the owner wasn't sure why. Bill concluded it had to be something simple and the owner had no knowledge of auto repair, or it was someone that knew the problem was serious and was playing dumb so as to unload the vehicle on a sucker. Bill put me in charge of calling on the car.

I contacted the owner and he indicated the car had crapped out on him about two miles from his home. He claimed to have no clue as to the nature of the break down. He convinced me that he was not feigning ignorance of auto repair. Due to extenuating circumstances, not only did he have to walk from home to show the car where it had expired, he could not do so until about ten that evening. As it was eight in the morning at the time of the call, I assured him we would meet him at the car at the prearranged time. He gave me detailed directions to the vehicle and sought assurance of my sincerity of interest in the car several times during our conversation. I assured him my intentions were honorable and I would be punctual. As the day progressed, Bill and I grew more intoxicated swilling Old Mr. Boston's Apricot Brandy. It's not entirely clear to me if we actually maintained just enough common sense to stay out of a car and off the highway, or if we simply forgot about our rendezvous with the broken down vehicle. In all probability it was a fortunate stroke of luck that I had lost the directions to the resting place of the car.

During the course of the next day, Bill inquired, "I thought we were going to look at a car yesterday. I wonder if that poor bastard walked down there to meet us? Rained quite a bit last night." After a good laugh, and a few belts of what was left of Old Mr. Boston, it was decided that I should call the guy with the car just to see if he still had it and was willing to talk again. Underneath the phone I had found the lost directions he had given me the day before.

Initially, he was a bit of a grouch complaining about the inclement weather he had endured while walking to the car, actually resorting to cursing at me over the phone. "Where the hell were you?" he castigated, "I spent an hour waiting in that car, soaking wet and without a heater! It was just lucky I flagged down a fella that lives on my lane and got a ride half way home!"

I knew at that instance that this was no ordinary guy trying to sell a car. I could sense the presence of a sheltered life that, up to now, had little or no exposure to sophisticated, practical joking. As that old Asian proverb says, "When the student is ready the teacher will come."

I responded with indignation, "What do you mean, where the hell was I? Where the hell were you and your damn car? I drove around most of the night and didn't see a white Chevy alongside the road; did you sell it to someone else? I thought we had a deal buddy!" When he asked about where it was that I had gone to inspect the vehicle, I read the directions back to him, changing a few details, pretending to have misinterpreted his instructions. He apologized for being upset and asked if I was still interested in the car. I insisted I most certainly was and another rendezvous was arranged for that evening. When no one arrived to meet this mysterious, auto peddler that time either, Bill and I were sure he would never speak to us again.

The next morning after the aborted engagement, I called the gentleman to complain that he was not on time. He was adamant in making counter allegations that it was I who had not been on time. It was resolved that we had somehow managed a second mix up on our timing, and yet another arrangement to see the car was negotiated.

He was understandably skeptical, but I assured him that we had given the car a thorough evaluation while awaiting his arrival the night before and that I was on the level about purchasing it. To consummate the deal, I gave him my phone number to call in the event he was unable to fulfill his obligation once again, thus placing the onus of the past failures on his shoulders. He began to protest that he had done everything he had committed to doing, but I cut him off, chastising him for rehashing the past and quibbling over details. The poor fellow could not fathom that another human being would actually go to such lengths to dupe another and derive any entertainment from such antics. It was simply beyond his realm of potential scenarios. I was beginning to feel a growing, moral imperative demanding that I provide the lost soul with appropriate instruction and indoctrination in the convoluted, encumbering nuances encountered when one enters into the used car transaction zone.

As could have been expected, Bill and I were a bit negligent with our events calendar and failed once again to appear at the prescribed meeting with the perplexed, auto merchant. When he called that evening I was ecstatic. He was upset having walked during the last week close to ten miles through all sorts of weather to sell a car that neither he, nor the potential purchaser, had an iota of interest in owning. He began by unleashing a litany of profanity that I had not up to that point felt him capable of.

"You sonofabitch!" he began, "I missed my ride to work last night because of you! You don't even want to buy it; I don't know why I ever believed you! The pay I lost is more than the damn car is worth!"

I'm sorry to say that when he expressed disappointment that I had let his belief in me down. Rather than feeling remorse or guilt, my gut reaction was that the guy was still on the hook. I responded with a hurt, self-righteous indignation. "Listen pal, you're not the only one with car problems. I was driving with my grandpa on the way to buy your damn car and mine broke down. I had to pack that old man on my back for over two hours to get him home. The old buzzard's got a weak bowel and bladder. Out of respect for him I won't go into the details of how that played out during his piggyback ride."

There was silence on the line until my friend resumed, "I'm sorry, it's just been a bad week, the car breaking down and trying to arrange rides to work and all, it's getting expensive. Let's forget about the car. I'll sell it to the junk yard, they said they will tow it and give me fifty bucks."

"Nonsense," I said, "We have a deal, right? That car is worth a hundred bucks if it worth a cent, said so yourself. I wouldn't hear of someone taking advantage of your good nature. Look, I have to be out of town for the next few days, but my grandpa can drive. I'll send him out tomorrow with the cash for the car and then I can pick it up when I get back. That way I'll have someone to show me the way. Maybe he'll have better luck figuring out your directions. Seems like you change them every time I talk to ya. Good thing you ain't a cab driver or something like that."

Why this individual would have believed me, or spent another moment of his time conversing with me on the phone, is still beyond me. "I haven't changed . . ." he paused momentarily and continued, " . . . Oh, never mind. If you're sure it's not too much trouble for your grandfather." He seemed oblivious to the reality that he was the only one to have experienced any inconvenience during our extended, business negotiations.

"Grandpa's a tough old buzzard and he loves to drive, just give me a time for him to be there. He drives an old, gray Rambler that smokes like hell. You can't miss him. He can close the deal and I'll pick the car up when I get back into town."

"OK!" my car salesman replied, "I'll have to walk to the bus stop and try and catch the last bus to town, go into work, and hang around until my shift starts. I should be at the car tomorrow around ten a.m., no later than ten-fifteen. That's tomorrow! In the morning!"

"Sure, good idea!" I answered, "That way you could find a ride home with a buddy or something, make sure you're on time. I'll have grandpa there at nine sharp."

"No! No, not nine, ten! Please, write it down! Ten o'clock in the morning, tomorrow morning."

"Hey pal, just take it easy, I got it. Just be there with the title and we can close this deal."

Suffice it to say that my Grandpa conjured from an overactive imagination, never materialized to buy the car. Some time later I happened onto the scrap of paper with the fellow's phone number who had gallantly attempted to sell the car. I gave him a call, disguising my voice so I sounded like grandpa. "Ello?" I bellowed into the phone, "This Grandpa, you have car? I'm coming on da bus to pick 'er up. Bring it home on bus, OK?"

Exasperated the car guy implored, "You can't take a car on the bus, the damn thing doesn't even run. You'll have to tow it."

"What's wrong with your toes?" Grandpa demanded.

"Not my toes, tow it, the car! That's how you get it home."

As I could no longer maintain my composure, I thanked the seller and informed him I was on my way to pick up the car, then hung up. At about midnight, I had grandpa call again. "Ello?" he said, "You got car for sale?"

The tormented fellow on the other end responded, "You must have the wrong number, I don't have any cars." then he hung up on Grandpa.

Lucky for this guy, we somehow lost his phone number after that last call and were not able to contact him any further. We had every intention of placing monthly ads in the paper offering enticing deals on automobiles on his behalf. I learned a valuable lesson about life here. Sometimes life is too serious to take seriously all the time, and there's a difference between a malicious attempt at a practical joke and one that's harmless. As long as feelings aren't hurt too bad and no real damage is done in the process everything and everyone is fair game.

There are many striking similarities between life and the used car racket. Sometimes you have to lay your money down, roll the dice and find out if you're going to be a winner or looser that day. As with so many other facets of life, you tend to get out of it what you put in. When I bought my first car I couldn't help but be reminded of the fun I took at the expense of that misfortunate fellow with the car broke down at the side of the road.

Following the enlightened path of my brother, I snatched a copy of the *Little Nickel Ads* hot off the press. I zeroed in on a vintage Datsun four-door. It had all the right attributes, a home in the high rent district, undiagnosed engine problems, and a price tag of two hundred bucks. Bill had this theory that rich folks had their vehicles serviced by competent mechanics and considerably devalued a used vehicle in general and those with cosmetic damage in particular. The ideal environment for a bargain hunting car shopper. I went to check out the car and was amazed at the condition. The vehicle had indeed been cared for, but it had developed a rattling noise in the transmission. I took that little Datsun home and drove it for three months, all the while intending to tear into it and identify the source of the racket it was making. My chronic procrastination came back on me with a vengeance when the transmission of my car exploded while I was barreling down I-5.

I just pulled into my driveway as that valiant little auto expired. At a loss of what to do, I remembered having seen a certificate of transmission repair in the paperwork that came with the car. On closer inspection I found that the previous owner, a Mr. Leroy Beshears, had paid one thousand five hundred dollars to have the transmission rebuilt less than a two thousand miles ago.

I got Leroy on the phone and presented my case. "Look," I said, "This shop doesn't know that I bought the car from you. If you take it in to have this warranty honored, no one will be the wiser."

To this Leroy replied, "I don't think I could do that, it wouldn't be honest."

I rebutted, "What's worse, you doing that or them taking your money for doing a shabby job?" He was adamant that he would not help, so I was on my own.

I called the shop and posed as Mr. Beshears. I informed them I was bringing my vehicle in for them to repair under warranty.

They had no objections and said it would take a few days to determine the cause of the break down.

When they called back, I was informed that the damage was the result of faulty parts other than those which they had serviced. I argued to no avail. I knew then and there that the time had come to accept my losses and walk away from the table with as much dignity as I could salvage. Holding my head high and drawing an inspirational breath I spoke, "That little car has been in my family for twenty some years. I drove it, my kids drove it and I want my grand kids to have it. Money is no object. You do whatever it takes to get her back on the road." The repairman assured me he would have it running better than new in a week or two. I had no intention of ever going to pick it back up.

Over the course of several months the shop quit calling me, beseeching me to come up with twenty five hundred dollars to reclaim a car I had paid two hundred for. One night at a social gathering I was relaying this story to a friend of mine who expressed an interest in purchasing this very same vehicle. I sold it to him for one hundred dollars and drove him down to the shop where the car was in a fenced area.

"Nile," I whispered, "Once you get over the fence, you'll have to pull this battery over with the rope." I had taken the battery out of the vehicle when I dropped it off for repairs. Nile scaled the cyclone fence with ease and as I was readying the delivery system for the battery that little Datsun roared to life. I had just enough time to jump out of the way as Nile crashed to gate to the fence and sped down the road.

About a month later I got a nasty letter from the city of Seattle. It seemed that my little Datsun had been involved in a rampage of vandalism. A dozen parking meters had been decimated, a fire hydrant damaged, and the vehicle came to rest under a beer delivery truck parked behind a down town pub. All told, I had in my hand a bill for close to three thousand dollars worth of damage. I wrote the city a polite letter explaining the circumstances and never heard anything back. I have often wondered, however, if Leroy ever got any calls from that transmission shop.

Chapter 7

*B*ill and Glad's four kids' ages spanned five to twelve years. Getting them ready for a road trip was a considerable challenge. By the time they were rounded up and herded into the car one was either crying, hungry, or needed to go to the bathroom. By virtue of his occupation Bill was attentive to the clock when it came to travel. A train runs on the clock and must depart and arrive on time. This commitment to leaving the station on time was about the only work related trait I could detect that Bill allowed to seep into his private life. When he selected a departure time he was serious about keeping to it.

For the majority of individuals I have known the line between their occupation and their private lives are more often than not, blurred, bent, or completely indiscernible. Bill seldom spoke about his occupation and on the rare occasion when he did he had a motive or goal in mind. In retrospect, I now understand why it was that he maintained such a definitive separation between employment and his other life as a family man. His view of work was that it was something that was required of a man in order to be a good father and provider. He resented the general, exploitative arrangement between the bourgeoisie and the proletariat. This is not to say he had any aversion to strenuous labor, quite the contrary. I have seen the man work his job and on a project for weeks-on-end, surviving on what couldn't add up to more than four hours of sleep a day. His resentment stemmed from the travesty of an economic system allowing an individual to place a monetary value on the time of another human being and in doing so, typically devaluing that time in comparison to his own. Bill considered the time we are given on this earth so priceless, he felt insulted and exploited by the capitalist arrangement. He summed it up with a favorite saying of his, "The only difference between a twenty dollar prostitute and an hundred dollar one is the amount of money they charge." What he meant was that we all strive to receive the maximum monetary return in exchange for our labors, but seldom come away without feeling we have been exploited to a certain extent. This arrangement necessitated that a man give up some of the time he would prefer to spend with his family in exchange for the money required to provide for his family. I assumed at the time that it was the desire of all men to stay home and be attentive to the needs of their families and not be required to go to the marketplace and sell their labor. I found out later he was in a minority, but I'm happy to say I'm a lifetime member of that and many other social, political, and philosophical minorities.

For Bill, the separation of work and family was the key to the preservation of his self-identity. Viewing the world of work in this way Bill extolled the virtues of an education in that it not only empowers an individual to choose a vocation which they find rewarding, but it also allows them a more equitable negotiation on compensation.

When he was home Bill was not willing to give up an un-reimbursed moment of time talking about his job, which he referred to as 'the corporation'. He never fell back on his job related experiences as a default mode for moments where he was at a loss for words. When he spoke he wove stories with quotes from ancient and recent history, giving the impression of a well schooled, international traveler. I think he finished high school and he did indeed travel extensively to the library and that last realm of unconquered frontier, the endless expanse that we refer to as our minds and souls. A natural pastor he formulated a myriad of theories about human behavior by extensive reading, philosophizing, introspection, and conclusion drawing from observations of and interactions with his fellow men. He immersed himself in the sea of humanity like a true preacher devoid of any ulterior motive of saving or converting souls; he did so out of sheer love of humanity.

He tried to go to college once. While I am not in command of the exact details of the story, my best recollection is that it went something like this. He spent about a week in a history class at a community college. As a result of his interactions in the class, and on the recommendation of the instructor, the college administration offered him a teaching position. I heard the story from a source other than my brother and never got around to asking him why he never took the position or continued with school.

It is interesting how events impact all of us differently. While in high school I knew that I would attend college for the simple reason that Bill emphasized the virtues of acquiring an education and helped me to realize my personal value and worthiness of a formal education. He was just as strong an advocate that his four children attend college as well, all of whom he would have gladly put through the colleges of their choice on his tab. Yet none of them were inclined to do so, and all turned out to be successful, happy individuals. I find it curious as to why Bill's advocacy of the acquisition of a formal, post secondary education persuaded me and not his own children, or for that matter himself, to attend college. But this would be a droll existence if all experiences effected each of us in the same manner. How would it be with us today if primordial man had heeded the warning of elders in the clan not to play with fire? Cooking might never have been discovered.

As we went through the convolutions required getting the crew in the Caddie Clipper, as well as the various support materials: blankets, water toys, food and drink, I caught a trace of frustration flash across my brother's face, we were slipping behind schedule. In short order all passengers and parcels were secure and we were on our way. With the top down and the radio blaring we pulled out of the driveway. About a block from the house Bill realized that the family dog Mister was in hot pursuit of the vehicle.

The best way to describe how this critter looked would be to recall the time Glad was looking as some newly developed pictures someone had taken. She handed me one with a strange looking, black object and asked me with all sincerity, "Why the hell would someone take a picture of a stump?" That stump was Mister. He had a peculiar habit of burying waffles in the gravel driveway, but not by digging a hole and covering it up like some cartoon hound.

Mister was more of a muzzle plower. He pushed the gravel with his snout, making little pyramids of gravel, entombing the morsel he had been tossed from the breakfast table. Someone in charge of the camera must have construed this to be a National Geographic moment and captured the ritual on film for posterity.

Bill turned around and took the dog home. We kids thought it funny to see that old dog run behind the car. A bizarre looking creature, Mister was a stubby mass of black, woolly curls which made it near impossible to tell which end was which until he either wagged his tail, opened his mouth, or relieved himself. As we attempted to embark again, someone called the dog and he was more than willing to give hot pursuit once again. Bill was pissed off this time, one of the few times I had ever seen him get mad at his kids. The gist of the scolding was that he was going out of his way to do something fun for us kids and we were unappreciative in that we were making things more difficult for him. Mediocre on the spectrum of chastisement, but from someone whom I had the utmost respect and admiration, it stung like a cat of nine. I wanted to proclaim my innocence; it had been my nice who had coaxed the beast to give chase. I resigned myself to guilt by association and slunk down in my seat.

The vividness and intensity of this recollection seems indicative to me of how the small stuff in life is really big stuff. In retrospect, this incident stands out more in my memory that graduating from college (I fell asleep and missed it), or the time I received a twenty thousand dollar, insurance check (I took a year off from reality and don't much remember what I spent it on). I'm committed to having a big stuff life, just some events are bigger than others.

In no time we were at the river. Bill was the first in the water. The Native American blood in our family line was most pronounced in him, bestowing upon his skin a natural, bronze, suntan tone that bespoke of a healthy vitality. He was fond of wearing Speedo swimsuits, not much different than going buck ass naked.

I remember one time we were at the beach on the Fourth of July. Why the hell my family always seemed to migrate to the ocean shore on this holiday I'm not sure. Bill had cut his foot on a chard of glass in the sand, which was remedied by a bandage held in place by a sock on his wounded foot. He was strutting down the beach, one blue sock on his wounded foot, skin tight neon banana yellow Speedo trunks, and oversized K-Mart sun glasses that resembled the chrome bumper off a sub-compact sports car. As he strode past a large group of admirers on the beach I couldn't resist screaming, "Hey, Buddy! Why the hell did you stuff one of your socks down the crotch of your swimming trunks?"

I modeled my keen wit after that of my brother Bill. During this particular visit to the ocean, we contrived to provide a bit of entertainment to the tourists wandering along the boardwalk. I had a kite with an ample enough supply of string for it to reach the cover of the low-lying, cloud cover. To the line I attached a light colored, sand pail, which at the proper altitude was rendered virtually invisible as it blended into the cloudy sky. In the bucket I placed several hotdogs. With the proper amount of maneuvering I could situate the pail over the path of pedestrian traffic, give the kite string some slack, and cause hotdogs to rain down on the unsuspecting passers-bye.

On the beach near the boardwalk we would put on a little skit for the benefit of the meandering tourists. My other brother, Scott, was wearing a full-length, hooded, white frock similar to those worn by actors in television depictions of Jesus. He would be saying a prayer over the sinner kneeling in the sand before him, our brother Bill. I'm paraphrasing but it went something like this, "And the fruits of the earth were bountiful, and man thrived in the Eden that God had provided. But soon man grew dissatisfied and restless, beseeching God to give some sign of his omnipotence. God obliged, proclaiming that manna would usher forth from the Heavens and behold; the gates of Heaven swung open and God rained forth hotdogs on his children and all creation."

That was my cue to let loose of the string and pelt the spectators that had gathered around with pork and beef projectiles. It was a Candid Camera moment. Some people would be amazed when the hotdogs would come plummeting down, they would stop to try and determine the origin of the franks. Other people would have the experience of a hotdog dropping from an empty sky right in front of them and never break stride or appear to give the event a second thought or glance. We spent hours repeating this performance and laughing like the drunken fools we were. If it was blasphemy then I'm sure that God has forgiven us by now. No one could laugh that hard and long and have a trace of malicious intent in his soul. I am convinced that this world would be much more to the liking of the Creator if more of us would spend more time laughing and enjoying the simple pleasures this life is.

It has next to nothing to do with this story, but I can't, in good conscious, leave this detail out. During this very same excursion to the beach a friend of my nieces and I were walking along the beach back to the beach house after the bars in town had closed. I pulled a stop sign out of the ground and was parading down the shoreline when officers of the law corralled us. I proclaimed my compatriot's innocence in the crime and convinced the police to let him go. In the process of putting the cuffs on me, I must have stumbled and clutched at the officer in an attempt to keep from falling. I latched on to his holstered sidearm and this was misinterpreted as an attempt to arm myself and make my escape. An accident which resulted in a severe thump on my head, compliments of the nightstick the other officer was clutching. When my partner from the night before came and bailed me out the next day, my bumbling collision with the police officer the night before had been embellished by those seeking to facilitate my freedom. They were all convinced that I had indeed disarmed the officer and discharged his pistol before being subdued. Keep in mind this story had been fabricated without any input or encouragement on my part. The best I was able to muster given the severity of the charges against me was to use my one phone call to place an order at Pizza Hut. I spent the night in jail, and was given a hero's welcome when I was released. The fabricated story my friends had made up sounded better than the one I had in mind, so I left things pretty much as they were.

I felt a little guilty that some guy I had just met got stuck making my bail. When I returned home I sold several, prized possessions and sent this Good Samaritan a check in the mail. I got a call from my niece a few days later, the one that had invited my benefactor to the beach. She wanted directions to my house, saying she was thinking about paying me a visit. Half an hour later she and my rescuer were knocking on the door.

Her friend and now mine took the check from his pocket and said, "I make lots of money in my business and my friends know it and hit me up for loans all the time. This is the first one that's ever been paid back without me having to twist an arm or two." With that he placed the check in an ashtray and set it ablaze. Then we proceeded to do the same to the town that evening.

Bill dove in and swam underwater for about thirty yards. I had lived on the very same river for a number of years and prided myself at being able to out swim anyone visiting my beach. One summer some flatlander came running down the beach whining that his boat had capsized upstream in the rapids and he would give anyone that could get it back to shore twenty bucks. I watched several muscle men types attempt to pull the overturned boat back to the dock, struggling valiantly but ultimately in vain, fighting the current. When I rose to take the challenge, I swam to the boat, about three fourths of the way across the river, snagged the bow line, then swam back at something like a twenty degree angle with the current, making landfall about a fifth of a mile down stream from the beach from which I had started. I tied the boat, walked back to the boat ramp, and picked up my money. To be a good swimmer you have to be as smart as you are strong and remember that swimming in a river is a lot like navigating that big treacherous river of love; if you jump in you had better have enough sense to go with the flow of the main current, and if you plan to fight it, you had best keep your feet on dry land least you end up on the bottom, a decomposing feast for the multitude of scavengers awaiting the demise of drown dimwits and dejected lovers.

I was wondering how someone twenty years my senior that spent next to no time in the water, as far as I could tell, was able to swim with such authority. As he breached the surface his muscular back glistened as the water rolled off. In that instant I was transported back to a memory of my childhood. Like I said, my chronological memory isn't that great, something could have happened two weeks ago and I might refer to it as two months ago or, just as easily, the other way around. I figure that as long as I'm not lying it's not that important.

I was about four years old at the Molalla River with Bill and a family friend by the name of Fritz. If anyone else was there I don't remember. I do remember being on Bill's back in the water and him swimming across what appeared to me at the time to be a raging unfordable torrent of frothing purgatory. Surrounded by perils and dangers, which were beyond my quantification or comprehension at that age. I can still revisit the safety and invincibility I felt while perched on his back in the face of all the destructive forces of this world that the river represented to me at the time. While saddled on the strong back of a man whom I instinctively knew was to me unique above all others, I had no real concept that he and I were brothers. All I knew was there was a bond of love and trust that no river could compromise or come between.

As I watched my brother swim across the river I pondered how it was with the world and me. It seemed that a man divides his time between three major realms, the present, past, and future. When you have relatively few experiences, your focus tends to lean in the direction of the present. As a young man, no longer a child, the future is where you live as you contemplate the accomplishments and great deeds you will achieve. When your pace begins to slow and the strength in your arm begins to fade, the past is the place where your heart and mind will increasingly travel for consolation. I sat in humble appreciation of simply being alive, enjoying the warmth radiating from the sun, the memory I was visiting, and the gratitude I felt for having such a man for a brother.

This also ignited my recollection of a more terrifying event that had taken place while on a camping excursion to the Pacific Ocean. Bill's son, Steve, had been swept out to sea by a rip tide. People were running around the beach hysterically when Bill arrived on the scene. Hearing that his son had been taken by the tide, he dove into the treacherous, frigid waters. Steve was just a dot on the surface of the ocean that could only been seen when a wave would raise him high enough on the horizon to be observed. Bill managed to reach his son and swim back safely to shore.

When I talked to Bill about the incident some years later, he said that by the time he had reached Steve the only thing he was thinking about was that he had no intention of letting his son die alone. He was convinced he didn't have the strength to make it back to shore alone, and certainly not enough to swim for two. He wasn't sure how he had made it back. All he could remember was being on the shore and people insisting that he seek medical attention. He refused on the rationale that all he needed was some rest and to throw up the salt water in his stomach.

Steve related his version of the story to me shortly after his father's funeral. He recalled being swept further and further out to sea and not being able to see any people on the shore, but then, just for a moment, standing on the shore was a man, larger than life, who suddenly disappeared into the water. Steve knew that man was his father and that he would soon be rescued. He figured his dad had pulled him out of every tight spot he had ever been in and he had no reason to doubt his fathers' ability to do so this time. When Bill reached his son, he was shouting, "Where's Craig?"

In the confusion on the shore, Bill was under the impression that his nephew Craig was also in the water. Steve assured him that he was alone. Craig was safe on shore as Bill and Steve were soon to be. Here was a man that was convinced he and his son were about to meet their doom and still he managed to be concerned about the son of his brother. Had his nephew indeed been in the water there would have been little chance for any of them surviving. They would all have drown while Bill fought those frigid waters with his last breath and ounce of strength, refusing to relinquish his grasp on the two lives he was determined to preserve. But, knowing Bill, chances are he would have tapped into some reserve of inner strength and managed to swim to shore. Bill never once made mention to me, or any other person that I know of, that he thought Craig was also in need of rescue that day.

On the drive home from the river I was sitting up front with my brother and his wife. The top of the Caddie was down and the rear speaker was blasting. Bill never gave any indication he had any interest or admiration for popular music on the radio. In this, and many other arenas, he was on call for his kids, dutifully pushing buttons and spinning dials at their respective, and always conflicting, requests. Offhandedly, and not addressing anyone in particular, he said, "I wonder how hard it would be for a guy to build his own swimming pool?"

I remarked, "Couldn't be that much to it as far as technical stuff, just a hell of a lot of digging would be my guess."

"Would be nice to have in your own back yard on days like this. Rather than spending half the day driving to the river a guy could just step out the back door and jump in."

Bill was not given to idle chatter or directionless conversation when it came to potential projects, I knew something was brewing just over the horizon of his unbridled imagination.

Bill continued, "We've got all that damn room in the backyard there that isn't being used for anything now that the horse is dead. The kids aren't interested in another one. They weren't all that crazy about the first one after the novelty wore off. Be a good spot for a swimming pool. It's ironic. If you look at the material things that rich folks have like a swimming pool, fancy car, nice house, they're all things that working class people like us build for them. Its an unjust system to say the least when a man becomes a skilled craftsman and by virtue of the rules of the society in which he lives he is prohibited from acquiring the finished product of his own hands." Up to that point in my life the only hard work I had ever really done was as an assistant to my brother during numerous, handyman adventures.

I chimed in enthusiastically, "Hell yes, that'd be great! Get a cooler full of beer to set beside the pool, float around on an air mattress all day in the sun. Sounds good to me." I was soon to discover that the leisurely stroll from the back porch to poolside was about as smooth as riding a unicycle down the Ho Chi Min Trail during the Ted Offensive.

Chapter 8

The basic plan for the pool was laid out on the kitchen table early the next day. The depth would increase from the shallow end of three feet to a diving depth of twelve. Linear dimensions would be eighty feet with a width of twenty-five. Bill and I staked out the perimeter and tied a string around the stakes to define the dimensions. I was expecting an imminent, earth moving experience. Yellow behemoths knocking over trees, gouging out craters in the earth, dynamite-blasting bedrock into oblivion as I, clad in stylish cut off Levi jeans and Ray Ban shades, sat in ecstatic anticipation of a marine, world-class, aquatic, theme park in the backyard.

Bill was poking at the ground with a shovel like a hunter nudging a gut shot bear. "If this ground is anything like that in the front yard, there's gonna be lots of rocks when we get down more than a foot or two. We should be able to get a good start on it with the rotor tiller, break up the dirt and move it out with shovels. Looks to me like it's about time to burn off this brush though. Make the digging a lot easier. No point in gumming up the tiller with weeds. Probably ought to clear a firebreak around the fence line, then burn the whole damn field early tomorrow morning. No wind and the dew will keep the intensity down so it doesn't get away from us."

On the surface, the plan seemed reasonable to me. As it included a fire of considerable proportions I could feel the warmth of pyromania percolating in my blood in anticipation of erratic flames licking at the boundaries of a potential, unintentional, urban disaster of catastrophic proportions. Not that I would want to burn down a neighborhood, but if it had to happen I wouldn't mind having a catbird seat to watch it unfold.

We went to work on the fence line: Bill whacking a path of brush and I raking the fallen fodder into the central area of the field. While I considered this activity to be mundane as far as generating any interest to the causal observer I began to get that creeping feeling along my spine you get when someone is watching you from behind.

I was reminded of the terror I felt when my third grade teacher, Mrs. Long, who happened to look more like Mr. Long than he did, would walk around the room during a spelling test, always approaching from behind. I can still hear those hard sole shoes; clip, clop, clip, clopping closer and closer, stopping just behind me. I stopped breathing at the erratic sound of her labored breath, bronchial damage, no doubt the result of screaming at young children for thirty some years. She had that old lady smell reminiscent of an olfactory insult my innocent nose once encountered at a funeral parlor, a smell that I found out later in high school biology was nothing other than formaldehyde. I always pictured her standing behind me in a black hood, holding a broad axe high above her head, awaiting confirmation from the principal to consummate my pending execution. Relief and respiration returned when all she did was whack me across the knuckles with a ruler for the sin of writing with my left hand instead of my right.

I leaned on my rake and looked about. In all, five houses bordered Bill's chunk of land. Interestingly, there just happened to be people in the yards of three of those homes and in the other two individuals could be seen peering out of windows. I remember thinking it quite odd they had nothing better to do on such a beautiful day than watch us labor in the noonday sun. I sensed a malingering dissatisfaction emanating into the atmosphere from the scrutiny we were receiving.

Before I could validate or eradicate my paranoia Bill's neighbor, George, came running in our direction. At first glance I could have sworn he had a miniature rain cloud under each arm, beautiful white fluffy ones, gorged with rain that extruded from them as he ran. When he came closer and I got a better look at him I could see that what I mistook for rain clouds were in actuality poodles.

Judging by his attire and the fact that he was as wet as his furry companions I could only conclude that all three had abruptly terminated a community shower. George raised show dogs, pitiful, neurotic creatures that had all the attributes that made a dog a noble creature bred out of them. All that remained was a purified pathetic gene pool; admirable to eyes more cultured and discriminating than mine. A dog that could star on a TV show but couldn't bury a bone on Monday and remember where to dig it up on Tuesday.

He was screaming something incoherent at Bill as he ran. Come to think of it, I can't remember a time that George actually approached Bill with anything that resembled a normal gait, remaining silent until he was within normal communication distance. Not George, and at least not when he was talking to Bill. He always ran, or walked, with an urgent briskness, deploring Bill to both cease and desist, or beseeching some sort of action.

As he came into audible range I could begin to hear his lament, "Bill! Bill! No fire, no fire! Too late in year, too damn dry. Remember last year? You burned neighbor's yard, big mistake, all those clothes on the line. Poof! Don't do again. Please! Bill." As George was pleading with my brother not to consort with flames or convert our quaint, quiet, little community into a real life version of the last chapter of *Daunte's Inferno*, George was alternating between directing his pleas towards Bill and then towards each of the protesting poodles he held under his arms.

"Now take it easy George," Bill began, "I fought forest fires for years when I was a kid, and if by some mysterious act of God this very field should burst into a spontaneous fiery inferno, then I'll do my utmost to preserve the neighborhood. I wouldn't be able to sleep at night if I knew I was responsible in any way for initiating any sort of activity which resulted in an insurance company having to pay for property loss or damage." Now at the time it didn't quite register with me what the hell Bill meant about the 'Act of God' part. Maybe he liked to play with fire as much as I did and considered it a God like endeavor by virtue of the creative and destructive power that it unleashed. I didn't really care because I knew that somewhere in my imminent future there lurked the fiendish flames of a ferocious field of fire.

George responded, "No, no! No accident, no act of God. Goddamnit Bill, you set fire! Every damn year the same thing." George was getting worked up, and when he did he kicked in a lot of body language and those poor poodles were the current recipients of his physical expressiveness. His boa constrictor hold on each of the creatures had grown tighter; the one under his left arm had slipped until George was holding it in a strangle hold about the neck, while the other had maneuvered to the point that its posterior was in the original position of its head. I could see that the one being strangled was attempting to vocalize its duress, unable to do so as a result of George's grip cutting off it's air supply. George seemed impervious to the critters' squirming and scratching attempts to get free. He also received several bites from the dogs, which caused no reaction on his part. I figured it was like being a beekeeper; you get use to being stung and it gets to where it doesn't bother you.

Just when it looked like he might snuff the life out of the inbred, pitiful fur balls, George dropped them as he began an animated demonstration of how Bill responded when the fire department arrived to investigate what was beginning to sound like a yearly act of God. As close as I could figure, George was pretending he was tending a fire with a long handled, garden tool and a hose, looking for all the world as innocent as Lucifer tossing a gallon of gas on a Girl Scout, weenie roast campfire. As he worked with his imaginary implement, his head and eyes darted from side to side, obviously impervious to the fire raging at his feet, concerned only about being discovered and apprehended. Then, pretending to be Bill speaking to the authorities responding to the blazing back yard, George shrugged his shoulders, rolled his eyes to the heavens and threw his hands in the air and said, "Well Chief, can't say how fire started, lightning? Kids and matches? Damn good thing I home."

I was extremely impressed with his pantomime skit and thought George had missed his calling; this guy was a great actor. Except for his limited fluency with the English language I could see my brother in the real life version. As he put the finishing touches on his performance I could picture in the bargain theatre of my mind the event as it unfolded: Bill stealthily starting the fire under cover of darkness; monitoring it's progress with a hose and shovel; then leaning on the shovel while talking to the Fire Chief, the conversation culminating with Bill feigning innocence, and placing a reassuring, consoling arm around the Fire Chief's shoulders. I enjoyed the sneak preview and couldn't wait to see the full-length feature.

I was awakened at 3:00am with the words, "It's time." I didn't know what it was time for, but I didn't question the validity of the statement. Duty called and I dutifully responded when it beckoned. As I was in the habit of sleeping in my cloths when they were relatively clean, when I was drunk, or when I was fairly certain an expeditious escape might be in order with limited notice, all I needed to do was slip on my shoes and I was good to go. I followed my brother into the darkness to the garage where he was mixing up some sort of evil brew in a five-gallon bucket.

"The best way to mix this stuff is to use about a quart of old motor oil to a gallon of gas, the oil adheres to the grass or whatever you want to burn long enough for the gas to get a good fire going. It slows the combustion of the gas down too, making it burn longer. Put it in these old paper milk cartons and if the fire department shows up, you just toss the incriminating evidence into the fire and play dumb." On top of all the other areas in which Bill was a well-schooled journeyman he was a professional pyro too. I sat in silent humility of his sagely experience and expertise and couldn't begin to express the camaraderie I felt with him at that moment. Bill continued, "The trick is to get the fire line burning as quickly as possible so it burns towards the middle, away from the neighbors, before they have a chance to call the fire department." He stopped for a moment apparently reviewing his memory for details of fires gone by and then continued, "Well, someone always calls. But the goal is to have most of it burnt before the fire department shows. We'll start on opposite sides of the field, start three or four small fires as quickly as you can, then toss the milk carton out into the middle of the field. I'll man the hose, you take the shovel and keep the fire out of the neighbor's yards."

I would have preferred an explosive, flash fire to a controlled burn, but what the hell, a fire's a fire and a big one is always better than a little one. As the individual little blazes grew on the perimeter of the field, they appeared to be lost souls erratically wandering in search of their brethren, drawn to the heat of each other's flames until the ultimate reunion, resulting in a synergistic, self-consuming juggernaut of an inferno intent on engulfing the world in flames. The last thing on my mind was doing anything to impede the progress of this spectacular display of pyrotechnics.

I wasn't sure if it was pleasure pumped by adrenaline or the roaring lion of a fire causing the faint ringing in my ears, or if it was the fire police on their way to spoil the fun. As the true nature of the noise became clearer I could see in the distance the reflection of the flashing, emergency lights flickering in the treetops. The fire trucks made there way to the scene, etching a geometric pattern in the darkness as the procession transversed the main streets and then the adjoining side streets to Bill's abode.

I held back in the cover of darkness at the far end of the field to see how the situation would unfold. I figured that if the cops were going to get involved, there was no point in Bill and I both going to jail. It's not that I minded going to jail. Hell, the first time I did I was sixteen; got locked up for jay walking. I was accompanying my girlfriend to an appointment she had at Planned Parenthood. Typically, I would have protested going along for a medical visit, but I had a vested interest here. I was lending moral support while she was getting fitted for a diaphragm.

I was killing some time out on a deserted, street corner in downtown Portland. It was the middle of the week and about ten at night. I ran across a street completely void of traffic and a cop streaks out of the darkness like a bolt of lightening, issuing me a lecture and a citation for jay walking. The ticket mandated that I attend a pedestrian education class utilizing a curriculum chock full of graphic depictions of what transpires when human flesh is mauled by rubber and steel on the pavement. I thanked the cop for the ticket. Why in the hell I would thank a cop for a ticket I don't understand. I guess it's because when I have to talk to one I switch into a kiss ass mode, and then forget to turn it off when it doesn't do any good. The time to be polite to a pig is when there is a possibility they will let you off with a sermon and warning. Once you get the ticket, what's the point? Anyway, I went back inside and found my girl and her new miniature trampoline ready to be field-tested.

Naturally the fact that I owed a debt to society for a criminal act of podiatry soon slipped my mind. She really was that kind of girl. Several months later some dim wit stole the tags off the license plate of my motorcycle. I had to buy a new one and for security reasons, I stuck it on the back of my helmet. Actually, I put it there primarily because the rules dictated otherwise. In short, I was once again guilty of being a wise ass. I got pulled over a few days after that and the cop asked about my expired plates. I pointed to the valid tag stuck on my helmet and told him the story about the stolen tags. He was sympathetic and understanding and just about to let me go with a warning and assurance from me that I would get the tag off my helmet and onto my plates, when his radio belched out a bench warrant for my arrest. I assured him that it must be a mistake and that he must really want one of my big brothers, like in the Billy Goat Gruff story. The big brothers had more meat on them. He checked on the particulars and my name came back as being wanted for a failure to appear at jay walking school. He apologized for the stupidity of having to arrest me for such a crime and made a feeble attempt at placing partial blame on me for not attending the pedestrian education class and misplacing my license tags. He declined to cuff me when I presented myself in the required posture. To his credit as a human being he used his radio to patch a telephone call; this mind you was a time prior to satellite-facilitated communications. The call allowed me to have someone come and pick up my motorcycle rather than having it impounded, saving me considerable time and money I didn't have, as well as the inconvenience of retrieving my motorcycle from impound at a later date.

The rest of the story parallels Arlo Guthrie's song from the 60's, *Alice's Restaurant*. They threw me in a holding tank with a bunch of guys sharing war stories about what they did to get locked up this time, last time, and the time before that. From what I could gather there was a healthy sampling of assault, larceny, and armed robbery in their illustrious pasts. I was keeping to myself when an intimidating inmate inquired, "What ya in for hippie?"

I mustered all the macho at my disposal and shot back, "Jay walking." An unnatural silence descended on the jail cell as if they had just served liver for lunch.

My inquisitor broke the silence by saying, "Ooooh, one of the baaaad boys." That was the end of it and we all went on telling our stories and talking about how we were innocent victims of an unjust system. That was back in the good old days when inmates were allowed to smoke, and we sealed our newfound kinship with the traditional tobacco ceremony. Lucky for me I had near a full pack of factory rolled smokes to cement our blossoming relationship.

It took several hours to see the judge who fined me all the money I had in my wallet and then released me. The cops drove me to the nearest public road and told me to get out of the car. When I asked about bus fare I was advised to get a job. When I pointed out that I had one and was on my way to work when I had been intercepted the officer slammed his door and sped off, spewing me with dust and gravel. Let that be a lesson to all of us.

The first emergency vehicle to arrive on the scene was the Fire Chief's. I though it interesting that he didn't park in the driveway, rather he drove around the side of the house into the backyard, dodging trees and stored paraphernalia with the precision of a marine storming a fortified bunker, maneuvering around and negotiating obstacles while dodging enemy fire in the process. After coming to a stop the Chief disembarked, removed his fire fighting hat and coat, then made straight for Bill. I was taken aback when I heard the Chief call out, "Goddamnit, what's the story this year Gribble? Boy Scouts rubbing sticks together? The horse smoking in the barn again? Let's have it." The last phrase was uttered with a tinge of resignation and recognition of the futility of trying to get to the bottom of the situation. The Chief had a notepad and stood poised to record the details of the incident.

Shovel in hand, Bill sauntered close enough to the Chief to respond cordially, "How the hell are you Chief? Can you believe this? Another fire. Just lucky I was home and not at work, no telling what might have happened if I'd been gone. My kid brother and I just happened to be out here just this morning, whacking down the brush along the fence line, probably kept the fire from spreading." Bill was gripping the shovel handle at his chin, level with both hands, leaning on it, while unraveling the details of a story which I had no prior knowledge of, except of course, the pantomime George had put on earlier in the day. I had momentarily forgotten about the fire and was focused on whether the Chief would swallow the story Bill was fabricating.

The Chief laughed sarcastically, "Hell, if you hadn't been home there wouldn't have been a damn fire. I'll write you up a citation and by God this time it'll stick." I took this as a sign the Chief wasn't buying Bill's innocent stance.

Unscathed by the Chief's rebuttal Bill stuck to his original ploy with renewed conviction. Ignoring the Chief's remarks Bill continued, "Well Chief, it's got to be those kids again. Playing with matches would be my guess. I chase them off any chance I get, but I can't stand vigil twenty-four hours a day. You know how they are. They got nothing better to do than play that game, plot and wait until the grownups drop their guard, the zero in for the kill." I was trying to recall when I had ever seen Bill run any kids off and drew a blank.

All I could come up with was the time he took a bunch of us kids with him to the city dump and almost ran us over. Piloting an old Plymouth station wagon, kids were crammed in the front and back seats while the cargo section of the vehicle was packed tight with sun ripened household refuge. It didn't make any difference when you were a kid and got a chance to go somewhere with my brother Bill you got in line and hoped there was room. He always went out of his way to do something special for you in the process of taking care of whatever business he had to deal with. On this particular trip he let us kids look over the abyss at the dump, down into the cauldron of garbage. He chose this moment to check the water level in the radiator. I can remember seeing him begin to remove the radiator cap and it appeared that the ensuing blast of super heated steam shot up the sleeve of his shirt and exited around the collar. Understandably agitated and pissed off he jumped into the car with the intention of backing up. Apparently the car was still in a forward gear because it lurched towards we band of garbage gapers in a manner I could only conclude would culminate in the majority of us bouncing off the massive, chrome bumper and over the ledge of the vast pit of refuge, plummeting to our doom in the sea of rubbish below. Bill managed to stop the unruly auto prior to our being catapulted to our deaths. His arm looked like a broiled polish sausage, but he still stopped at the Tastie Freeze and bought a round of ice cream.

I remember talking to him about such trips when I was older and a father myself. I was relating a story about how I had promised my young son a trip to the ice cream shop, and as the day's events unfurled I began to get crunched for time. When I mentioned to my son that we would not have time to stop for a cone I saw on his little face the gravity and disappointment he felt. I realized my priorities were askew and I made time to stop and get the ice cream I had promised.

As we reminisced Bill summed things up by pointing out that, "When you are young your world is fairly small and controlled by the adults around you. If you watch children to see how they respond to relatively small acts of kindness, you will realize that in proportion to what you do and the results you produce, you'll never make a better investment than the time you spend with children, bestowing upon them those acts of kindness most adults would consider insignificant." I made a vow at that time to treat my own kids to ice cream at each and every opportunity.

Even now, with my second family, years later, my two little girls like to play "Ice Cream Store." They stand on a chair on the front porch outside the kitchen window and place orders with me, the ice cream guy, who by the way, is required to wear a special apron from Yellowstone Park while dispensing cones. One day they'll be to grown up to play game and we will cherish those memories.

Bill running kids off? Ha! His house was the central hub and nerve center for all kid related activity in the neighborhood. And just to keep things stirred up Bill touted, "Well Chief, I would never attempt to dissuade you from your duty, but, as I recall, the last few citations didn't amount to much. Judge threw them out when we went to court. Lack of evidence wasn't it? You were their, come on, help me out with my memory, it's not that good anymore."

"There didn't seem to be a damn thing wrong with your memory when you got up to talk to the judge. Seemed to me like you had gone out of your way to memorize a lot of legal crap that has to with my damn job." Putting his pad away he continued, "So you expect me to believe that a bunch of kids got up at three a.m., crept into your backyard, and started a fire? A fire, which incidentally appears to have been lit from all four sides, just for the hell of it? If my memory serves me, this has happened before." The Chief was ranting, pacing back and forth with his head in one hand as if he were struggling to resurrect a crucial fire fighting technique. He continued, "No, wait, it'll come to me. By God, that's it! I've been here before, not once, not twice, but let me count, seven times in the last ten years?" He threw his hands up to the heavens as he proclaimed this statement to the sky. "Last year it was an outdoor cookout, a wiener roast. A fire big enough to cook a herd of elephants and your story was it's a cook out. I talked to the cops too. They said you recited some ordinance that technically allows a fire in the city limits for outdoor recreational cooking. You a lawyer or something? Christ, you'd think you'd have something better to do with your damn time than play with fire."

Pleadingly without any conviction, the Chief asked the question of no one in particular, "I don't suppose there's much point of having the police respond, they'd be in the same squeeze as me. I'll tell you one thing though wise ass, you light one of these midnight infernos and it causes any collateral damage and I'll see your ass fry."

As the Chief climbed back into his truck, Bill called out, "See ya next year Chief!" The Chief turned on his lights and siren, and then sped out of the yard doing as much damage to the landscape as possible in the process.

While the emergency crew sped off and Bill and I starred hypnotically at the concentric flames converging in the center of the field Bill said, "That Fire Chief was a bit on the grouchy side. Maybe we ought to invite him over for a pool party sometime, give him a chance to cool off and relax." I tried to picture the overweight fireman on an inner tube, decked out in swim trunks, fire boots and hat, adrift in our new pool. I concluded I would rather have a nest of moray eels share the water.

The fire burned quickly and cleanly, and in no time at all the lot was clear of the year's growth of brush. We made sure it was dead out before retiring for the night. There is something entrancing, almost intoxicating about a fire to the male of the species. If a fire breaks out in the kitchen, a woman with set upon it with salt and baking soda while a man would be just as apt to toss some kindling on it. From a candle to a blast furnace, if combustion is involved, boys and men will be tempted to meddle in it. It's like the allure of fireworks. How often have you seen a female with powder burns after the forth of July? There is definitely something in the collective past of the human species, which links the male of the clan to things of a pyrotechnic nature. Might be a good research topic for a book.

Chapter 9

$\mathcal{I}$'ve always liked the early morning. The air is cool, clean and crisp. It's like nature has had a chance to rejuvenate and clean up from the degradation of the previous day's activities of the human race. Let's face it, humans are the dirtiest critters on the earth. We flock together and befoul our habitats with our waste and byproducts of materialistic activities. Pigs don't do that even if we pen them up. In the absence of the background noise that accompanies man's incessant marathon to either catch or beat the clock, in that predawn bastion of solitude, you can experience an invigorating communion of your heart with the world of nature in a humble reminder that we are truly a part of all that we see around us. Our fates are mutually intertwined and the fate of the world is ultimately our own. There's no smell of auto exhaust permeating the air, and if you are lucky enough to live near substantial swaths of natural or cultivated flora and fauna, a discerning sniffer can discriminate between those scents which belong to the breeze and those which are byproducts of man's activities—rose blossoms or coffee brewing.

There was a bit of a chill in the air and I was looking forward to some physical activity to warm up. As I rolled the tiller out of the garage, I was hoping the endeavor on which I was about to embark would be physically demanding enough to be classified as a workout. I've always been a physical fitness fanatic. Come to think of it, lots of people would have considered me a fanatic in many other respects and probably still do. Did I mention that I at one time was a health food fanatic? Not so much anymore, but there was a time when my eating habits would have been classified as down right peculiar.

I would get up at the crack of dawn and make sure my bicycle was ready for the trip, check the tires, brakes, and fill the water bottle. As for fuel for myself, I would mix the following ingredients in a blender for a power drink: ¼ cup of brewers yeast, ¼ cup of cold pressed, soy bean oil, three tablespoons of honey, two raw eggs, and a splash of whole unpasteurized milk. The concoction went down your throat like San Francisco sliding into the Pacific Ocean. There was a definite technique to drinking the sludge; you never let your teeth come together while consuming this concoction. In those unfortunate situations in which this would inadvertently happen, the flavor locked inside the granules of yeast would activate your taste buds like peeing on an electric fence. Brewers yeast is the raw material they make natural vitamin B supplements out of. Ever get a whiff of those babies when you pop the top? The pungent smell is a mere hint of how Brewers yeast tastes. It's reminiscent of the taste you would expect from a slab of liver after letting it sit on the counter a day or two, ripening in the sun. I don't have any hard evidence that this brew was the fountain of youth, or that it actually produced any discernible positive enhancements of the human condition or metabolic function. The truth of the matter is that I can't say at this point why the hell I drank something that if given the option, most people would prefer to dine with Count Dracula before allowing such a swill to pass their lips. I can only guess that my reasoning was I had bits and fragments of information about the health benefits to be derived from the individual ingredients I was mixing, so the logic goes, why not mix them all together? Didn't they end up that way in the end? Somewhere along the line I made the determination that one of those Molotov milkshakes was to be the last, and as far as I can tell it hasn't made a damn bit of difference.

I fired up the tiller and made a pass along the length of the anticipated, pool site. The tiller shook, jerked and bucked, in much the same way as a large fish does the dance of death while squirming on a gaff hook. After an hour or so I had a strange sensation that I wasn't actually attempting to break sod. No, I had somehow drifted off my path and accidentally commenced tilling the concrete on the sidewalk. The combination of soil that had been compacted by years of human activity and never thatched, cultivated, or otherwise groomed by human activity, had produced a sod shell on the soil that was impervious to the tiller tines. I began to think that once again I might be in for more work than I had bargained for at the onset.

After a few more hours of this, I shut the tiller down and contemplated the situation, reconnoitering my present situation. Have you ever done some sort of repetitive, physical activity, which after you stop, your body still continues to perform the motions? When I shut that bucking, Briggs & Stratton bronco down my arms involuntarily floated back up to the level of the handgrips, and I could still feel the rippling convulsions they delivered coursing through my body. A close examination of my recent attempts at cultivation revealed dismal results. The ground had not been sufficiently broken up to even begin considering removing any dirt with a shovel. I figured that if I could just break through that protective mantle of sod, the digging would be a breeze. It was time for more rudimentary, primitive implements of excavation, a pickaxe.

The total surface area of the pool was going to be around two thousand square feet. That figures out to something like three hundred thousand square inches. In extremely stubborn sod a pick can turn over about five spare inches of sod per pick. If you do the rest of the math on a calculator, you come up with an astounding fifty five thousand swings of a pickaxe, not to mention the work required to actually move the dirt once it had been loosened up. Even at that depth the dig would only be a few inches deep. If calculators had been invented back then I might have had reservations about my decision that the pick was a sensible alternative.

It's funny how technological innovations can give us a more objective, comprehensive picture of the potential challenges our goals, dreams and aspirations actually entail or conceal. Global satellite weather information could well suggest that putting off that trip to Hawaii one more year night be prudent. Information on projected mortgage rates at MONEYLOVERS.COM may imply that the time just isn't right to take the plunge and buy the home your family has dreamed of for years. A truly objective assessment of the typical family's, financial situation would indicate that in the long run you not only could not afford to have another child, but you can't even afford those presently in your nest. Or your health for that matter. Information and research abounds, everything is bad for you, quit eating, breathing and drinking. Had I all the techno tools of today thirty years ago I would have done a lot more planning and researching. As a result, I would have in all likelihood, never found the time or the most opportune interval to actually aspire to do much of anything. I'm glad I did somethings, even though a lot of things in the end turned out to be rather stupid endeavors. I'm glad I did them before I came to the realization and enlightenment much later in life that what I had actually done was either pointless, illegal, or impossible.

As was the case in most situations, Bill had a philosophical perspective towards the process of embarking on projects where realistic completion was questionable. An informal student of human nature and activity, he studied the actions of his fellow man and pondered the rational and ultimate results of their actions. He explained it to me this way, "The worst thing I can imagine experiencing in this world would be to be stretched out on your death bed regretting not having done something in your life that you desired to. Take digging a swimming pool for example. We could put it off until next year because of the weather, then put it off another year because of work, then next a sick kid. All too soon I'd look in the mirror and see an old man not up to the labor required. Then I'd have to look myself in the eye and admit to myself that the dream had come to an end; I'd never dig that swimming pool. I see people all around me living in tomorrow as if their will always be one. Even if you can't drag every dream into reality, there is considerable satisfaction in know you gave it a shot."

His advice to me was to make your dreams come true today and not expect tomorrow to do your work for you. To his credit he was one of those few people who actually took the advice he gave. When he found out he had prostrate cancer it was around the time he and his wife were about to take a long planned trip to Rome. His doctor wanted him to stick around for more tests and Bills response was, "No one gets to stick around forever Doc. I plan to see the Sistine Chapel before this rides over." I am not advocating that anyone should put off medical attention to take a holiday, but Bill had his mind made up about how he was going to deal with his illness and he wasn't about to compromise the quality of life he had left to increase the quantity of it.

When Bill arrived home from work I had spent approximately eight hours with a pick and the tiller. I had bleeding blisters, heat stroke, and a throbbing headache, which felt like a mother gopher was burrowing into my brain stem with the goal of nesting her brood next to my cerebellum.

As we inspected the project Bill remarked, "Pretty tough going?"

I replied, "The tiller would have done a better job if I had taken the wheels off it and drug it behind the car. I gave up on it and went to work with the pick. It was all I could do to get a pick in this ground, forget about a shovel."

I was proud of the blisters on my hands, but that was not the kind of thing that a man would brag to another about or deliberately draw attention to. I always thought of things in that light, "How would my brother behave in a similar situation?" There you have the reason I was working without gloves. Bill and I had been working on some other project and he had remarked that I was like him in that he couldn't work as well with gloves on. Prior to that statement I would have been more than happy to have a pair. From that day forth I would have rather slid down the trunk of a cactus naked rather than toil with a pair of gloves on. I stuck to that commitment until just a few years ago when I moved to a colder climate where I cut several cords of wood a season.

Now when he asked if the going was tough it wasn't just idle banter. He was acknowledging that it would have been just as hard for him. That was the thing about talking to my brother. He never came out and said it in so many words, but you knew he was looking at you and talking to you as an equal, as a man. When he implied that a task was tough or challenging he was not addressing any limitations on your part, it was an affirmation that you had done a commendable job and put forth an honest effort, never subliminally implying that he could have done a better job or conveying any covert dissatisfaction with your performance.

Given the fact that at the time, as far as I knew, there wasn't much of anything my brother couldn't do if he set his mind to it. I considered this a hell of a compliment.

We've all heard those stories about the guy that could tear a telephone book in half, right? I saw Bill do it. I was around eight years old and we were having one of our famous family get togethers. I was obliquely eavesdropping on an adult conversation which centered on feats of strength; who had or could do what. These individuals were arguing about who was the strongest, alternatively struggling to rip an old telephone book in half. As Bill walked by he asked to see the book, tore it in half, then handed a half back to each of the original protagonists. I remember looking at him like he were some Greek God mingling with we mere mortals. If he had told me at the time he was going outside and uproot the apple tree and shake the ripe fruit form its bows, I would have grabbed some baskets to gather the bounty in and a hard hat to keep form getting hit on the head when it rained apples. I was convinced that here was a man for whom no goal was too lofty.

Bill kicked some dirt and asked, "What do you think, are we going to be able to move enough dirt this way and make any head way?" He never asked a question or your opinion in order to appease some social amenity or convention. I can remember as an adolescent being involved in those discussions with adults who held sway over me, masquerading as if they had some magnanimous intentions of taking my opinion into consideration in the process of making a decision which was theirs to make. In reality they had come to the table with the decisions already made. I still deal with people like that today as an adult; it's an insult and in the end a waste of time. These people solicit the input of others for the sole purpose of buttressing a point they are trying to make. When you talk to people like this the only time they give you any credence is when you regurgitate what they have shoved down your throat and then feast on it with them. When Bill would invite your opinion the sincerity that he had not made any decision at the juncture was evident. I saw my brother as a juggernaut that could accomplish any goal and obliterate any obstacle that stood in defiance of achieving it. For him to value my ideas and actually incorporate them into his overall strategy in battle was, and still is, an affirmation of unsurpassed magnitude.

I was careful when I spoke to him when it came to making any statement that a task was too difficult or impossible. He had a simple saying when it came to automotive repair which summed up his philosophy on doing that which on the surface appeared could not be done, "If they put it together in Detroit, I can tear it apart in Portland." There were many projects that I assisted him with when I was convinced in my heart one of us would either be killed, maimed, or driven to dementia before completing. If these words were in my heart, they would be miraculously transformed and mutated into an affirmation that success was within our grasp as they rolled off my lips. My brother never used the word "can't" in my presence. I extrapolated from the absence of this word in his vocabulary that it was a four-letter word not to be uttered.

I can remember the time I went to visit him at a home he acquired later in life. It had a duck pond on it. On this particular day I came to visit, in the middle of the pond sat Bill's D8 cat, an earth moving machine of monstrous proportions, sunk into the pond muck up to the tops of the tracks and slowly submerging further like some yellow mastodon gallantly struggling to gain freedom from the clutches of a tar pit. When I inquired about the predicament Bill was not inclined to engage in idle banter, he was on a mission to rescue the yellow beast from slowly sinking into the oblivion of the duck guano pit.

Bill was placing any and all materials he could scrounge around the farm under the upraised bucket of the cat, then lowering it in an attempt to create a firm enough foundation, which would then allow him to slide some railroad ties underneath the tracks in hopes of gaining sufficient traction to allow the cat to escape its present entrapment. Beings as I had some clothes on which could have arguably been classified as non-work attire and a fifth of whiskey in my hand, this was one of the few situations in which I declined to offer up my services to my brother while he was locked in combat with some formidable opponent. In reality my attire was nothing more than a superficial excuse; I was convinced that if there ever was a lost cause, this was it.

I excused myself and went into the house where I found my brother Doug. He too was well dressed and in possession of a gallon of Christian Brothers Brandy. We discussed the futility of Bill's endeavor, watching out the living room window as successive dimensions of lumber disappeared into the goo at the bottom of the pond. Doug and I agreed that the only viable solution would be to have another cat pull the entrapped one from the clutches of the quagmire, or better yet, drain the pond and let it dry out. Bill's wife informed us that he had been stuck for more than seven hours now.

Several hours later, about the time Doug and I were congratulating ourselves for our objective engineering assessments of the futility of Bill's pathetic rescue attempt, we heard the diesel monster roar as a plume of blue smoke and a wave of mud spewed forth from the pond. As the plume engulfed the pond Doug and I awaited the eminent explosion we knew would soon follow from the strain on the old cat. As we watched out of the primeval cloud came Bill, triumphantly perched on the back of the creature he had rescued from obliteration. I was reminded of a line from the Stienbeck book *Old Man And The Sea* when the old fisherman was struggling with the fish and he declares to the gargantuan Marlin he was battling that a man is meant for destruction, not defeat!

To put things simply, I was already convinced that he was crazy about the whole pool idea and that made me an even more severe case, stumbling about in the back yard with a pickaxe like some deranged pirate who's buried treasure map had been distorted by saltwater, frenziedly probing the earth in a dispirited search for his lost treasure.

"Don't know," I responded. "I spent the better part of the night and morning bustin' up that sod and haven't moved any dirt with a shovel yet." I was using my hands to illustrate my day's toil with an ulterior motive; I was hoping he would notice the blisters on my hands, but it didn't work.

Bill continued, "Doesn't look like that tiller is biting deep enough, needs more weight on it. I'll bet we can rig something up to make it work a little better."

We wheeled the tiller into the garage and went to work. Bill had some square chunks of metal that he had salvaged from the railroad, they were used to secure the rail ties to the bed, each of which weighted about forty pounds. "We can weld a few of these to the frame of the tiller, give it more weight to make those tines dig in." I had no cause to doubt his logic, so I waited patiently for the task to be completed. Now Bill wasn't much of a believer in the finer points of engineering. He swore that such things, like having your rear tires balanced, were a scam perpetrated on us by corporate America. In the case of the rototiller, however we soon found that the original design had meticulously balanced the weight of the devise to minimize vibration and bucking. As Bill attacked the terra firma of our future pool with the newly modified earth cultivator, he looked a lot like a rodeo clown who had grasped the horns of a rampaging bull, trying to maintain control and stay out of the path of its thrashing hooves.

After an initial test run Bill exclaimed, "I think we both have put in a long day, let's pack in up and take another whack at it tomorrow morning." Music to my ears, I was dead on my feet. The only part of my brain registering any activity was the old brain, which was commanding me to breathe and kept my heart beating.

Early the next morning Bill organized a work crew, he would run the tiller, his eldest two daughters would gleam the rocks from the freshly turned soil, and I would come behind with the wheelbarrow and gather them.

So it went for several days. Then one morning when revelry blew, malingering set in. His daughter's social calendars conflicted with the work routine and precluded their participation in the project. Bill was not inclined to extract manual labor from his children, so they were excused from the chore without malice. As the only volunteer left on site it fell to me to remove the rocks from the dirt in preparation for the soil to be efficiently moved with a shovel. Initially, it was fascinating work. I would clear a swath of freshly tilled soil of rocks; Bill would make another pass over the exact same section and spontaneous, inorganic reproduction would take place. The earth would give up a volume of granite equal to that which I had laboriously removed in the past half-hour.

The novelty wore off after several days, coinciding with the ever increasing melody being played by the twitching nerves and muscles in the taught, strained sinews of my back.

I was beginning to wonder at this point how badly I wanted to have a swimming pool and what price the God that governs such human endeavors would extract from us. Much later in life I found this axiom repeated and validated in research and biographical literature about individuals considered successful. A common strand was a strong belief in self, and a dream, and an unwavering commitment to a goal. One of the greatest body builders of all time, Arnold Schwarzenegger, summed it up when he spoke about his decision to win the title of Mr. Universe. He visualized his goal to the extent that he could 'see' himself as Mr. Universe in the mirror while posing at the gym. The brutal toils and disciplines required to reach that pinnacle of human development were mere details of the trip to achieving his ultimate objective.

As I slaved at my brother's side, I pictured us as modern day characters out of Stienbeck's "Of Mice and Men," in which the main characters George and Lenny had a collective dream of owning a little piece of paradise and raising rabbits. When the feeble minded Lenny would begin to loose sight of the dream he would beseech George to tell him about the rabbits and in the process revitalize the vision. In the Pit (that's the name we gave to our excavation) Bill was George and I was Lenny. When I needed reassurance that we did indeed have a goal in mind worthy of the physical punishment my body was enduring Bill was able to invigorate my resolve. He seemed to revel in every failed endeavor; relish minor inconveniences that exploded into insurmountable impediments to progress. He met each new challenge with an uncompromising, unfailing self-assurance that in the end all things are possible to those that believe and persevere. I tagged along and began to look at the tasks in the pit from a more optimist orientation.

On the offensive I attacked the ground with a renewed vigor, keeping in the forefront of my mind a visual goal of me floating on an air mattress, guzzling ice cold beer, surrounded by scantily clad high school girls, compliments of the considerable number of friends my nieces would be able to deliver pool side. I guess that's why it didn't bother me that much that my nieces were not partaking in the brutal labor. They would fulfill their obligations by providing pool accessories. A sexist attitude to be sure, but I was unenlightened at the time and a slave to my hormones. Drifting further into my daydream I could smell the aroma of banana essence and coconut, suntan oil mingling with the sweet sent of innocent, virgin flesh as they surrounded me, rubbing the oil from their bodies to mine, massaging the ambrosia into my willing flesh. Coaxed by their flagellating fingers, I rose from my lawn chair, floating weightless. Just as I was about to be kissed in unison by my bewitchers, I came crashing down on the cement pool apron and came tumbling back into reality by Bill's cursing, "Mother fuckin' sonofabitch!" which shattered my transcendental state.

Now I can remember making that transition from a child, in front of whom grown ups refrained from swearing and other such vulgarities, to that of someone who was an acceptable recipient of such verbalizations. At the time it was a 'man-thing' and I was complimented by it.

I remember it like it was yesterday. I was riding with another brother by the name of Gary and someone in another car cut him off. He unleashed a flurry of profanity targeted at the driver, the car she drove, and the rat dog perched in her lap with its head protruding from the driver's side window. When he had finished he didn't apologize to me or give any indication he was remorseful for cursing in front of me. I could feel the testosterone coursing through my veins and pubic hair sprouting in strategic places. At the age of eleven there was no doubt in my mind that I wasn't a kid anymore. I didn't make a serious attempt at expunging swearing from my vocabulary until at least the age of forty-three when I became the father of a daughter.

Swearing to me is a lot like something I read in the novel *From Here to Eternity*. In the book there's this army officer who allows everyone to address him informally by his first name except for one sergeant. When the sergeant can't take the inequality anymore, he asks the officer why he lets everyone else use his first name. The officer replies, "Because when you do it, it sounds disrespectful." That's how it is with swearing and me. For some people it is a bonafide component of their vocabulary, for others it's a vulgarity meant to illicit a reaction.

Then there was the time Scott and I were riding in the back seat and Bill was driving with old Kermit riding shotgun. We were stopped at a crosswalk, yielding the right of way to several young girls waiting to cross the street. Kermit rolled down his window and shouted, "Get out of the road you fucking sluts." Scott and I had never heard anyone talk like that before, let alone spewing such vulgarity towards children. Kermit smiled stupidly at Bill, apparently seeking some sort of recognition for his oratorical prowess.

Bill responded with a sharp jab with his elbow into Kermit's floating ribs, causing him to buckle over, at which time Bill grabbed a hand full of his greasy hair, shoving Kermit's face into his groin proclaiming, "Anyone with a mouth like that, there's only one thing he should do for a living." We couldn't wait to get back to school and tell our friends the story. Hell, I'm still telling it.

Bill was still swearing, stomping in the dirt, holding his face and probing his mouth with a grimy hand. "I chipped a damned tooth." He said. It was no surprise to me, having watched as the vibrations emanating from the out of balance tiller radiated up his arms and ripple across every fiber of his back. One could well have expected to see a trail of broken, pulverized teeth like corn seeds in the furrow he had just finished plowing.

As Bill fingered the damaged tooth he spoke, "Looks like we need to rethink this. Probably going to need a backhoe." I didn't really care what he got, just as long as the pick and shovel were out of the picture. Now, if he had said that the amount of work done was acceptable for the time invested, I would have dutifully come back out with my pick the next morning. I might well have rebelled in my mind, but my heart would not have allowed my body the luxury of accompanying the notion. As it were, the pick and shovel were retired for the day and so were we. I was looking forward to soaking my tormented hands in hot water laced with Epson Salts.

Chapter 10

Bill had a great job for a guy that liked to do home-improvement projects. He was on call so he could work on stuff at home until he received conformation of where and when his next work assignment would be. Consequently, he had no regular sleeping pattern, taking catnaps which never culminated in more than three or four hours of rest in any given day. The only time this seemed to have an adverse affect on him was that first few minutes he was on his feet after getting out of bed. He would stumble about, eyes rolled back in his head, mumble incoherently, giving every indication that he had just risen from a crypt to join some sort of night of the living dead convention. He also made this noise down in his throat, a kind of a clicking sound with his mouth closed. Initially, it was not something he did on a conscious level, but as the noise drew more attention over the years from his children and the ever-present children of friends and family Bill considered the time opportune to weave a story.

The first time I asked him what that noise was and he replied, "Oh that noise? That's the little pig that's still hiding from the big bad wolf."

"Hiding? Hiding where? Which little pig?"

"He's hiding down my throat. You remember the three little pigs and how the only little pig that didn't get eaten up by the wolf was living in the brick house? And how that pig cooked the wolf and ate him? Well, that wolf has a cousin that has been after the brick house pig ever since. One day the little pig was walking down the street right out in front of our house. He was on his way home packing a bag of groceries and that wolf's cousin was waiting for him out under that bush. The bush right out there." Pointing to a shrub in the front yard. "The wolf jumped out and tried to grab the pig, but that little piggy threw the groceries at the wolf and ran as fast as he could into our house, looking for a dark place to hide. He snuck into my bedroom while I was sleeping, and it was so dark that he thought my mouth was a cave and he jumped in. He's been living down there every since that day."

I didn't question that these were the undisputed facts because my infantile mind was running at maximum capacity struggling to generate an image of that pig and the dimensions of a creature that could squeeze down a man's throat. I remember being perplexed about whether the pig removed his shoes and hat before making this extraordinary journey.

"Can I see the pig Uncle Bill?" I called him Uncle as a small child I think because in our immediate family I had about twenty nieces and nephews who were fairly close to my age. They spent a lot of time at Bill's house, as I did, and we all called him Uncle.

"Sure," he said, "Just look down my throat. Bill opened his mouth wide and bent over. At the time I could have sworn that I did indeed see a vague outline of the little pig's hat down there in the dark.

"Why does that piggy make that noise?"

"That's what he does to let me know he's hungry."

"Why doesn't he do it when your mouth is open?"

"He can see the light shining down my throat and he's scared that if he says anything that bad old wolf will hear and come looking for him."

I was proud of my brother's humanitarian sacrifice on behalf of the little pig and proclaimed his virtuous protection of that terrified pig whenever the opportunity arose. It made for quite the story during show and tell at school.

He was a good storyteller, so I naturally gravitated in the same direction; upholding a family tradition. There was the time I lost a tooth at the age of five. The tooth fairy left me a fifty-cent piece under my pillow. The damn thing hurt like hell, bled like a severed jugular and I was absolutely sure the ordeal was worth more than fifty cents. My brother Gary lived at home at the time and I was inclined to innocently rummage through his personal effects while he was gone, admiring those things a man possesses. I liked how his stuff smelled of Old Spice cologne and Camel cigarettes, marveling at the piles of coins causally strewn about his room. During one such exploration I stumbled upon a money pouch in his dresser drawer. Inside I found a multitude of folding money unfamiliar to me. I figured that in such abundance one bill would not be missed, so I helped myself to a twenty, which I commenced to show off to the neighborhood, proclaiming it as my reward for the lost tooth. When word got back to my mother about this windfall I got put on the hot seat and interrogated. The way I had it figured was that no one had access o the tooth fairy's accounting books, so who could say how much money she had left me? I stuck to my story only to be astounded and bewildered that my mother somehow knew that I had taken the money from my brother. I later admitted to it under the duress of Gary administering a spanking. As I recall, even after confessing he continued the corporal punishment and blistered my butt. It was then that the seeds of doubt were planted in my mind about the existence of the tooth fairy.

When I lost my next tooth I set a trap. I put on a contrived, theatrical performance highlighting the fact I had lost the tooth and that I intended to leave it in a plastic wristwatch case to see if the tooth fairy could find it. What I left out was that I had also attached to this case the end of a segment of string, the other end secured to my big toe. When someone snuck into the room my security devise did its job and I caught them in the act. Judging by the pittance left behind, I am quite certain that fairy was annoyed at being discovered.

Over the years however, I came to accept the fact that my mother would often know things about me and my actions when logic would dictate that she would not be privy to such details. This came home to me the only time I tried to lie to her about something other than in the context of a practical joke. I had been out carousing with some of my pals in high school. We had skipped school, gone cruising, and came back toasted. Mom asked the typical questions: where had I been and what had I been up to? I gave her some bullshit story she didn't question, but she registered her disbelief and disappointment with a look; a look that conveyed the hurt I had inflicted by dishonoring the trust between us. It was the first and last lie I ever perpetrated on my mother. We never spoke about the incident because there wasn't anything to talk about. She had communicated to me that which she needed too and my lesson was learned.

As the old girl got older it got easier to put-one-over on her. She was living in a retirement home and I felt duty bound to make life a bit more exciting for her when the opportunity arose. Early one morning, about three-thirty, I had nothing better to do than give Mom a call. When she answered I hurriedly asked, "Have the police been there looking for me?"

She replied, "No."

"Good," I said, "When they show up, tell them I was with you all night." Without an explanation I hung up the phone. A few days later I went to visit her and she asked me what kind of trouble I was in this time. I had completely forgotten about my prank call.

"Mom," I began, "I didn't see that old lady in the crosswalk. Honest! She had no business out walking at night in a black dress."

"Was she hurt bad son?"

"I don't know, I never stopped. Do you have any idea what something like that could do to my insurance rates?"

I told her I went back to the scene of the crime later on and couldn't find a body so either she walked away, was drug off by scavengers, or she got caught up in some tree branches. Mom just shook her head and said, "You'll never get away with this."

Seeing that she was concerned I tried in vain to convince her I was joking, to which she replied, "It won't do any good to lie to me about it." She never mentioned it again, and I didn't either. I sincerely hope that she forgot the unfortunate incident before she passed away.

Mark Twain said that the only thing he ever did in his life that he was proud of was to take care of his parents when they got old. There was a lot more I could have done for my mother, a lot less too. I was the last of her children to see her alive. It was an interesting relationship. After spending a summer in the Pit, Bill had indoctrinated me with his philosophy about the true nature of happiness and how it was not a commodity which permeated the atmosphere of the nearest shopping mall. It was rather, an internal orientation towards the world, a perspective that precluded any material assault to diminish it. I think the way he said it was, "A man's body dwells in the material world, his spirits flourishes in his soul."

From this philosophical orientation I approached my relationship with my elderly mother. We were in agreement that there was a good chance she could very well die soon after one of my visits. However, in reality her physical presence here on this earth would have terminated, but in my mind she would continue to exist. I knew that at the moment I learned of her demise I would be confronted with the most important decision of my life. Would I succumb to a life of mourning, or would I rise above my selfish interests and honor her memory in the fashion she deserved and wanted?

The old girl died two days later. My son at the time was ten years old and his mother was inclined to think of death as something to shun and shield youngsters from. I felt he should be allowed to attend the funeral of his grandmother, MiMi, if he so choose, which he did.

As we drove to the funeral, my son asked me about what had happened to MiMi and why she had to die. I don't recall the exact words but it went something like this. "MiMi was like a big strong tree in the forest. She spent her lifetime sowing seeds on the wind and giving shade and shelter to the little trees that sprung up around her. When she could no longer provide in this way for her children she made one last contribution to those she loved best. When a big tree dies and falls in the forest it goes back into the ground in which the living trees are still growing and makes them stronger. MiMi died and a little bit of her went into everyone that knew and loved her. So she'll always be with us in our hearts."

After the funeral and the wake, my son and I were driving back north to our home. Neither of us had said much of anything for close to an hour when my son turned to me and asked, "Dad, when are we gonna have another one of them funerals? That was more fun than Christmas." Exactly the send off mom would have wanted when she checked out.

I loved and honored my mother in accord with the example Bill set in his interactions with her. He was always polite, respectful and reverent. We never had a discussion about the appropriate way in which a son should be oriented towards his mother. Like so many other things I learned from him, this was a process of osmosis.

Along with a healthy dose of respect for our Mother, I also picked up a streak of the prankster that was my brother. I always told mom that the only thing she had that I wanted after she died was her two gold teeth. I kept telling her that I would have them made into earrings. One day I came to visit her and she was asleep in bed. I went back to my car and came back in with a pair of pliers which I snapped in her face, waking her up. She shouted, "Damnit! I'm not dead yet!" To which I responded that it was hard to tell if she had been asleep or dead, so I thought I had better latch onto my legacy before the mortician showed up. I was hard to see the old girl wasting away, but I made a point of going to visit every chance I had. Even when I wasn't the best company I could tell she appreciated just spending some time, and if I could get her to laugh (which I was pretty good at), so much the better.

The next morning as soon as Bill became lucid it was clear he had been reworking the pool plan in his sleep. He was on the phone tracking down a backhoe to rent. I remember thinking how great it was gonna be to have a machine around to do the backbreaking work. Like I said, Bill was a guy that did a lot of home improvement and repair projects. Over the years I followed him around as he worked diligently on tasks ranging from rejuvenating a toaster to constructing from scratch a thirty five-foot motor home. I had come to realize that my brother was truly a man of many trades and talents. When it was plumbing in need of attention, he got on the phone and got supply quotes for "Bills Plumbing." When he was building the horse a shed, his lumberyard calls were in the name of "B&G Construction." I basically assumed this to be proper vernacular in the world of do it yourself projects. On one particular occasion dealing with automotive repair I overheard Bill conversing with an auto parts store. He concluded his conversation saying, "I'll send a man down to pick it up." It was only my brother and I at the house and I was wondering who the hell he was planning to send because I wasn't a man and nowhere near old enough to drive. Bill explained that when he shopped for parts or supplies he presented himself as a business owner on the phone and an employee of that business in person when making a purchase. That way he could dicker and negotiate the best price on the phone and then if complications developed when closing the transaction in person, he would pretend to be a dumb employee running an errand for the boss. He figured that with his "business" discount he typically saved 10 to 20% on his expenditures. I think he liked playing the game more than he did saving thirty-seven cents on a head gasket. Suffice it to say that the backhoe was procured under the name of "Bills Excavation & Septic Service."

After all the running around Bill got home with the backhoe at just about dusk, and I naively assumed that the plan of attack would be a big meal, a good nights sleep, and then hit it hard as soon as it was light enough to commence working safely. Bill however, was operating under some radically different assumptions.

A socialist in his soul, he hated money because it represented what he considered to be the exploitation of working class people. He was fond of saying "In order for a human being to amass substantial material wealth, that individual must make the transition in personal values which culminates in placing a higher value on monetary and material things in this life than on the people in it. People that have a lot of money love it more than they do the people around them."

He further elaborated on this theme claiming that, "In order for a man to receive a dollar for which he did not work, another must work for a dollar he did not receive." An interesting footnote to lend fodder to this argument is the economic expansion of the U.S. economy during the 1990's, the longest in history. Many economists attribute this miracle to increased worker productivity and relatively stagnant wages. People working harder and longer so that the rich can get richer, a great arraignment providing you reside in the top 5% of the food chain. And when this miracle economic bubble burst Bill would have predicated the results. Those people responsible for the economic expansion, the people who actually produced the wealth, were the ones who lost the most.

While Bill's assertion was a lofty statement for the average person to make, most people would be relatively safe making it while resting assured they would never accumulate the critical mass of wealth which would precipitate this dilemma, confronting them with making the decision between worshiping money or adhering to a more fundamental Christian, if you like, relationship with the human race.

One can not amass a fortune and be oblivious to the potential a mere fraction of it holds to relieve untold human suffering. Easily achievable with negligible adverse impact on the quality of life of the donor. Can you imagine the belt tightening that would take place if an individual with a fortune of $500 million gave half of it away?

Much later in life Bill had the opportunity to prove his conviction on this issue. He fell beneficiary to a windfall of about a quarter of a million dollars as the result of a work related accident. In a span of a few years he basically gave all the money away either in loans never repaid, or in outright gifts to family and friends. He took pride not in the deeds he had accomplished with the money, but in the fact that the money had not corrupted nor taken control of him. Other than providing for his personal basic sustenance of brandy and bread he spent the money on the needs of others.

I remember the day he received the check and the day he sold a parcel of property he had acquired in Eastern Oregon because his bank account was tapped out. He was wearing the same pair of holy K-Mart tennis shoes. He was of the opinion that the love of money or any pleasure derived from its mere possession was akin to the relationship between an addict and his heroin. He made a concerted decision in the way he lead his life to never become dependent on money as a source or facilitator of serenity or happiness in his life. Bill considered his home to be a bastion against the woes of a capitalist society and a world that, more often than not, seemed to ascribe little value to the common man and even less to the downtrodden. He insisted that troubles be left at his door because he would only allow the halls of his home to be filled with love and happiness. And they flocked to his sanctuary by the droves. Even those that claimed to need financial assistance were there for something more fundamental.

They were searching for the secret. How could this man of relatively humble means derive so much satisfaction out of spending his day feeding his ducks and rabbits? It was deceptively simple, Bill ascribed significant value to each and every breath he drew. He refused to live in spurts, enduring a mundane existence for eleven months out of the year and then attempt to compensate for that disillusionment during an extravagant vacation. For Bill life was here and now, each day a different type of fruit requiring varied approaches to extract the meat and juices it had to offer.

The backhoe was rented by the day and Bill had every intention of doing all within his power to make sure that Bob's Rental Company did not somehow secure an unfair advantage in the money game as the result of something as insignificant as the rotation of the planets in the solar system in which we happened to reside. As I watched him change into his work coveralls I felt a little twitch in the bottom of my stomach and wondered for a moment if there might be more than one little pig that survived the big bad wolf's feeding frenzy.

"Got something you're gonna work on?" I asked Bill, knowing full well what he would have to say.

"That backhoe is going to run close to $200 a day so we can't afford to let her sit. It's got lights on it and there are five cars here that run. We can park them around the deep end of the pool. That will give us plenty of light and still leave room on the shallow end to get the back hoe in and out." We were on our way to a midnight, excavation extravaganza.

My interest in this endeavor grew exponentially when I was christened with the responsibility of readying the cars for the project. I checked the oil, water and gas, and then positioned the vehicles. Bill could have done this himself in twice the time, but he knew how deeply rooted the automobile was in the American rights of passage mystique. His trust and belief in my ability to execute such tasks laid a solid foundation on which I began to rebuild the shattered self-esteem and confidence which public education had systematically tore down in ten years of public schooling. After maneuvering the cars into position around the pool, I had to make the rounds, starting each one for about ten minutes on the hour to ensure that none of the batteries would go dead.

As boredom set in with the monotony of this my mind, not needing much of an invitation, began to wander into fantasies about being a valiant hero in some catastrophic military conflict. I pretended that I was a wounded soldier in combat, the last one left alive in my platoon, even though I wasn't really sure what a platoon was. Some important guy, a general or a president, in a plane circling in the dark skies above, intermittently illuminated by the flashes of antiaircraft fire, needing to land on the air strip that my compadres and me had not only dug out of the inhospitable foreign soil with our bare hands, but had also defended from the godless hordes in a horrific battle that had left everyone in my platoon dead, and me barely alive. The cars around the pool site were actually army jeeps and troop carriers I had lined up along the airstrip to guide in the plane carrying the guy who would ultimately change the tide of the battle and win the war for the good guys. I pulled myself in and out of the cars without the use of my legs that had been riddled with machine gun fire and rendered useless. I died as soon as the plane touched down safely, my hand on the accelerator feeding fuel to the engine producing the power to illuminate the runway. When the important guy got off the plane he and his congregation investigated the lighting innovation, which had facilitated their safe landing. There I was dead, covered with dirt caked blood, in the front seat of an army jeep with lights on and the motor running. The important guy brushed the dirt from my face, closed my eyelids on blood shot, glazed eyes which bespoke duty, honor and country, then saluted and said, "I won't let you down soldier." I always wanted to be an unsung hero who was really responsible for winning a war.

As the night wore on I looked for ways to keep myself entertained and awake. I set the radios in each car to a different station, so I could hear different programming as I moved from vehicle to vehicle. As the radios were competing with the oscillating roar of the backhoe as it gouged out mouthfuls of earth I was obligated to set the radio volumes on maximum output. A variation of the radio game was to tune each receiver into the same station and, when a song was playing, I would try to sing and stay on time while moving from car to car. I was quite content with this, as I had not yet learned that quality entertainment must be purchased, the fun derived proportionately increasing with the amount of money expended, ideally utilizing a credit card.

I can never mention credit cards without this incident creeping into my consciousness. Bill was conversing with a socialist friend, Burl Howard, teasing him about not making extravagant expenditures and being a gluttonous consumer.

Taunting, Bill inquired, "Burl why don't you get with it, get some credit cards and start buying, you don't need any money to have stuff."

Burl responded sardonically, "Yes Bill by all means, I could buy things I don't really need, with money I don't have, to impress people that don't really like me anyway. What a grand idea, I'll get right on it!" Can't argue with logic like that. Burl Howard; there was a character for you. I always wondered how guys like that end up being part of an extended family like he was a part of ours. I asked Bill about it one time and this was the story he related. Years ago Bill was drinking beer at a bar by the name of "The Wheel" and this burley sailor by the name of Burl, was spending money like the drunken sailor he was, tipping the bar maid exorbitantly and buying round after round for the house. When his money ran out so did his bottomless glass and his popularity rating. No one offered to return his generosity by buying him a drink, nor did anyone come to his defense when he was thrown out of the bar into the street. No one except Bill. Bill took this stranger home and extended him a measure of human kindness that he felt all men deserved and in return, all men were morally required to offer up.

Their friendship endured some thirty years until Burl died. As time and booze extracted their due from Burl he became ostracized from the few friends he had managed to secure in his life. Incontinent and broken down he was still a welcome guest at Bill's home. When someone happened to question why Bill would allow an old drunk to sleep and piss on the couch Bill bristled and shot back, "My respect is for the man that he was, not that which he has become." The old boy tried to quit drinking one time and the shock to his system sent him into a coma and he died shortly there after.

Interestingly enough, Bill was left the executor of Burls humble estate. As the smell of death always excites and attracts scavengers the relatives who shunned Burl in life arrived on the scene demanding they be given the few sticks of furniture the old man had left behind. On principle, Bill defended Burl's will and last wishes, thus ensuring the buzzards didn't descended on the old man's belongings. Burl's last wish was that Bill retain his humble home for as long as another old friend of the family who had lived with Burl wished to remain a resident.

The lady to whom Burl referred lived in the home for several years. Bill installed an oil furnace to replace the wood stove one winter. His neighbor complained uproariously that the fuel tank for the stove protruded into his airspace by a foot or two, demanding that Bill remove it. Bill hired a surveyor to determine the exact property line and found, to the chagrin of the complaining neighbor, that several feet of his house were actually on Bill's property. After a week of threatening to saw that portion of the house off that infringed on his property Bill acquiesced. He had a lawyer draw up an agreement that the property would be leased to the neighbor and renewal would be contingent on the party in question maintaining a civilized relationship with the lady living in Burl's house. Playing it safe, the neighbor cut off all communications and other contacts with the occupant of Burl's home.

I am convinced that a man cannot bestow a complement onto his fellow man of more nobility than entrusting him to attend to the final disposition of his existence here on earth. In his time Bill had this honor thrust upon him by three friends, one of which was our brother Doug.

Abiding by his last wishes, Bill had Burl cremated and when he went to pick up the remains the director of the crematory, with much reverence and ceremony, began to market ash urns to my brother. Bill respectfully declined all models requesting that the ashes be turned over to him in the container in which they were removed from the furnace and presently stored, assuming they were in a temporary generic vessel such as a paper bag or a coffee can. When the director said that was not possible, Bill excused himself and returned with a shoe shine box, placed it on the directors desk, and simply said, "Put him in there." He put Burl in the trunk of the car and promptly forgot about him. There the ashes remained for several months.

I just happened to be a Bill's house when one of his daughters who was about thirteen at the time, was digging in the trunk of Bill's car. I noticed that she had opened what appeared to be a shoeshine box and was running her fingers through what resembled some kind of extremely fine sand. As Bill walked by she held up a handful of the substance and asked her father what it was. Without breaking his stride he nonchalantly responded, "Oh that? That's Burl." Being of a delicate constitution his daughter promptly screamed threw the handful of Burl into the trunk then bolted for the bathroom, vomiting as she ran. She spent about a hour in the tub, succeeding in scrubbing several skin layers off in the process of trying to cleanse herself of the realization that she had contaminated her physical being with the remains of another. It was not an issue of desecration of the slumber of the dead, with her it was strictly a hygiene concern.

She had some rather peculiar inclinations and ideas when it came to sanitation and cleanliness. When she was a kid she didn't know where chicken eggs came from. When I finally convinced her that they were delivered via the posterior end of a chicken, she took a vow to never eat them again. She was about eight at the time and to my knowledge she has not ingested an egg in the past thirty years. The only person I ever met that refused to throw up in the toilet. She found it quite impossible to get her face that close to the bowl, so if she got sick at your house she would puke in your sink or bathtub, whichever one passed her inspection as being the most sanitary receptacle in your facility. Considering the number of children she has birthed into this world and cared for, I have to admire her rising above her revulsion of human excrement and changing all those dirty diapers.

From my vantage point behind the wheel of an auto the digging taking place had a surrealistic appearance. The earth moving apparatus was the back half of an articulating tractor contraption. Bright yellow with air craft, landing light intensity, bug-eyed headlights, it looked like a gigantic version of one of those bugs you see on TV that drills its abdomen into the soil with the intention of depositing its brood of eggs. This activity was taking place against a larger backdrop filled with dust, diesel and gas fumes, and the bellowing of the backhoe contraption, interspersed by the unintelligible blaring of five, auto radios which were audible intermittently when the digging machine was not under a strain. I imagined I was on the first manned mission to Mars and this marauding, yellow beast was an inhabitant of that planet defending its turf from our alien intrusion. All of our sophisticated weapons were impotent against this creature, as it was wreaking havoc upon our exploration units, crushing them and pummeling the remains into the Martian tundra, working its way to the command module which had to be protected if we were to entertain any aspirations of returning to earth. Being the heroic martyr in all of my fantasies I naturally rose to the challenge in this crisis. My keen analytical mind noticed that the monster had not crushed one exploration unit that was in its path towards the return module. The monster had avoided contact with this particular unit for some unknown reason. As I went to start the motor of the Pinto because it's lights had begun to dim I slipped back into my Martian mission. True to the character of a Hollywood hero I had absolutely no concern what-so-ever for my own personal safety when I went into action. Making my way to the rover that had been spared from the crushing jaws of the unrelenting onslaught of the yellow demon, with the intention of discerning what, if any, secrets this unit held about any strategy for repelling the assault of the Martian mangler. My cucumber cool assessment of the rover gave no indication that there was anything unique to it that could be construed to be a deterrent to the decimation wielded by the destroyer; nothing that is except the rock and roll music streaming at a barely audible volume from the audio system. Music which, by the way, mysteriously had not distorted beyond recognition, compliments of the Martian atmosphere. That's what's so great about an imagination. Even the rigid laws of physics have no regulatory power there. This phenomenon appeared to be our last hope to salvage the mission and save ourselves from the pending plunge into the abysses. In an instant I was back on board the command ship, patching my personal stereo into the emergency address system, which would transmit on all receivers and external speakers. The Beatles song, *Yellow Submarine* was blasting back on earth on the radio of Bill's bowhead whale of a Cadillac, while it was simultaneously incapacitating the Martin marauder, rendering it helpless as it fled erratically to escape the music.

Chapter 11

*B*ill and I both had a tendency to be myopic in focus and oblivious to the outside world when fully engaged in a major endeavor. I can't really say if this is a genetic predisposition, or if I acquired it by assimilation; the result of working beside my brother on this as well as many other projects. I don't know if he was given to flights of fantasy such as I, because this is the first time I've ever talked to anyone about any of mine. Suffice it to say that we were one hundred percent focused on what we were doing, completely void of consideration for anything or anyone not in intimate contact with the dust particles that were beginning to congeal in our respiratory systems. That's probably why neither of us heard the neighbor George as he screamed at us from across his fence at 4:00am on this Sunday morning.

George came around the fence fuming. I saw him as he approached, illuminated in the indirect, stray light from the combined candescence of the ten, automobile headlights from our job site. A striking figure as he strode across the front yard, decked out in what had to have been his wife's bathrobe. I had never seen this man after dusk and was intrigued by the disarray of the hair upon his head. During the daylight hours George sported an immaculately manicured doo, skillfully sculptured to cover an ever-increasing bald spot. I marveled at his more natural appearance as he stomped towards the edge of the excavation site. At that instant, the realization hit me that his hair bore an uncanny resemblance to the fungi which grows in long, angel hair like filaments inside a Halloween jack-o-lantern left on the front porch until Thanksgiving.

I surmised, by virtue of his convulsive gyrations, George was screaming in an attempt to capture Bill's attention over the din of the guttural roar of the Detroit demons devouring fossil fuel. As he flailed his arms spasmodically at his sides he bore a striking resemblance to a gooney bird gallantly struggling against the superior force of gravity to take flight from a stationary position without the aid of the required preliminary running start.

When Bill finally caught sight of George and killed the engine and I had made the rounds shutting off the cars, there was no one at the helm of George's cerebrum to execute the same courtesy. George has slipped into a more primitive mode.

"You crazy sonofabitch!" George began, "It's the middle of the night! For Christ's sake, my dogs get some rest!" As George was bellowing and flailing his arms up and down, I could indeed detect the yapping of a pack of perturbed poodles, irate at having their beauty sleep interrupted.

Now George and Bill had some history when it came to unusual goings-on in the neighborhood, giving George just cause to be upset. As a neighbor, Bill could best be characterized as an eccentric and urban farmer. By town standards Bill had a big place, about two acres, the back being fenced in for a horse for his children. When we built the fence the neighbors were pleased that Bill was manifesting some civilized attributes in the form of bringing some semblance of containment to his weed patch. But things moved in the other direction when Patty the horse arrived to take up residence in the newly fenced pasture. An anonymous, irate neighbor complained to the city and a health inspector was dispatched; I suppose to investigate if the equestrienne posed a threat to public health. Bill had done his homework and he knew that an archaic zoning clause did allow for large livestock in his locale, provided they were necessary for farming. The health inspector was promptly informed that Patty the horse was indeed a plow horse, a vital, productive member of a farm family. The befuddled health inspector withdrew with her clipboard.

A few weeks later a city building inspector arrived on the scene. It was evident that the man felt his brethren bureaucrat in the form of the health inspector had been snubbed and incapacitated by a mere peasant, a precedent which could not be tolerated by the system. He was a man with a mission seeing it as his solemn duty that all residents of the county under his jurisdiction abide by each and every rule, law and ordinance that pertained to construction.

With all due respect, the inspector inquired, "Mr. Gribble, it seems that you have constructed a barn for your horse here and I can't find a prior building permit on file with the city. Had we received the proper forms at our office you would have been informed that such a structure would not be permissible under current ordinances. Do you have any records that could help resolve this problem?"

Bill responded, "Actually that's not a barn, it's a tool shed. I've explained to that damn horse that she has to stay out of it, but the old girl must have some mule blood in her line somewhere. Got a mind of her own she has. I chase her out of there every chance I get, but hell, I can't move into the tool shed and guard it all day and night. Got a mind of her own that horse does."

Fidgeting with the compliment of pens in his pocket protector and nervously flicking the tip of his snake like tongue at the corners of his mouth, the inspector continued, "Come now Mr. Gribble, the structure is clearly a barn for that creature and ordinance 74.503 requires that I certify all building plans and issue a permit prior to the commencement of construction of any structure built for that particular utilization."

Bill retorted, "I'm no real, architectural expert and a mediocre carpenter at best. I built that tool shed to keep my shovel in, but like I said, the damn horse has taken up squatter's rights. Be my guest, if you can convince her to stay out of my tool shed I would be most grateful." As Bill walked away without any parting formalities the frustrated inspector was continuing to make his case that the building in question was in reality a barn. Bill had done his homework and knew he did not need a permit to build a facility with a primary purpose of storing non-commercial tools and hardware. The inspector sulked off never to be heard from again on that specific issue.

When the novelty of the horse wore off and the kids lost interest the responsibility for its care reverted back to their parents, which meant Glad fed and watered it. I recall at a particular family celebration—our family never needed much of an excuse to get together and raise some hell—several adults were in the back yard at Bill's drinking vodka mixed with orange juice, a concoction known as a screwdriver. On this occasion these grown-ups decided that they would share their beverages with the horse, which greedily lapped up the offering. I'm not sure if the relationship was causative or coincidental, but the next day poor Patty the horse was on her back, feet sticking straight up in the air; dead as a door nail. After the funeral, Bill proceeded to contact all of the local business establishments that might have need of a rigormortised equine. To his chagrin and dismay he found that the rendering plants would charge him to come and pick Patty up and process her into paste, dog food, whatever it is they manufacture from a dead horse. Rather than contribute to this blatant, capitalist exploitation, Bill concluded that the only thing to do would be to bury the horse in the back yard. The task was initiated in the wee hours of the morning to minimize undue concern or publicity on the part of the adjoining neighbors.

As he was toiling with a pick and shovel in an uncooperative soil, his plot was discovered by a neighbor who diligently activated the early warning phone tree, alerting the surrounding community that Bill was up to something again. Reconnaissance teams were dispatched to provide stealthy surveillance in the name of protecting the neighborhood from whatever Bill was conjuring this time. I'm not really sure why he got away with it, but to my knowledge no official from the health department, nor any other governmental agency charged with monitoring and enforcing lawful and civilized behavior on the part of the citizenry, ever responded to a complaint and investigated. I could only conclude that they were glad the horse was finally dead and no longer a source of dissent in their respective areas of responsibility.

Taking a cleansing breath and realizing he had been cursing, George struggled to regain his composure and adopted a more diplomatic demeanor. "Bill, what in Gods name you up to this time? Sewer plugged again?"

Bill stepped down off the backhoe and greeted George, "Hi neighbor! Sorry about all the noise, me and my kid brother are digging a swimming pool." As he spoke he put his hand on George's back. The majority of people who touch you while communicating, outside of that intimate circle of loved ones, do so because they read in some self-help book or article that it ingratiates you to the person whom you are attempting to sway to your point of view or exploit in some other fashion. With Bill it was a natural, spontaneous expression of his love for the human race in general, and the recipient of his attention in particular. I witnessed the initial hostility in George's body, the confrontational inflections in his voice, and the aggressive belligerence on his face all begin to dissipate into neutrality upon receiving a greeting from my brother.

"A pool . . . A pool?" George exclaimed, "But how, I mean. It OK? The city?" I could tell that George still had one foot in bed and wasn't sure if he had completely left dreamland.

"To hell with those pencil pushing pricks, no one's going to tell me what I can do on my own land." Bill was the epitome of an urban frontiersman.

"A pool?" George said again, making sure he had understood. He said it for a fourth time, but this time I could tell he was exploring the future options of having a neighbor with a swimming pool, quite an extravagant addition to a humble neighborhood such as this. "That's great Bill! But the middle of the night? Is it necessary? For how long?"

"Oh, we shouldn't be at it for more than five days I figure. I plan to hit it hard and get the lion's share of the digging done as quickly as possible, rather than dragging it out for weeks. I don't want to disturb the neighborhood for any longer than I have to." Now I heard these words pass my brothers lips and I was pretty sure that he was not prone to fabricating fallacies. I was also pretty sure that if an individual was not predisposed to performing activities which had extremely high potential to irritate and aggravate, the laws of probability would dictate that Bill would spend proportionally, considerably less time involved in just such activities. I was convinced that Bill relished bucking the system and all social conventions. It was not maliciously targeted at any individual, but it was a statement of individuality and a challenge to the bureaucracy of blind, unquestioning adherence to uniformity and mediocrity. There was however, always the potential for collateral damage to and conflict with, those blind adherents. "Servants of the system," as Bill called them.

Bill hated blind conformity. One morning we were eating left over turkey, dressing, and sweet potatoes smothered in gravy for breakfast. Bill began, "This is a sick system. It's natural for a man to eat whatever food is in abundance in a specific geographical location during that particular time of the year. Deer don't insist on eating spring blossoms during the winter. They eat what nature provides at the time or die." Pointing to the plate of food in front of him he continued, "Take this food here, you would never see this served during breakfast on TV or see it on a box of cold cereal. Bacon, pancakes, and orange juice are considered breakfast items because commercial agriculture has decreed that all shall consume only those commodities arbitrarily designated as breakfast items, during the prescribed hours allocated to the peasants for the purpose of consumption of breakfast. Take a small child and set this meal before him and he'll dive into it like a hungry pig. Once indoctrinated by the system, a couple of years in school, he'd rather eat plywood than consume a 'dinner' item before five p.m." I can remember agreeing with him, but I couldn't fathom why he was so rabid and passionate about why anyone cared about what people ate any time of the day.

Later on, I learned in school about how important breakfast was propertied to be, the most important meal of the day, right? Not so! It has been determined by scientific, dietary inquiry that no one meal of the day is any more important than another. It has also been discovered that the breakfast cereal industry has been the champion advocate of breakfast as the most important meal of the day. The only evidence substantiating that this meal is the big one is the millions of dollars the cereal industry spent on propagating this falsehood. In other words, the most important meal that you consume is the one you eat when you are hungry. Just ask my three-year-old.

"We'll have the deep-end down here" Bill said, as he ushered George on a tour.

George was warming to the idea of a pool by now, "A diving board?" George asked the question as if he were sitting on Santa's lap, asking for an extravagant, Christmas present that he had longed for but felt a twinge of selfish humility while making the request.

"Sure thing George, right here! And not one of those ridiculous ones at water level either, we'll put that baby up about six feet, maybe even a few feet higher, so you can do some real diving."

George was no longer warming to the idea of a pool, he was ready to become actively involved. "But you have to go deep Bill, you need at least ten feet in the diving end." Now he was hooked, not only was he accepting the idea of a pool, he was weighing in with technical advice. I could picture in my mind George the foreman: bathrobe; fuzzy, pink, piggy slippers; clipboard; and hardhat.

"Plan is to go twelve. Already down about three feet George and haven't hit any major boulders. If our luck holds and the digging machine doesn't breakdown twelve feet won't be any problem."

George was a machinist, and if you have ever met someone dedicated to this vocation you would know they see the world and process information in much the same way as a computer does. The only difference is that a blue print does not come sputtering out of an orifice on the human version.

Later in life, one of Bill's daughters married a machinist, hell of a nice guy. I was helping him nail some trim around his garage door one-day. I finished the side I was working on and noticed that he was about a quarter done with the one he was working on. As I was talking to him I noticed the spacing of his nails appeared to be meticulously uniform. Some time after the job was completed, I slipped outside into the garage and found a tape measure and commenced a closer inspection of my nephews nailing job. An eight foot section of trim with eight nails each spaced a foot apart, not one more that $1/8^{th}$ of an inch off. That sort of precision just gushes out of a machinist like pure water from an artesian well.

In the span of thirty seconds, George had the plans and specifications for building a diving board. "Have to use stainless on board Bill, nothing else hold up to chlorine. And anchor bolts must go deep in apron surrounding pool, extra rebar and cement, have to dig down at least two feet deeper than apron, three square feet. The way I would do is like this." George picked up a stick and began drawing in the dirt as he spoke. "You make foundational base out of rebar for anchor bolts, look like the arms of star fish, you weld to bolt head. You get elephant on that board and not uproot it."

That's the kind of guy Bill is. He can get started on a major undertaking and people seem to be sucked into it, like getting too close to a neutron star with your space ship, or like Tom Sawyer painting a fence. George had forgotten that originally he had come outside at four a.m. wearing his wife's bathrobe to complain to Bill about the noise. He had been smitten by the pool project and it was incrementally taking control of his better judgment.

George continued, "I can make them for you neighbor, I think I might have scraps, make good sturdy ladder."

At the age of forty-five, Bill looked to be a man in his early thirties. Two hundred and thirty pounds with a thirty-four inch waist, his shoulders broad, and his upper arms bulged where his triceps and biceps strained to burst from his shirt. An intimidating and imposing figure, he underwent a radical transformation when he smiled. As Bill smiled, shook hands, and graciously accepted and thanked George for the offer of assistance he was transformed into something more that the mere physical presence of a human being. He became boundless and was the soul of a man expressing a humble appreciation and acknowledgement of another entity. As with so many other social edicts such as saying, "Thanks!" my brother uttered this word and his sincerity could be discerned in his voice, seen on his face, and felt in the warmth of his embrace or handshake. Personally, I had experienced this previously without giving it much thought, but found it fascinating to observe at this time and be reminded of the power and complexity it encompassed. His sincere smile and genuine gratitude confirmed and strengthened the relationship between brothers and friends; an affirmation that the recipient was worthy of this gift simply because of whom he or she is. It meant so much to George simply because it was an honest conveyance of that which makes all of us human.

When Bill told you thanks it came from every fiber of his being. You could be absolutely assured that there were no social niceties he felt obligated to adhere to. This is not to say he was some sort of daisy sniffer that never got pissed off, he was just as honest and convincing in that modality, it's just that he didn't go there very often. The point I am trying to make is that of the few memorable acts of human kindness for which I have been responsible, not one of the recipients was able, or willing, to express the level of sincere gratitude that I received from my bother for some fairly menial mundane task such as cleaning up his garage.

I think he was able to accomplish this because of his ability to transcend this material world and focus on the spiritual intent of the individual, valuing this intent much more than any potential material accomplishment, which might result. Bill would have argued that a man attempting to rescue another from the top of a burning building and inadvertently knocking that person to their death, would be worthy of the same admiration as the man who managed to save someone in a similar situation.

Given the nature of his personality people came to him in times of need. Some needed money, some advise, then there were those that sought shelter from the storm; needing a place of sanctuary and spiritual revitalization. When it came to money Bill didn't have a bankroll for long, but he did belong to the credit union and had no qualms about borrowing money to help someone else out. I was in a financial jam one time and I called him up to see if he could loan me three hundred bucks. I got a check in the mail a few days later with a note reading, "If you asked for three you probably need five." The check was made out for five hundred dollars. He didn't have that kind of money at the time but that's the kind of man he was. It took me close to six years to pay off that debt; a couple of bucks here, a couple there. In the end I worked it off clearing brush and stumps on a little spread he had up in the woods.

I expressed to him some time after that my regrets for not having serviced my debt in a timelier manner and he busted out laughing. When he regained his composure he exclaimed, "Brother, you're one of the only ones that ever bothered to pay me back." He went on to explain, "It didn't take long for word to get out that old Billy G. Goodpants," a nick name he used for himself, "was an easy touch when it came to borrowing money. No interest, no paper work and no nasty phone calls when you don't make a payment." His tone was sarcastic on the fringes as he went on to elaborate, "I really don't give a shit about the money, never expected most of the people I loaned to would pay all of it back in the first place. I guess I was more concerned about acknowledgment that the friendship I had extended to people was of a similar value to them as it was to me and that giving your word, especially to a friend, meant something. It has been my experience over the years with family and friends alike, rather than trying to reach a compromise and a mutually acceptable resolution of a debt owed me, most people choose to forget that I have ever loaned them a dime."

A socialist at heart, Bill liked the axiom, "Each man should contribute in accordance with his abilities, as each should receive in accordance to his needs." By this he meant that he was more interested in appreciation and reciprocity when it came to any financial loans he made. If a man was unable to meet financial obligations, let him give in accordance to his other abilities. I remember one guy he had loaned money to that built him a deck. Bill bought the materials, food and booze, but in the end they both considered the debut absolved without a formal agreement.

I asked him why the hell he didn't quit loaning money if he had such bad luck with ever getting paid back. He replied, "The way I look at it is if a man comes to me in need of something that is within my capacity to provide, I'll pony it up because it's the right thing to do, not because of the potential, or lack thereof, of future compensation for the act. It's kind of selfish in a way, but sometimes I think I do it more for me than I do the people I'm lending the money to."

To this day, I am in awe at how people spontaneously become involved in Bill's projects and his life. Bill is one of those guys that takes pride in never asking for anyone's help. You know the type, they consider it a flag of dishonor to actually admit they can't do it all. I'm the same way. I'll spend five hours working on something rather than asking my wife to hold the flashlight, so I can get the job done in half the time. The funny thing about it is I have seen what an affirmation it is to Bill when someone comes to request his assistance, and believe me, those doing so are too numerous to mention or count. You would think he would have made the generalization that if the experience of being asked for help was a positive rewarding one for him, the rational thing to do would be to pass that pleasure on when the opportunity manifested itself. I can only guess that we are a lot alike when we start working on something; I get so engrossed in what I am doing, or more often trying to do or trying to figure out what the hell I am doing, that I really don't stop and think how my chances at expeditious success and completion could improve with outside assistance.

As George departed I noticed that he veered from the path to his house and opted to enter his shop which was attached to the back of his house, the poodle kennel running the length of the house and shop. The lights went on in the shop and a short time thereafter I detected the intermittent, blue explosions of light, which were indicative of welding activity. I could picture George in his present welding attire: a women's house coat and slippers, complimentarily, accessorizing welding gloves, helmet, and other appropriate protective gear. Would have been a great poster for a transvestite, pinup boy calendar.

I was drifting in and out of consciousness about the time Bill shut the backhoe down. "Let's take a break," he said.

"*A break?*" I thought, "*What the hell ever happened to sleep?*" We grabbed a bite to eat and took a short break.

Now, when it comes to food I admit it brings out the beast in me on both ends of the spectrum; go without it too long and my disposition degenerates into that of a grizzly bear with insomnia in the dead of winter. Feed me too much and, like a gorged lion, I'm ready to sleep a couple of days. Bill is a dinner table philosopher. I think he figured that if he was biologically required to eat he might as well use the time efficiently and productively. As we sat eating at five-forty-five a.m. he expounded on his perspective of life and time.

"It's funny how people are driven and controlled by that invention," he began as he pointed to the clock on the wall while gnawing on the leg bone of the turkey we had been working on for the last several days. "People let that thing tell them when and what to eat, when and where to sleep, work, and play. The only clock or calendar of any real importance is the one that begins when you are born and terminates when you die. For all of us there comes a time in our lives when we realize that life on this earth is a finite commodity and that our days are numbered. With that realization comes the opportunity to live each of those days to the fullest in accord with that which you consider to be of importance and value in your life, or relinquish your ability to self determinate to the fickle winds of chance. This life is like a bag of priceless, gold coins that each of us is issued while visiting this world, playing this game we call life. The rules require that you spend a coin each day and barter with the world for what you will receive in exchange. If you choose not to barter and in return receive nothing, you still must forfeit a coin. Now if a man knows that he will loose a coin either way; why not get the most out of your expenditure? If you are trading a coin for money, get the most you can because you will never find anyone to pay you what it's really worth. If you are bartering for memories, make them memories that you won't mind reliving over and over because that's what you will be doing during the home stretch of this game, a game all men are required to play, all men finish, but no man wins." I was with him completely on that one, but his point was somewhat diluted by the image he presented while delivering his point. The man was still gashing his teeth on the grisly knee joint of an otherwise slicked clean, turkey leg, with a generous mantle of gravy and dressing plastered around his mouth.

Bill was working that following evening, and I was still thinking about racking up memories that would sustain me when I was knocking on death's door. Somehow I had managed to win the heart and accompanying favors of the most beautiful girl attending my high school. Not sure how it was arranged, but on a fairly regular basis I would ride my bicycle to a school close to her home, sneak around in the field behind her house until she gave me the signal that her parents were in bed. She left the basement door unlocked. I would arrive at about ten p.m., spend the entire night mating, exit at dawn, and then dutifully ride my bike to school for an unproductive day. On this particular night, I was making my departure from Bill's basement and I ran into him in the driveway as he returned home from work.

As was indicative of my youth, all of those covert activities that I assumed only a few friends and I knew about, were common knowledge to the significant adults in my life. Rather than waxing morality, Bill weighted in on the health and safety considerations stating, "If her dad is the red neck you have made him out to be, you might want to think about what he would do if he caught you making a midnight visit. You really run the risk of taking a slug of lead from a guy thinking he is protecting his home and family. I know what my first reaction would be in a similar situation." No sermon, no judgment. It's hard for an adult to interact that way with a young person, and it's even harder when they share the same family.

I thought long and hard about what he said but the call of the wild was too strong for me to resist with mere common sense. I set out into the night to violate the daughter of a man that would have not thought twice about plugging me, had he known I was cavorting in his basement with his little girl.

This brings to mind a time that Bill had me do some undercover work for him. One of his daughters was a little on the wild side in her early teens and Bill was concerned about with whom and where she was spending her leisure time. She was allegedly spending the evening at a local youth hangout, an under twenty-one-pool hall. Bill gave me a few bucks and dropped me off close by. He was worried about his daughter being sexually active. I guess he figured that if she wasn't at the pool hall she must be getting laid, but I didn't necessarily see the connection. She wasn't there and when we returned home Bill was agitated to say the least. Ranting is a good way to put it, proclaiming to his wife that no daughter of his was going to engage in such activities while living under his roof.

Glad gave him a reproachful look and responded, "What the hell do you want her to do? Go out and in the woods and get pine cones stuck in her ass like I did when you and I were young?" So much for the taboo theory.

In the end his daughter did become pregnant at the tender age of fifteen. I remember the father of the child coming to Bill's house one night shortly before the child was born. This strapping young man timidly took one step on the front porch as Bill came charging out the front door like a she bear bolting to the defense of her cubs. The poor kid, by the look on his face he had resigned himself to an imminent ambulance ride, complements of the thrashing he expected was to be administered. The right hand of my brother lashed out at the young man, but it was an open hand of friendship, not a clenched fist of anger. As was my brother's way a visitor to his home was showered with hospitality fit for royalty.

This kid spent the evening at the house and Bill treated him with the kindness and respect that were his trademark when interacting with guests in his home. The situation was awkward for the boy and his daughter, but Bill seemed unscathed. It didn't matter to Bill if you were a tramp from the street or the Queen of England, once you crossed the threshold of his abode like all visitors you were treated with the same level of graciousness.

But that hospitality can at times have unexpected results. There was the time Bill put on a deep fried shrimp feed for Christmas. I showed up late and all that was left of the party was Bill, who by the looks of things, had been the life of the party. I was helping clean up the kitchen and he asked me to save the oil in the fryer. I couldn't find anything to put it in so I poured it into an empty rum bottle. Well it just so happened that Bill's neighbor showed up, he had just gotten off work. Bill set about the kitchen mixing his friend hot buttered rum, accidentally grabbing the jug with used cooking oil. Not wanting to offend his host, the neighbor gagged down the fishy tasting drink and tried to make an escape. Bill was not one to allow a guest in his house to have only one drink. He insisted that his friend have another. I could tell the man knew he would not win this argument and resigned himself to ingesting one more oily, buttered rum.

Speaking to Bill on the subject on the hospitality he extended to the man who had impregnated his daughter later the next day, he related his "package deal" concept about people. What he meant is that people are in some respects like cars; when they're new there's not much to dislike and everything works pretty much the way it should, just like little babies and small children. The more miles you put on one however, the more dents, rattles and irritating malfunctions the vehicle tends to acquire. Depends a lot on what sort of road it's been driven on and what sort of maintenance schedule has been adhered to. The point he was making was that as a direct result of living life, everyone is going to pick up a few characteristics or experiences, which will not set well with your personal standards or ideals. You have to take the good with the bad. Bill's advise was that when you felt like passing judgment on someone else, take some time out and spend it in front of a mirror. He wasn't putting on pretenses when he opened his door and heart to the father of the child in the womb of his little girl.

The kid ended up being a deadbeat low-life, so much so that when Bill's grandson came of age and got to know his biological father for what he was, he took his grandfather's last name. Mark, Bill's grandson, is living proof of the fact that we often never know the true value or meaning of the events in our lives when those events take place. Different seeds take different paths to germination: some produce plants that bare fruit perennially, some bare only once and then die, and some only produce flowers. Mark and Bill have a special love for each other that grew stronger right up to the moment Bill died. Mark was more like a second son to Bill, arriving later in life when Bill was able to see that he had spent considerably less time with his own son than he felt he should have when the boy was small.

Conventional wisdom at the time would have advised that a girl so young should have an abortion and finish growing up before considering bearing children. It was a gamble which the odds dictated would end in failure and remourse. In many ways this child born to a child pulled our immediate family together, strengthening many of the bonds which make for a healthy family unit. The blessing this child was to all of those with whom he made contact while growing up is a testament to the frailty of human judgement. Unfortunately, few families and even fewer pregnant teens are fortunate enough to have a father figure in their lives such as Bill. Without his unwavering assistance and moral support, my nice and her child would have been anonymous statistics added to the dismal roles of typical single parent families headed by a female without a formal education or employment training.

In many ways, I guess Mark, my brother Scott, and I, shared a similar relationship with Bill. All three of us were young boys adrift in the world without a father figure worthy of holding very tight to. Bill heeded the call and can be considered to be the single most important person in our respective journeys to becoming men.

Chapter 12

While digging in the deep end of the pit the backhoe strained against a large rock. Attempting to maneuver and get the right leverage to remove the bolder the ball joint that connected the digging end to the control and locomotion end snapped. The machine lay there like some gigantic arthropod with a severed spinal column. After a considerable dissertation on the inadequacies of the digger, interspersed with cursing of a general nature, Bill got on the phone to the rental company.

Now, I enjoyed listening to Bill talk anytime, but business on the phone was a real treat because he could shift communication gears into the communication modality that the situation begged, smooth as a log truck driver with a bad clutch. Always polite and diplomatic to begin with, this was not necessarily the conduit he found the most successful. As he relayed the information about the breakdown the person on the other end seemed to be implying that Bill was responsible for returning the equipment to the rental facility for an evaluation to determine if the failure was due to normal usage or inappropriate operator actions.

Bill politely inquired, "And how much might I ask, do you think that piece of equipment weights?" There was a pause that I interpreted as the person on the other end stating they didn't know. Then Bill continued, "How then, do you suggest that I remove your defective machinery from an eight-foot-deep hole in the ground and return it to you, to have it inspected, to determine the cause of its breakdown in its present state of incapacitation?" When he was informed that he might need to rent another piece of machinery to move it, Bill replied, "If I am going to rent anything else it will be a cat to bury your backhoe in the hole in which it has met such an untimely demise. You choose: you can get someone out here to fix it, or you can be here at noon for its funeral." On the top rung of the ladder of communication Bill gave everyone the same amount of consideration and respect that he commanded for himself, that was until he was given some indication that a shift in position was in order. On the bottom rung he could be a belligerent, intimidating sonofabitch who wasn't inclined to make idle threats. As he hung up the phone I could see on his face that he wasn't bluffing.

Before he could explain the details of his conversation the phone rang. I surmised that the previous individual's supervisor had been briefed on the details of the conversation, which had culminated in the ultimatum on which the fate of the disabled backhoe precariously hung. Bill was diplomatic and curt, finishing the discussion in less than a minute. When he hung up all he said was, "They'll have a repair man out here inside of four hours at no charge and we'll get an extra twelve hours of rental time." During the duration of the week in which we had this digging machine Bob's Rental would provide on site repairs a total of three times. After the initial confrontation all further visits were initiated with a short phone request.

In this and all other situations in his life it was the principle that meant the most to Bill. The idea that some anonymous business or cooperate entity could treat an individual as some sort of subservient, inferior being invoked a rabid response by my brother. When he retired Bill bought a little piece of land on the outskirts of town, called it his duck ranch. Several years after this purchase a multinational conglomerate commenced laying a natural gas pipeline that ran from Canada, passing through the states of Washington and Oregon, intersecting Bill's duck farm to the south land. Bill had nothing better to do than encumber the progress of this gas line with endless haggling with the company about equitable compensation for an easement across his property. When Bill surveyed his neighbors and found that the gas company had bullied each of them into a less than reasonable compensation package for the right to cross their properties Bill felt it his duty to extract the maximum amount of restitution for their acts of corporate arrogance. He held the project up for several weeks refusing to allow them to cross his property, then settled on a tidy sum with the company, only to call the deal off at the last moment when the planned pipeline intrusion would require cutting down a majestic Douglas Fur next to the pond. In the end, the gas company agreed to place a ninety-degree turn in the pipeline in order to circumvent the fur tree.

Bill took great pride in knowing that preserving the tree had cost the company more money that the sum total of all the easements in the neighborhood. He joked that when the inspectors came out to check on the pipeline detour, he would like to stroll out with his chain saw and cut down the tree. He had no real affection for the tree, what he did have was an intense hate for any business organization that somehow felt, that by virtue of amassing a fortune, they were entitled to some sort of superior status in this world over the rights of an individual.

Like I said, Bill was quite an artist on the phone. My whole family has always had a phone fetish of sorts. I remember one time Bill and Doug, both in their late thirties, were playing practical jokes on the phone. As a kid I played on the phone with my friends making prank calls, but to see two grown men engaged in such an activity took away a bit of the consternation which I intermittently felt about growing up. During this episode, Doug gets on the phone and calls the Hilton Hotel speaking in a pathetic English accent. "Yes, the is Mr. James Edwards Blair III. I'm an emissary for Royal Dutch Shell Middle Eastern Operations and Explorations. We are considering holding our quarterly meeting in your area and I need some information about your facilities. We will need food, lodging, and meeting rooms for one hundred twenty five individuals for a minimum of two weeks." You could tell by Doug's expression that the individual on the other end had taken the bait. He continued, "We will be hosting several important dignitaries from the major oil producing nations and will require they be served the ethnic foods to which they are accustomed. Will that be a problem? Good! Good! In particular, there is one individual, a member of the royal family of the United Arab Emirates, who apparently has a voracious appetite for fried sheep genitalia. Some sort of traditional cuisine would be my guess. Is that something you would be able to procure in fresh abundance? Wonderful, wonderful, I can see it is going to be a pleasure to do business with your establishment. Now one last thing, it is the custom in the land of the gentleman of whom we speak to have his food sampled in front of his table by the staff who has responsibility for its preparation. A traditional ceremony to ensure the purity of the food consumed by the royal family. Would you be willing to do this? You would?" At this point, using his God given voice Doug said, "You would stand in front of one hundred twenty five people and devour the fried penis of a sheep? On second thought, I don't think I like the idea of doing business with a guy who eats sheep dicks! I'll call Motel Six instead. Thanks anyway."

As we had not had any sleep the previous night this seemed an opportune time to take a hiatus. Sun worshiper that I was, I decided to settle into a reclining lawn chair in a quite corner of the yard and soak up a few rays. As I drifted in and out of fitful sleep I dreamt I was a slave in ancient Egypt, toiling without relief in the blazing sun, constructing a swimming pool of gigantic proportions for that great King Rutin Tootin who was immortalized in several Three Stooges classics, most notable being, *I Want My Mummy*. The thing was shaped like a serpent, big enough for leisurely navigation by the royal barge, with pyramids interspersed on the edges, diving boards on their peeks. When Bill woke me to begin our task anew, for a moment, I could have sworn that he was wearing the head garb of an Egyptian slave taskmaster brandishing a hemp lash or a cat of nine tails. As my visual acuity cleared I could see that the object he held in his hand was a garden hose.

"They got that damn thing fixed" Bill said, "Can you believe those capitalist bastards wanted me to pay for it? The contraption is over four years old. If they rented it once a week for at least three days, that means they have taken in a minimum of $93,600 in rental fees. They could buy a new one right now and still be money ahead." As I stumbled to my feet and tried to clear my head enough to figure out why it was going to cost Bill about ninety three thousand dollars to water the lawn he continued, "I thought we could hose down the dig and try to keep the dust cloud down."

The days wore on. I alternated between keeping the vehicles running, packing five gallon pails of rock and dirt, and spraying water on the surface of a hole that was looking a lot more like a swimming pool with each successive mouth full of dirt exhumed by the diesel belching demon. In between I used a rake and shovel to clean up the dirt and rocks the digging machine left it its wake. On this particular evening out of the corner of my eye I caught a freeze frame of something moving in the dark. It was George charging across the lawn adorned in pajamas, which could have passed as a leisure suit for Bozo the clown. This particular outfit was smattered with little yellow duckies and brown and white chicks, frolicking with multicolored balloons in their beaks and bills. This sleeping attire was oversized to accommodate George's unique physic, best exemplified by an equatorial bulge. I was reminded of a clown I had seen once as a child in the circus; the guy who had his pants filled up with water by a fellow clown, causing them to expand at the waist line, somehow holding a reservoir within his trousers without loosing any water down the legs.

Rather than hollering at Bill, George was making his way towards me. "No, no, not again, not tonight too! This noise, this digging! All night long. Has to stop! My poor babies cannot sleep. They very sensitive." George was going on about his dogs as though they were family members with delicate, complex, medical conditions. "The stress of noise, no! This must stop. It causes rashes, then the scratching. The scratching, then out comes the fur. Bill promised only digging for five days, only five!" I wasn't sure if George was repeating himself because of the background noise, to emphasize his point, or maybe he was a bit off his regular game by virtue of fretting about his powder puff pooches. Regardless, it was evident that he was in need of venting his concerns to Bill.

Unresponsive to my pleas for attention, I felt I had no recourse but to give Bill a blast from the hose. An extremely effective mode of communication, he was off the digging machine in no time and made his way up the bank to where George and I were standing in no time. Bill asked, "What's the idea of the shower smart ass?"

Before I could think of a snappy response, Bill had engaged George in conversation. "Sorry for disturbing you another night George, this damn thing broke down again and we lost a lot of daylight digging time. If the dirt keeps moving at this rate, this will be the last night. Take a look George. The depth and grade are basically done, all I'm doing now is trying to square up the sides the best I can."

While Bill led George on another tour, George valiantly tried to make a stand, "Bill, my dogs, the noise, you postpone this . . . ."

Bill continued, not consciously ignoring George, but oblivious to the here and now as he became immersed in that world in which dreams begin their transformation into reality. Bill was being seduced deeper into his swimming pool of the future, not unlike a process of self-hypnosis, and George was just close enough to be caught in the vortex. "Just think George, on those hot summer days, no more hiding in the shade like a couple of old, worn out, blood hounds. We can put a cooler full of beer right there and we'll be on our air mattress in the water floating like two feathers on a cool summer breeze. Hell, we'll never need to go on vacation again, right? The only reason I ever do is to be in the sun and near the water, now it'll all be right here, and the comforts of home to boot."

"But Bill . . . ." George spoke these words as if he felt obligated to make one last valiant interdiction to make the point he had come armed with. I got the impression that he felt he would loose face with his high-stung fir balls that were closely monitoring our activities and eavesdropping on the present conversation if he failed to lodge a formal complaint about the disturbance. George's words however, were void of authority and without conviction, a meager echo of the complaint he had come to make. The echo grew fainter in George's head as he envisioned himself in the summer of the future yet to come which Bill was enticing him to visit. George could see himself poolside, his poodles dressed in suggestive scanty swimsuits, serving him umbrella drinks, and rubbing his back with coconut oil.

Bill continued, "And over at this end we'll have a deck, table, lawn chairs, and a big enough umbrella to cast some shade on that corner of the pool, just in case a guy wants to get out of the sun for a while without getting out of the water."

I could see by the course of the conversation that George was being sucked into the confluence at the mouth of the river of reality and the ocean of unbridled imagination. With enthusiasm George added, "Yea, and that getting out of the pool Bill, you know you don't want hoping in and out at the sides, no. That concrete finish too rough, scratch you all up to hell. You need ladders to get out, and back in for he who don't dive. I like having one each end of pool, diving you don't need to swim all the way to other end to get out."

"Good idea George, I never gave it that much thought, but right you are. I'll have to do some checking into prices at the pool supply joints." Bill said.

"Nonsense, I make them. You pay for materials. I draw up the plans, give you a price sometime tomorrow."

"Sounds great to me George." Bill said, "At this rate we'll have this pool ready for a christening before the good weather is gone."

George wandered back home contentedly, having completely forgotten the burning issue that had initially been the impetus for his journey to the hole instillation project. As the night before George did not return to his disturbed place of rest, he made a bee line to his shop were the blue white explosions of arch welding light flashed on the window panes once again, kindling a ferrous fire which would soon give birth to quality, pool side accessories.

Bill and I continued operations. I was tolerating the mechanically generated noise well enough, but I was reaching the breaking point with the pack of poodles that were yapping in a continuous K9 chorus, reaching an unnerving crescendo each time I would walk by their pen. You know how we all have those quirky, insignificant situations, which for some unknown reason you can't ignore or tolerate? For me it's incessant barking by a dog, that in all likelihood, has no more idea as to why its barking than I do; out of habit or plain stupidity. As the night was warm and the poor creatures appeared to have accumulated copious carpeting of dust on their pedigreed pelts, I thought that a shower might be in order. So it went for the duration. Each time I would come by their pen, I gave them a good douching down. Almost immediately their level of complaining was dramatically reduced, so naturally I concluded that it was the dirt and heat which had been the source of their collective irritation.

Somewhere just before dawn, Bill drove the hoe out of the hole, disembarked and stated, "I think that just about does it. Let's clean this rig up and get it back to the store. We should be able to get it there before they open this morning. The way I have it figured, with the additional twenty four hours they gave us on this contraption, I should get close to a hundred bucks back for the time we didn't use." I never saw Bill loose an argument, and if it came down to it, he was always willing to fight for what he believed in. As this situation played out, I was later to find that rather than demand the money he felt was his due, Bill ultimately agreed to a compromise in which he was allotted the residual credit for future rentals.

Chapter 13

After returning the hoe, Bill and I spend some time milling around the excavation and talking about the details of finishing the project. As he kicked a few dirt clods into the deep end, Bill said, "Well, we've put in close to two months of work in the pit. Here's to a job well done." Bill handed me a beer from the six-pack he was holding. I'm sorry to say that at the time I felt that a beer was a sign of transitioning to manhood. I'm even sorrier to say that this cultural myth is still perpetuated in our society thirty years later. Irrespective of the inappropriate nature of the event, I really shouldn't have been drinking at that age, it was still an intimate moment I shared with my brother, adding yet another strand to an ever thickening hawser which bound our hearts together.

The next task in the pit was squaring the walls and leveling the floor to make ready for the cement. It seemed a simple enough task on the surface until I discovered that in the pit all things are not what they seem. Take for instance a small rock sticking out that began to protrude from the deep end of the floor while I was in the process of leveling it with a shovel. The more I leveled, the more rock I found. As it was strategically located in an area where structural supports for the concrete frames would be placed, the rock had to go. I had given up on the rock ever being moved long before I broke the handles of three shovels in what I considered an exercise in futility, but I continued to toil dutifully for the better part of a day attempting to unearth the bottom of the boulder. In Bill's absence I often slipped into lethargy of pessimism and in spirit gave up on the pit. I did not however, allow my body to give in to that allure. I kept the shovel picking away at the dirt surrounding the boulder.

When it appeared that we had uncovered the majority of the rock Bill exclaimed, "I think we can get a choker around this thing about now. The engine in that old caddie's got damn near four hundred cubic inches. If I don't loose traction, I'll bet we get it out." My brother and I were a perfect match to take on challenges of this caliber. He was unwaveringly positive that anything could be done and he voiced this perspective. I desperately needed to hear such evocations because I always seemed to focus on the pessimistic attributes of the job at hand. While Bill was elated about moving the son of Gibraltar, I was wondering what good would it do when inevitably the granite gargantuan would have to be elevated four feet in the air in order to remove it from the shallow end of the pool. I resigned myself to silent faith in the infallibility of my brother. His take on the situation was that sometimes if you look at each step of a task from start to finish you might well dwell on those that at the moment seem insurmountable. This can lead to ignoring the fact that the single most important step of any task is the first one. Bills plan was simple; move the damn thing first then figure out how to get it out of the pool.

Over the years I have learned the value of the character trait of unfaltering belief in one's ability to conquer adversity. As a very young man I remember talking with Bill about this subject. He told me, "Everything in this life has a price tag on it, so to speak. This is not to say that all things have a monetary value. All things in this life have an individual, specific price tag, and it may well be a different price for you than it is for me. Let's say that you and I both wanted a bottle of whisky right now. The price I would have to pay would be the time and effort it would take for me to drive to the liquor store, the expenditures associated with transportation, and that which the system extracted from me in exchange for the amount of money I spent. Your costs would be different. You aren't old enough to drive so let's say you pay a friend five bucks to drive you to the liquor store. You hang around the front of the store for an hour waiting for someone you perceive to be willing to buy you, a minor, a jug of booze. You confront the individual, give him ten bucks for the jug, and pay him five for his services. Let's say he then walks out of the store with your whiskey, gets in his car, and drives away. You are presented with a new dilemma, do you cut your losses and head home, or do you want that booze bad enough to try again? You make the decisions about how important the things are in life that you aspire to. If it's important enough to you, then no price is too high. You might even go so far as to rob the liquor store, the price being the risk you may be shot or arrested and sent to jail. You can have anything in this life you want, provided you are willing to pay the price."

As a junior high school teacher, I find myself using this philosophy time and time again in my classroom, making a concerted effort however, to find more appropriate scenarios than attempting to acquire whiskey as a minor. I don't allow my students to use the words smart or dumb in my classroom. I tell them that if they are capable of finding their way to school and then into my classroom, they have passed the intelligence test for my class. The rest is work, which can be harder for some than others. I explain to them they all have the potential to be an "A" student in my class should they desire to, but the price tag for that "A" will be different for each individual. Some students will be able to get an "A" and spend one hour a week on homework, some will have to spend ten hours a week, some will need to come in before or after school for extra help, some will need to study for tests, some will not. The prize is within the grasp of all, provided they are willing to persevere.

When I look at a class of young people I see unlimited potential and realize that what I learned in the pit was this: the only limitations which pose an impenetrable barrier are those we construct in the privacy of our hearts and souls; those little, self defeating lies we whisper to ourselves when we begin to question our abilities, thanks in large part to the judgments passed on us as developing learners by the educational system and society. These dirty, little, self defeating lies exacerbate that which has been identified as weaknesses which, in reality, are nothing more than a mix of inexperience and immaturity; natural states for young people to pass through at various depths and durations of time.

Bill had a saying that he heard from our father who had been an amateur boxer. Dad said, "There's no disgrace in getting knocked down in the ring or in life, it comes with the territory. The only time a man had anything to be ashamed of is when he doesn't get up off the canvas and back into the fight."

When Bill had woven the choker cable around the rock, in what he assured me was a secure manner, he proceeded to attach the other end to the frame of the caddie. Bill explained that his plan was to get the car out on the paved street to ensure maximum traction in order to facilitate a smooth, successful extraction of the bolder. This necessitated using a substantial length of cable, about one hundred feet. I did not at the time understand the physics of stretching a pliable object and that any energy expended in doing so was merely stored temporally, awaiting the proper circumstances which would allow said item to return to a homeostatic state. Suffice it to say that I now know all I need to know about this aspect of the laws of physics as a direct result of the experience that was soon to follow.

"Better stand clear when the cable takes on tension" Bill hollered, "Just make sure it's not kinked while we stretch it out tight."

From my vantage point in the garage I watched as the events unfolded. The caddie was screaming under the strain, blue smoke pouring out of the wheel wells. I was wondering, pessimistically, what would happen if the cable slipped or the rock actually came loose. Would Bill's reflexes respond quickly enough for him to stop the forward lurch of the car before it leapt across the neighbor's front yard and came crashing through the wall of their living room? Would the bolder become dislodged and catapult to a resting place more inconvenient than its present one?

Before I could generate any more optimistic scenarios I heard a sound reminiscent of a cartoon classic; you know when Yosemite Sam shoots a cannon and you get the initial explosion and then the whistling as the projectile travels through the air? That's the noise the cable made when it snapped. It broke somewhere near the rock and it came lashing out of the pool like a rattlesnake tossed on a hot stove. It's funny how many different things can happen in a split second. As the cable lashed out indiscriminately it tore into George's rose garden. In one clean sweep, his entire garden was leveled to about knee height.

It appeared that the serpentine cable was on a mission of vengeance against the vehicle that had dared to disturb its slumber. Fortunately for Bill, the cable rapped neatly around the power lines running parallel to the street, sparing him a lashing from the erratic whipping of the angry cable. The frayed end of the cable came to rest on the cyclone fence, which was the line of demarcation between Bill and George's property. This fence also comprised the front portion of the poodle palace, and unfortunately, one of the more curious creatures came to the fence to investigate the ruckus and stuck its wet nose on the electrified fence. The 440 volts in the line came straight from and complements of the Bonneville Dam Power Administration. The unbridled power made short work of the critter, I heard a crackling noise and saw a flash of flames enshrouded in a plume of residual smoke where the poodle had been standing, but I didn't have time for a more thorough investigation of the smoldering remains at that point.

I was running on my way to see if Bill was OK, screaming, "Don't get out! The cables in the power lines!" Momentarily anticipating the worst, I pictured my barbecued, brother's remnants behind the wheel of his Cadillac, the only material object I have any recollection of to this day that he had a kind word for. I had the funeral all planed out and began composing on the slate of my mind a fitting eulogy. The funeral service would be held at the edge of the pit, I would insist that his remains not be disturbed from the hallowed site of his untimely demise. He had given his life in the line of duty. In recognition of his dedication, I would demand that he not only be encrypted in his caddie, but the two of them would be laid to rest in the hollowed earth of the pit.

Before I could put the finishing touches on my graveside eulogy, I could hear a familiar voice cursing from the caddie. "Stay in the car Bill!" I was still screeching, "The cable's caught in the power lines! It's hot! I saw it French fry one of the poodles."

Bill looked at me with a quirky smile and said, "Stand back."

I was terrified that he planned to grab the door handle in a gesture of defiance to the power company for the inconvenience they had caused him. I dutifully stood back and half closed my eyes, not wanting to witness a repeat of the recently cindered creature next door. Closing my eyes only made things worse. As they closed Bill metamorphosed into a six-foot poodle positioned behind the wheel of the electrified Cadillac.

Bill backed the car into the street and began to slowly drive away, instructing me "Give that cable some room, no telling where it will fall, give me a signal when it's free of the power lines." Adding, "Don't worry about the power, as long as I'm in the car the rubber tires keep me from grounding."

I figured he knew what he was doing, so I did as instructed. When the cable snagged in the transformer connection I began jumping up and down flailing my arms looking akin I am sure, to a turkey on Thanksgiving imploring farmer John to consider substituting a ham for the holiday feast. My gyrations were of no avail, the cable grew taunt until the connection on the transformer snapped off. The cable and caddie were free, but the power line recoiled, coming to rest on the roof of George's house.

I couldn't have been more than eight years old when George moved into the house next door. I use to spend a considerable amount of time carefully observing his activities as he groomed his newly acquired nest. He spent endless hours nursing seeds, bulbs, and sprigs of new growth from meticulously manicured flowerbeds. I remember daydreaming about what he was really up to. As he was of Philippine nationality and I was naive about other cultures by virtue of extremely limited multicultural interactions and had no education on the subject, I came to the conclusion that he was a sorcerer, commissioned by the parents of mischievous children who did not mind or who did not eat their parsnips. These children I concluded, were delivered to this man of black magic who extracted from their bodies all their essence which their parents considered noble and desirable, disposing of the worthless tailings in the infamous incinerator that must have resided in the tin building out back, where the sparks and blue flames could been seen dancing on the windows as yet another poor child met the fate of those that don't wash their hands and face. With a child's mind I surmised that this maternal attention given to the objects he was placing in the ground could mean only one thing; these things had to be seeds that would produce children, the new good kids to replace the one that got thrown into the oven out back after being apprehended for failed, feeble attempts to turn F's on their report cards into B's. I would sneak over to the fence when I thought it was safe and scrutinized the flora and fauna for signs of human characteristics. I soon came to the realization that the new good kids must only bloom at midnight, during a full moon. I tried for years to stay up that late whenever I would spend the night at Bill's but I never made it.

George was meticulous and maternal in all aspect of lining and refurbishing his nest. This was most notably illustrated in what he considered the crowning pinnacle of his restoration, the hand hewn California redwood shingles adorning his roof. I had never seen shingles before and was at a complete loss as to why anyone would want or need to have them on the roof of a house. There was just something about it, an intrinsic flaw that resonated with the lessons learned by the little pig that build his house of twigs. I revisited all of this as I witnessed the power line's hot end spewing sparks on those shingles, sparks that randomly gave birth to lazy, little flames which reached out to each other forming an ever increasing ring of fire.

Frozen by indecisive terror I didn't know where to run and whom to run to. Bill was down at the end of the street apparently dealing with the remnants of the cable. Should I call the fire department before conferring with my brother about the origins of the present potential catastrophe? Bad idea, they were quite perturbed on the last visit, and this appeared to be the collateral property damage the Chief had warned against. Should I pretend this was all just a movie? Sit back and enjoy the show and wait for the next scene to evolve? Or should I beat on the door and disturb George once more?

That was it, better get him up and out of the house before the fire does. I was beating on the door making as much noise as I could without giving out any incriminating details about the situation when George threw the door open, wearing what I hoped was a man's girdle I said matter-of-factly, "Your house is on fire George, run!" Without questioning my rationale for neither this warning, nor its validity, he ran.

He ran right to his precious poodles, calling them by name preparing them for all he knew, was the fast approaching clutch of the grim reaper. "I will free you my babies, no worry." He was trying to sound confident and supportive but his voice broke and took on a timber of terror when he reached through the fence and removed Fi-Fi's rhinestone studded collar from the smoldering embers which had not so long ago been a perky little powder puff of a poodle.

I didn't know much about George's religious affiliations and wasn't much interested at this juncture. He began to cross himself repeatedly, invoking the protection of a laundry list of saints and angels, each being assigned to an individual poodle to protect from the demons that had smitten Fi-Fi with the fires of damnation and surely had the rest of the pack on a hit list. Something deep inside of me released a collective sigh of relief to have heard this unequivocal assurance that George was a religious man and not the Warlock of my youth, lusting after the livers of innocent children to satiate his demonic appetite.

"What happened? Lightening from heaven?" George didn't seem to be addressing me specifically so I declined to reveal any of the precipitous details to which I was privy. He was fumbling with the latch on the kennel, encumbered by the poodle collar clutched in his fist, becoming more distracted as the flames dancing on his roof began to demand more of his attention. I imagined that they were little fire imps square dancing to the fire kings fiddle music. As the tempo and volume increased, so to did the area the flames commanded.

By this time, the poodles, high-strung creatures to begin with, were, as a result of the chaotic commotion, worked up into a frenzied froth of fidgeting fur. By default they collectively channeled their displeasure with the present situation towards the most convenient human, which unfortunately was George. I heard the gate creek as it swung open and those poodles set upon poor George like wiener pigs nursing from an upright sow, each of the seven creatures attaching to different sections of George's body with their needle sharp teeth. George screamed like a peacock and bolted without any evident direction or destination in mind, motivated by a more primitive motive, escaping the pain being inflicted by the multitude of poodle teeth piercing his hide.

"Drop and roll, drop and roll George!" I was hollering as I ran to George's aid, hoping that he had at some time had a personal fire prevention class, making the assumption that in the confusion he might possibly associate the present pain he was feeling with the flames engulfing his house. As I chased him down, I was reluctant to try and detach any of the poodles by pulling them off, fearing that the damage inflicted would surpass that by letting nature run it's course, but then my first aid training got the best of me. I tackled George to the ground, rolling him until the last parasitic poodle released its grip.

George was a pitiful site, disheveled hair, body covered with abrasions and bite marks, wearing his lingerie, which I noticed had delicate light pink roses embroidered on the lace trim, definitely not one of those for older men that I had seen advertised in the back of Sunset Magazine. No sir. That was a woman's girdle I was sure, even though the only one I had ever seen was in the Sears catalog. I had anticipated that George, being a merchant marine and an old military man, would have, by virtue of prior training and instinct, manned his battle station and commenced fire suppression maneuvers. To my chagrin, he leapt over the fence with the agility and grace of a gazelle and proceeded to give hot pursuit to the pack of poodles, which had formed a posse heading down the street in the direction of Bill and the caddie. So I was alone with a roof fire growing larger by the moment and I had to decide, let her burn, wait for Bill, or call 911. I opted for the 911 call.

Things had been happening so fast that I never had the chance to tell my brother the mitigating circumstances that had contributed to the recent house fire before the arrival of the authorities. Bill had spoken to the fire fighters and seemed sincere when stating that he had no information or ideas about the origins of the tragic blaze. The Fire Chief was adamant that Bill would hang this time and must have had something to do with the blaze. After giving it some thought I decided it might be a topic best left fallow, kinda let it age awhile before a public, press release.

Chapter 14

Several hours after the inferno was brought under control and extinguished by the fire department, and I had detailed to Bill just how the fire had started, I noticed that the poodles had returned to the charred remains of George's abode. I was concerned however, that they had returned without their master. "I wonder what happen to George?" I asked Bill, "Does he have any family near by that he would have gone to stay with?"

"That wouldn't be like George" Bill replied, "He would never just take off without coming back to see the extent of damage to his home, I'm afraid that something might have happened to him."

I could see the headlines, "Deranged Man in Girdle Chasing Pack of Poodles Hit by Bus." I was contemplating the legal technicalities about my guilt in the whole affair and being indited as an accomplice to murder (or at the least an accessory to manslaughter or arson.)

Bill took a brief phone call and when he hung up he asked me to take care of the dogs while he went to pick George up. I didn't ask where George was, but I had extrapolated from the conversation on our end that wherever he was, he was being held against his will, presumably by the police, and would only be released to a competent individual willing to take responsibility for his abstaining from chasing small animals in general, and his doing so in women's undergarments, in particular.

Aside from material possessions there just weren't many things that Bill disliked, but dogs happened to fall into that category. Maybe it wasn't that he disliked them, it was more that he couldn't see the utility of the creature. He never came out and said it in so many words, but now I understand that his disdain was not for the creatures, it was for the bizarre relationship that most Americans have with them. I understand now that he considered it an abomination and an affront to humanity that many civilized people treat their dogs with more compassion and respect than they do their fellow humans. At the time I felt his philosophical orientation on the topic was a bit skewed in the radical direction, that was true until I read an article in the paper about how much money the U.S. population spent on pet pampering in one year compared to what it would have cost to provide food and palatable drinking water in order to save the lives of three million children who died for lack of them during the same time frame. You guessed it, if the American population collectively gave up their pets and channeled those funds into a humanitarian effort these children would have survived.

Bill had requested that I dispense kindness to these critters vicariously, atonement for the guilt he felt for his role in the calamity that had descended on George's life. George loved those dogs and Bill felt the need to do anything he could to assist George in the process of coping with the situation and restoring a semblance of order and stability to his existence.

Shortly thereafter Bill and George arrived home. Wherever George had been he appeared to have suffered some additional injuries, which I assumed resulted from the force needed to subdue him. All of his injuries however, looked to have been cleaned and bandaged very well. Bill led his wounded comrade to the spare room in the basement where George's, faithful poodles awaited. I could hear them yelping and was quite sure that I could hear George too, yapping happily with the pack.

"George will be staying with us until he gets back on his feet, the firemen gave me this safety deposit box, it's got all of George's paperwork on his insurance here. I'm gonna get on the phone and see what I can do for him."

I went outside to take a look at the fire damage. The fire department had done a hell of a job saving the majority of George's house. It looked as though the interior of the structure had suffered relatively superficial damage from cinders, ashes and water. From my naive assessment, I concluded that a new roof, paint and carpeting would restore the habitat its previous state.

After my inspection I wandered aimlessly out to the pit, peering over the ledge. I had to laugh when I discovered that the boulder had been dislodged from it's resting place and moved from the deep end of the pool, to a new perch smack dab in the middle of the excavation. I wasn't sure if that was progress or not, but what the hell, it wasn't underground anymore, and we made it move.

The next day when the fire situation and its accompanying complications were resolved and under more control, it was back to the pit. The game plan according to Bill was that we would attack the boulder with sledgehammers and chisels, bust it up into manageable chunks and pack it out. If you have ever hit your hand with a hammer when you meant to hit a stubborn nail, you have had a mild introduction to the thrill of smashing it with a sledge that weights twenty times as much. After the first whack your hand takes on an independent survival reaction. Your brain tells your hand to hold the chisel still, but your hand remembers that the last time it did what you told it to the reward was a crushed fingernail bleeding profusely from the cuticle. So you end up like Charlie Brown trying to kick the football Lucy is holding. No matter what the preliminary agreements are, in the end your hand, like the football, always moves.

In the pit, there was plenty of sweating going on. Simultaneously, there were a lot of other things going on, at several different levels that as a kid I was able to feel but not define, digest, or initially profit from. I could discern however, that I was being transformed by the experience, a metamorphic change mentored by the man I admire most in this life, my brother Bill.

Thirty years down the road I have made some progress with the revelations resulting from seeds planted in my soul during my stint in the pit, but I cannot lay claim to having achieved an all encompassing, nirvanic pinnacle of understanding as of yet. I often feel as though my life is a fertile garden upon which a multitude of seeds have been flung over the years by those individuals who have passed in and out of my boundaries, leaving behind encapsulated secrets which they were unable to reveal in there entirety all at once. Often times these seeds lay dormant, forgotten over the years, germinating abruptly of their own volition, strategically blossoming and baring fruit at those times when my soul is engulfed in turmoil and indecision and in dire need of some kind of inspiration or direction.

I figured it was time to revise my game plan, I would bide my time until Bill gave up, which was not going to happen, or one of us came up with a better idea or a disabling injury. I began to feel one of those seeds my brother had planted, but I didn't remember where or when. I began to realize that often times in this life what it is you are doing is not nearly as important as whom it is you are doing it with. It was enough for me at that point in time that I was working beside a comrade. When I heard Bill scream, and was abruptly jerked back into reality, I must admit I was hoping for a serious enough injury for a monetary reprieve from my labors. Sure, I enjoyed the adventure my brother was spearheading, but I was tired to.

"Sonofabitch!" He bellowed as he danced around in the pit holding his left hand as if he had a hand full of pissed off Yellow Jackets demanding their freedom. "To hell with this" he continued, "We're gonna have to blast."

Chapter 15

$\mathcal{W}$henever I hear those words, two separate remembrances come to mind. Most people would have a hard time distinguishing one from the other. In the Stooges immortal movie, *The Sit Downers*, Curly gets his feet stuck in two blocks of cement. Moe comes to the rescue and after failing at more conventional interventions with an electric drill and sledgehammer to set Curly free, Moe concludes, "I'll have to blast." When Curly questions the decision, Moe responds curtly, "What would you do?" To which Curly freely admits, "I'd blast."

The other story is from a little farm that my brother Doug lived on in a country town by the name of Mollala. I'm not sure why I can remember things from my distant past and not remember where I put my glasses down two minutes ago, but that seems to be the way it works. Anyhow, I wasn't in school yet so I had to be about four years old. I can remember my brothers Bill and Doug engaged in an intense discussion that involved considerable planning review and revision. They were drinking beer and drawing in the dirt with sticks. When they had reached a mutually acceptable agreement they departed for a brief period of time. When returning they were both running, which I interpreted as a couple of grownups playing tag or some such game. They arrived at the front porch of the house were I was perched on a fence rail about three feet off the ground. Doug and Bill seemed highly agitated, bubbling with the kind of nervous expectation you get when the grown ups make you wait until you Grandma gets in the living room so you can open your Christmas presents. First I heard the explosion and before I had time to process the significance or the origin of it, the concussion wave hit me, knocking me off the fence rail.

I remember sailing through the air as if in slow motion. I could hear glass breaking all around me. The air was filled with small shards of glass which refracted the sunlight, surrounding me with thousands of minuscule rainbows. I was reconciled with reality when the wall, which I had been catapulted into, brought my free flight to an abrupt halt. When I came to rest on the front porch I thought sure everyone would rush to my aid checking to see if any damage had been done. I was disappointed to see that my brothers ran in the direction from whence they had recently come, leaving me in a crumpled but unscathed heap on the porch.

From my vantage point I found it quite interesting that all the windows on the house were broken, and not the typical broken windowpane. Every pane was completely gone, with no trace that there had ever been a sheet of glass covering the gaping frames. Being a small child no one bothered to inform me of the initiating cause of the blast that had catapulted me from my perch on the fence rail.

It was not until years later that the details of this event were revealed to me. Apparently, Doug wanted to increase the water flow in a little spring he had on his farm. He and Bill concluded that blasting would be the most effective means of doing this. Taking the Bohemian approach to blasting, they figured that if they did not dig a blowhole to deliver the blast underground, they could compensate by increasing the over all blasts yield on the surface. They placed an entire case of dynamite on top of the spot where the spring bubbled up from the ground. The compacting force of the blast most likely fractured the substratum and sealed the ground surrounding the spring so tightly that the spring never again gave up a drop of water.

So when Bill mentioned blasting, I was excited and a bit apprehensive all at the same time. At the time it didn't seem at all out of sorts that my brother would be in the possession of high explosives and be contemplating their use in an urban area. It's hard to believe in this day and age when whackos blow up McDonalds to protest the genocide of the potato population of the world, that there was a time when people could access, with relative ease, dynamite for more legitimate means.

When Bill returned with the explosives he demonstrated the stability of the sticks of dynamite by banging two of them together. I wasn't sure that this was such a good idea because my instruction about proper handling of explosives up to this point had been delivered from Daffy Duck, Bugs Bunny and the likes. Bill assured me that the stuff would not go off unless coaxed to do so by a blasting cap. He was right, but I declined to handle the sticks or bang them together. I figured there was no point in me tempting the hands of fate or challenging the gods of high explosives.

As he was affixing the charges to the rock, he was explaining to me why and where the ensuing shrapnel would end up. The theory was that by virtue of strategic placement of the charges, the boulder would explode on the horizontal plane and the walls of the pit would contain the shattered boulder making this a safe situation for blasting. I had no cause to doubt what appeared on the surface to be a rational explanation of dynamite dynamics. He ran the ignition wire into the garage where we sequestered down in the furthest corner with a car battery.

"You want to touch it off?" Bill asked me.

I enthusiastically took the wire from him and responded, "Give me a count down."

"Five, four, three, two, one, fire in the hole!" I responded and touched the bare wire to the positive terminal of a car battery. There was a momentary delay before the detonation, but that delay only served to highlight the explosion. A deafening eruption that sent shockwaves through the air, actually inhibited breathing for a short spell. Not waiting for the dust to clear, we ran out to check on the success of the blast. The boulder had been rendered into chunks that could be muscled out of the pit or removed with a come-along wench. I couldn't tell if Bill was jubilant because of the effectiveness of the explosion or if he was amazed it had actually worked the way he had calculated.

As we were congratulating each other on a job well done, I came to the realization that if you looked at the boulder like a puzzle, all the parts in the pit would not constitute a rock half the size of the original boulder. But I had complete faith in my brothers' ability to execute such actions in a professional manner. They way I looked at it, if he didn't know what the hell he was doing, he would have been dead long ago, or at least maimed to the extent that his ability to initiate endeavors such as installing a pool in the back yard would have been greatly reduced or extinguished altogether.

I asked Bill about the possibility that some of the fragments might have been blasted clear of the pit and he dismissed my concerns, confident that the amount of dynamite he used could not have created sufficient inertia to cause a projectile of any real concern to exit the pit. Considering the remote possibility that one or two insignificant chunks had escaped, the chances were even slimmer that they would be noticed by anyone. The way he explained it, people shot guns in the air to celebrate all the time: Independence Day, Christmas, New Years, and Ground Hog Day. Those bullets never came down and killed anyone. Why would a few pebbles fare any worse? In his day that may well have been the case, rural armed revelers discharging firearms in the air harmlessly. With the advent of armed hordes of teens roaming more urban areas, the incidents of civilians being struck by bullets returning to earth has been on the increase during holiday celebrations. But this isn't a story about now, it's about back in the day.

By this time several of the neighbors were outside conversing about the explosion. An elderly lady from across the street made her way across the road to talk to Bill about the situation. Bill reassured her that the noise was of no consequence, in all likelihood nothing more than a sonic boom from a military aircraft. Bill was careful about not coming right out and telling a lie, but I had begun to notice that he was artful in steering people in the opposite direction when he did not necessarily want his actions to become public knowledge. Bill gallantly escorted this woman back across the street, holding her arm and remaining to chat with her for several minutes before returning to the pit.

"About time for a break don't you think?" Bill said. Something told me that this was more of a strategic pause so as to not draw undue attention to the pit production while there was heightened concern in the neighborhood about unexplained events. We discovered upon entering the house that all of the windows on the eastside facing the pit had been blasted from their frames, and the shrapnel was spewed randomly about the rooms. A closer inspection revealed that some chunks of rock had become embedded in the walls opposite the windows. Lucky for us, George's house was the closest to the blast and the previous day's fire and ensuing fire suppression activities had shattered most of his windows facing the pit. There were neighbors across the street that had sustained some minimal damage but apparently considered it the price of living on the same block with Bill.

Over lunch we were discussing ideas about removing the boulder fragments from the pit. We settled for a ramp and wheel barrel, got all the small stuff and used a come-along on whatever was left. We had the rock out of the pit in no time. Quite a successful endeavor for a days work.

On the local news that evening there was a short segment about our neighborhood. It seemed that several residents in the area had suffered what was alleged to have been meteor strikes, grapefruit sized visitors from outer space which fell from the sky with sufficient velocity to penetrate a three story building in one case. Investigators from Portland State University's space science department were reported to be on the scene investigating. When we heard this report and I looked at Bill for some reassurance that we were not on a fast track for incarceration he merely stated, "collateral damage."

Bill had a way of seeing opportunities in what most of us would construe to be obligations or burdens. Unlike the majority of people I have met Bill never felt any consternation from having to choose between his beliefs and obligations because for him they were the one and the same. We all have those dilemmas, I believe I should do this or that, but my job or position in life obligates me to doing something else. I remember him telling me a story when I was a young child about the people he worked with and how he watched them change over the years. He spoke of men who had strong union beliefs in their hearts but felt obligated to pretend for the sake of job security, to be loyal to the cooperation. One by one over the years these men, bit by bit, renounced their moral convictions as they pertained to the relationship between labor and management. In the end they were transmuted by their own volition into that which they had pretended to be, and had previously, sincerely despised. He warned me that a man must be vigilant and avoid pretenses at all costs, because no one knew what their individual threshold was before they actually mutated into that which they were pretending to be. And once the process had begun, your true identity and individuality was blurred by the charade to your own eyes, posing the very real risk that once lost, you may never rediscover your true self in the self inflicted delusion. Kinda like that old warning we all heard as kids not to cross your eyes, because of the risk they may stay that way forever. Now this scared the hell out of me and I spent the next several months trying to determine if I was really me or just some body I had pretended to be and had forgotten about it. I now realize that what he meant was to be true to your heart and always be what he called, "Your own man."

Chapter 16

My brother was an amazing confluence of contradictions; as generous as any Buddhist monk sharing a bowl of rice and as miserly as a spinster using both sides of a roll of toilet paper. We had the dimensions of the pool roughed out and it was time to build the forms; walls that ran parallel with the walls of the pit with a distance of twelve inches in between. These form walls would hold the wet cement of the pool walls until such time they cured and dried. Bill explained to me that professional masons used something called form oil on the side of the forms that contacted the cement. Bill was convinced that this was an unjustifiable extravagance that could be dispensed with. We filled the back seat of his Cadillac with all of the plastic containers we could scrounge from the garage and then preceded to tour the local gas stations, soliciting waste oil donations for our project. The majority of station attendants were happy to oblige and we had our quota in no time.

Interestingly enough, a trend seemed to manifest as we went begging exhausted motor oil. When the individual in charge of the station was obviously an employee and not the owner they were more than happy to avail what, if any, waste oil they had that was accessible. On the other hand, the few people we conversed with that were owners all declined to allow us to scavenge their waste products. Bill engaged one of these individuals in a discussion about this irrational intransigence.

Bill began, "What, may I ask, is it that you do with this waste oil?"

The proprietor replied, "A guy comes around once a month and picks up the drums."

"And, are you paid for the product?" Bill asked. I had learned long ago that Bill always practiced that old, general, lawyer's rule; never ask a question if you don't know the answer.

The owner answered, "No, with all this new EPA shit I have to store it a certain way and pay to have it hauled off. Same with antifreeze."

"So you seem to be telling me that you would rather pay someone to take the old oil away rather that have someone like me take some for free?" Bill stood there feigning confusion, waiting for an answer.

Searching nervously for a rebuttal to defend his stand, the owner replied, "It's a franchise policy not to give anything away. If we started there where would it end? We'd be giving gas away."

Bill inquired, "Have you a toilet for your patron's use?" The focus of this cross-examination looked a bit relived, assuming the interrogation was over and Bill was in need of relieving himself.

"Why, yes. Right over there."

Bill interrupted, "And in these facilities you have running water, towels, and soap?"

"Of course we do." It seemed to hurt the poor fellow's feelings that someone would question the sanitary amenities in his commode.

Bill continued, "And you do pay for these products, right?"

The man nodded his head. "So if I walked into your bathroom right now I could use all the soap, water and paper towels I wanted for free? All products you paid for, and yet you have a policy that prohibits giving away useless oil that you would rather pay to have removed?"

The station owner was looking around in a desperate manner, either for someone to lend support to his crumbling position in this debate or a customer requiring service. He had no inclination to continue this present conversation. Unconvincingly, he blurted out, "I'm a busy man and can't be wasting time arguing with you about business practices which you evidently have no understanding of. If you'll excuse me I have to get back to work." As he strode off with an air of superiority, the befuddled, business tycoon made straight away for the men's restroom. Bill remarked that it was an unusual location for the command center of such a prestigious business establishment.

We had the forms built in no time, and an impressive sight it was. The pit was catacombed with a factorial, geometric design created by the bracing buttressing the forms to withstand the weight of the concrete when it was poured.

Taking a well deserved siesta for the rest of the day Bill attended to the details of having the cement delivered early the next morning, my only responsibility was to wet the dirt in the pit down the night before. In the world of amateur excavation, copious amounts of water are typically used; keeps the dust down and softens up the soil, thus making it easier to move. Always looking for ways to cut corners Bill delegated to me the responsibility of investigating the feasibility of manipulating the public water meter in such a way as to elude paying for the extra water we were using and avoid detection at the same time. Now these meters are secured with a wire, affixed with a special lead seal, making it easy for the meter reader to determine if a meter has been tampered with. I began my task with an expansive complement of tools, not knowing which would be the key to success. Interestingly enough, I never had cause to take any of them in hand. While I was removing the cast iron cover from the compartment in the ground that housed the water meter the ten-pound cover slipped from my grasp and fell on the face of the meter, breaking the glass and rendering the meter inoperative. When Bill asked if I had met with any success I assured him the meter was out of commission, neglecting to supply the details of how this was accomplished.

Sometime later that same month as Bill and I were occupied with dredging the pit, the water meter reader happed by on his official rounds. Taking note of the damaged meter and a construction project in the immediate vicinity he approached to investigate. I was preoccupied spraying what was left of the poodle pack and the meter reader must have surmised that this gluttonous consumption of water was the rationale for the broken meter. As I saw him approach and realized the nature of his visit apprehension began to stir in my stomach, wondering how Bill would handle this situation and what, if any, consequences would result for my breaking the meter and failing to bring my crime to light. The meter man introduced himself and began a superficial conversation about the pit. It was evident he engaged in this introductory conversation out of social convention and that his ulterior motive was clamoring just below the surface, demanding to be given center stage.

He began, "Building a swimming pool? It's going to take a lot of water to fill that up once it's finished."

Bill responded, "Will probably have to fill it up in stages over a couple of months."

"Yes" said the meter maid, "A project like that could really put a dent in a guy's water bill." I was watching this conversation and I could see that the water meter guy was twitching after introducing the water bill into the conversation.

"Most of the time if a resident's meter registers that big of an increase in consumption we suspect a broken line or something. That's what I needed to talk to you about Mr. Gribble."

Bill put down his sledgehammer and looked up out of the pit to where the meter reader was standing and asked, "You think I've got a leak in my line somewhere?"

"No, no leak. But even if you did the water department would not be able to tell because of the damage done to your meter." The meter reader stood there as if he expected some emotional, hysterical confession and accompanying pleas for forgiveness.

Bill, loosing no composure, casually shot back, "I don't really know much about the condition of the meter, in fact I've never even bothered to look at it. The only part of my water system that is any concern to me is that portion attached to my side of the meter. It's my understanding you are responsible for the meter and the rest of the system back to the source of the city's water supply."

"That is basically true Mr. Gribble," began the reader, "But you must take some responsibility when your meter is destroyed and there is an obvious advantage to you in having it out of commission." He nodded his head towards the pool as if he expected Bill to admit to the crime.

Without rebutting this statement Bill began his own line of inquiry. "Where does all of this water come from anyway?"

"From the North Fork of the Clackamas River." The meter guy began, "Then it's stored in the reservoirs up there on Mt. Scott. The entire Portland community is supplied with water by a gravity feed system, except for the West Hills, there's a pumping station over there." The meter reader seemed to regain some composure and confidence talking about the water supply system, a more comfortable topic in comparison to the informal allegation of vandalism he was alluding to.

Bill replied, "It's great to live in a country which abounds in a wealth of natural resources like clean water. It's an added benefit to live in a country where those resources belong to everyone, except of course if you are poor or an Indian. What I can't seem to figure out is how the City Water Department came to be the sole proprietor of this very same water. Does the city own all the water in the river or just the water they can manage to siphon off? And for that matter, at what point does ownership begin or cease? Let's say that over the course of fifty years I purchase from you one hundred gallons of water a day. That would be about 365,000 gallons a year. Round that off and it's about 2 million gallons over a fifty-year period. At some point in the cycle of water flowing to the ocean, evaporating and condensing into a cloud which rains on the water shed you, in all likelihood, would be selling me water that already belongs to me."

On the defensive the meter man began, "Now, no-one has claimed that we own the water. We only charge what we must for the delivery, building and maintaining infrastructure that supports the system. The reservoirs, dams and such."

"You had best do some reading my friend," Bill said, "The infrastructure of which you speak was constructed during the depression by the public works administration. The City Water Department came along after the project was completed. As for the delivery are you claiming that the Water Department has some kind of controlling interest in the gravitational force utilized to deliver the water? You did say the system was gravity fed."

Realizing he was loosing ground on the argument, and that his advisory appeared to have nothing better to do than spend the day debating, the meter guy made his point, "Mr. Gribble the meter is damaged and I'm afraid I will have to report that it appears you may have had a motive for inflicting the damage."

Bill laughed, "Report what you like, but I can hardly be held liable for the vandalism that takes place in the neighborhood. Hell, about three weeks ago some damn kids set my field on fire. Just about burned me out. If I were you, I'd call the police and report this. I would also suggest, if you want to know how much water I'm using, you would be better off if you quit whining and doing paper work and simply replace the damn meter." Then Bill added, "Oh, and by the way. If in the future you should ever be fool enough to set foot on my property and make accusations questioning my integrity, you had best be prepared to backup your mouth with something more than a clipboard."

The meter reader beat a hasty retreat to his little motorized cart, fumbling over an incoherent apology as he went. Bill patted me on the back and said, "Nice work! Make sure you keep and eye out for that guy. Whenever you see him put in a new meter give it the same treatment you gave the old one. I would advise doing it at night. No witnesses."

Now the moral lesson of that encounter stuck with me (about how the water belongs to everyone.) Just by chance a few years later I was in attendance of an outdoor musical festival being held at Mt. Scott Park, on the very same mountain which housed the reservoirs for the Portland area. It was a blistering hot day and the cool waters of the drinking supply for the good citizens of Portland beckoned to me. I gave in and scaled the ten-foot cyclone fence and negotiated the strands of barbwire at the top. I was enjoying my refreshing pause when I was accosted by a blast from the bullhorn of a Portland Police Department cruiser. "You, in the water, get your ass out now! Don't you realize that's the drinking water?" I could tell the officer was befuddled by what he was witnessing.

"Not to worry," I shouted from my seat beneath the oxygenator shooting a plume of water fifty feet in the air. "I promise I won't pee until I get out! Hell, it was a long swim out here and if I try to swim back right now, I just might drown. I know you don't want a stiff like me floatin' in your water supply. I promise, I'll get out soon as I can." It was a calculated risk, but I was pretty sure that I detected a hint of appreciation in his voice, just a whisper in there that given the right combination of circumstances, he might be sitting next to me.

"You do that! I hope this isn't the first bath you had today." With that the cruiser went about its business. Who said all cops are bad?

When the cement trucks rolled in to deliver their respective loads of gray mud, Bill and I were sharing a state of mind akin to two young kids watching the school burn down. We were giddy and ecstatic to actually see our project coming to fruition. As the last bit of cement topped off the wall in the deep end I though I detected an alien noise escaping from the pit. I shrugged it off, attributing it to what I considered to be an unhealthy imagination laden with an inordinate blanket of pessimism.

The trucks had rolled away and we stood in quite admiration of the fruits of our collective labor. "The rest is easy." Bill said, "Just finish work. We can pour and shape the floor ourselves."

Suddenly, we both heard a creaking sound like the lid of Dracula's coffin opening, almost like a moan, emanating from the pit. Have you ever noticed how the human mind works when you experience something for which you have no ready explanation? You start out comparing whatever it is you just heard to all the similar things you have encountered in your life. If you fail to come up with an acceptable match, your imagination kicks in because you just can't ignore it and pretend it didn't happen. The only thing I could come up with was that we had been digging in hallowed ground, an Indian burial site, or maybe we had unearthed the remains of some early explorers who had desecrated the ground by violating the eleventh commandment, "Thou shall not cannibalize thy brother." I looked at Bill, not speaking, but begging for some explanation grounded in reality.

"Just the forms settling against the weight of the cement. They're braced to the hilt, no chance they will give way."

With that assurance I redirected my gaze to the pit. This time the moaning of a timber straining against a superior force erupted from the pit, accompanied by a barley detectable movement of a form in the corner of the deep end wall. More noise, more movement, and then the cement began to seep between the forms.

There was nothing to do or say, so we stood paralyzed and watched our engineering feat unravel. The major supports of our bracing consisted of two, twenty foot, twelve by twelve beams, buried six feet in the ground, standing like two guardian trees in a geometric forest. First one, then the other began to give ground to the relentless pressure of the cement struggling to break free from the confines of the form wall. When the two critical supports were eventually unearthed from the security and stability of the soil, the secondary support beams snapped like chicken bones in a fox's jaws. It took all of thirty seconds for the contents of four truckloads of cement to gush from the broken forms into the bottom of the pit.

It was at that particular moment I decided I was just a kid on summer vacation and I should be having some fun, not toiling in the dirt like some gold crazed miner wandering the wilderness in search of an elusive mother load.

Our discussion of the cataclysm we had just witnessed lasted less than a minute. It centered on how we should have braced the tops of the main supports with a beam anchored at both ends in the ground outside the pool. The conversation felt like one of those when a close family member dies unexpectedly. It's the only thing on your mind, but you haven't had an adequate amount of time to process the information in order to talk about it comfortably and constructively. I was listening to be polite, but I was already at McIver State Park, lounging in the sun and swimming in the Clackamas River. What the hell, why should I work so hard to build a swimming pool when God already made one I could use for free?

I let Bill know that I had made a prior commitment to some friends to accompany them to the doings at McIver Park. We both knew I was lying, just as we both knew it was a mental health issue for me to put some distance between the pit and myself.

Chapter 17

The Vietnam War was in full swing and the American Legion was planning their National Convention in Portland Oregon. Governor Tom McCall organized a rock festival dubbed "Vortex I" out at McIver to lure the hippies out of town. Pissed a lot of people off who had never been allowed to spend the night in the park when the Governor let a bunch of long hairs stay there for three days smoking dope and running around naked, fornicating and defecating in the woods like chipmunks. The taxpayers even picked up the tab for the bands that played and the free food. I needed the distraction of this three-day party in the sun. I had spent the better part of the last three months toiling in the pit, summer vacation was almost over and school was lurking in the wings. I needed to squeeze in some screw-off time and this was it.

But it didn't work out that way. During the first evening when I was just beginning to unwind, something horrible happened. The park was closed to automobile traffic except for those responsible for logistic support for the festival and county patrol cars, all easily recognized as official vehicles. The only civilian role I saw during three days was a black and white Cadillac Coup DeVille. A dead ringer for the only other one of its kind I had ever seen, sitting in Bill's driveway. I knew it was an omen, like spotting a raven clutching a lock of your hair in its talons after you received a trim out of doors. You just knew that bird was on its way to the nearest dungeon or cave where a witch was concocting a brew to deprive you of your procreative prowess. That Caddie was telling me that it wasn't over. There was still toil awaiting me in the Pit.

I spent three fitful days in the park with fifty thousand people, free music, food, love and the likes. I made a concerted effort to have a good time to no avail. There was unfinished business in the pit, I didn't know what it was, but I was sure it was there, waiting.

When I returned from my sabbatical, I didn't want to look at the pit and be reminded of the toil that had been expended in such an unqualified failure. Deep inside however, I knew I had to pay my last respects, get some closure on the whole thing, and get on with whatever it was that I was going to do, or far more likely, whatever new project it was that Bill had cooked up in my absence.

After the forms had broken and the tidal wave of cement had deluged into the pit I had been operating under the assumption that there had been finality in that fiasco. You can well imagine my curious chagrin when I heard the familiar music that only emanates from the rhythmic labors of a gandy dancer striking a chisel or spike with a sledgehammer. As I peered over the edge of the pit I observed my brother laboring away. My best guess was that he was breaking up the congealed cement that blanketed the bottom of the pit, transporting the chunks via wheelbarrow, up a ramp at the shallow end and out of the pit. There wasn't much point of asking what he was doing; the real question was why the hell he was doing it? I mean really? Was he planning to bust up fifty tons of dry cement and pack it up hill? It didn't make much difference. He was working and I was not. I took off my shirt, descended into the pit, and joined in.

And so the days passed into weeks, breaking up cement and hauling it out of the pit. We eventually removed all of the spilled cement and rebuilt the form walls that had given away.

It was then one of the foundational cornerstones of my belief system was quarried and in the process of being set in place. A belief that there's no such thing in this life as an insurmountable obstacle. Time and experience have not made me all that much wiser regarding the solution to these impediments, but I can take solace and inspiration by looking back at the obstacles I have overcome in the past that seemed hopeless when first confronted. I still have days when I have no idea how the hell I'll get through them, but I have complete confidence that if I don't find a way, a way will find me.

Bill was above all, a civil man, never passing prior judgment, always giving a new acquaintance the benefit of the doubt, meeting any man on the terms of engagement which they chose. He called it the latter of social intercourse. At the top rung you looked a man in the eye and both talked straight. On the bottom rung was where you dealt with things physically, settling things with your fists. Bill always tried to start on the top of the ladder, but he had no qualms about stepping off the bottom rung and resorting to fighting, provided the other individual began the descent on the ladder first. He also liked to quote General Eisenhower who once said, "I can beat any man alive in a fair fight as long as I get in the first punch." If Bill thought a man was descending the latter with the intent of stepping off the last rung, Bill was apt to get there first.

Such was the case when the county building inspector arrived on the scene. A slightly built, anemic looking fellow, wearing a suit off the rack which fluttered so freely in the breeze, it appeared as though it were still on the rack. His glasses were too large for his head and his clipboard seemed a burden that he bore proudly.

"Mr. Gribble?" He spoke, "I'm Mr. James with the planning department, might I have a word with you?" I could tell by the tone in his voice that he felt he was in uncharted territory, about to embark on an expedition into the unknown. I could sense his concern that rules were being violated, trampled upon and disrespected, feeling it his moral obligation to all of humanity to assure that all citizens adhere to the municipal code which governs land use within the city limits. I also thought it quite possible that by this time Bill's picture was hanging in the office of every city and county bureaucrat with a detailed description of his radical, antisocial nature and complete disregard for the rule of law which regulates land use and construction.

Bill had an interesting perspective on playing by the rules. As Union Local President for the railroad for which he worked, he was a prime target for conversion to the corporation. During a visit to the company headquarters in Arizona during one such episode, he was being wined, dined and otherwise courted by the suit and tie guild in an attempt to win his defection to the side of management. When I heard this story the first time I wondered why he even bothered to accept the invitation.

His union convictions were his religion and no amount of money or gold lettering on an office door could have swayed his commitment from the cause of labor. I now know it was because he reveled in playing the game, being in control of the situation, and stealthily deceiving and manipulating his adversary-management of the corporation. Get them right to the edge where they were celebrating a victory, then piss on the campfire right before the hotdogs are done. Bill gave every indication that he was seriously considering the management job being offered to him, and asked for some additional time to consider. The meeting was being held in a plush hotel, the company footing the bill for the bed, bread, bar and a car. While touring the locale Bill spied a dozen railroad labors toiling in the blistering midday summer sun. In a suit, tie, and luxury company car embossed with the company insignia he was at first viewed with a reserved suspicion by the work crew, suspecting he was an agent of the corporation. They lost this fear when Bill extended a personal invitation to lunch and refreshments, complements of the Southern Pacific Railroad, in appreciation of the dedication and manual labor that is as Bill said, the lifeblood of the railroad. Making two trips to the hotel from the work site Bill delivered the dirty, sweaty labors to the eatery of the hotel and informed the Matre De that they were to be provided with all their hearts desired and the SP railroad would pick up the tab. The men drank and ate, not as men do in the clutches of mere physical hunger, they consumed with a ravenous gluttony, spawned by the irony of providing the labor which generated the wealth allowing parasites to lounge in such luxury without breaking a sweat or soiling their manicured nails. The men ordered the most expensive items on the menu and drank vintage booze at the bar, not bothering to return to work.

When confronted by his corporate sponsors about why he had authorized such latitude for a despicable shock of working class vermin, Bill responded, "They were hungry and thirsty." This was one of several cooperate incursions into the camp of labor to attempt to facilitate a defection on Bill's part, all of which met a similar fate. Bill made it clear to the corporation that the only thing he had that was for sale was his labor.

That was an example of how a few working stiffs benefited by his confrontational posture with management of the organization for which he worked. A better example of why he chose to dedicate himself to improving the lot in life of the common working man is illustrated in the following story.

There was this fella that worked for the SP Railroad he had a girlfriend and they had two little boys. Partners for over ten years they had always intended to get married but just couldn't seem to get around to it. One night this guy is out on the town, had too much to drink, and opened his door just in time to get run over by a Mack Truck. Killed him on the spot.

After the details of a funeral had been attended to this poor woman found out that neither she nor the children of the deceased were to receive any of the pension fund disbursements they would have been entitled to had she and the children's father been married in the eyes of the law. A friend suggested she speak to the Union President, Bill.

Bill understood how the game was played. He also knew how to play hardball. It just so happened that he was an ordained minister in the Universal Life Church. He had responded to an ad in the National Enquirer and for ten bucks he became a preacher. He informed this distraught young woman that he intended to perform a marriage between her and her dead boyfriend. At first she was not sure there was any substantial difference between entering matrimony in this unholy manner and consorting with the devil, but in the end did what she thought was in the best interests of her children.

For his part, Padre Bill submitted the post-dated forms to the main office of the Universal Life Church with an apologetic explanation for his tardiness claiming that he had been spreading the word of God far and wide and had tarried too long in remote regions of the hinterland, and had not been able to submit the marriage license in a punctual manner. He also enclosed a substantial monetary gift to the church. A few weeks later the marriage certificate arrived in the mail, indicating that the dead, railroad brakeman had been married the day before his untimely demise.

There was considerable skepticism on the part of the administration of the SP Railroad about the authenticity of the marriage document, causing wide spread consternation when word spread that one Reverend Bill Gribble had consummated the questionable union.

There were threats to contest the matter in court, but when legal counsel for the Railroad Retirement Pension Board questioned Bill, he responded, "The Bill of Rights stipulates unequivocally that the government shall not infringe on the right of freedom of religion. Do you propose to dictate to the American people which religions are valid and which are not? If you do, take this case to court, if not, pay up." The widow and her two little boys got the survivors benefits. Bill got the satisfaction of knowing that a family had been rescued from becoming indigent, and at the same time he relished giving the corporation a swift kick where it hurt them the most, the pocket book.

Phrasing better than I ever could, Bill said, "I like to stick the knife in and let the blood run out on the ground."

As Bill lumbered out of the pit, I flashed back to that old science fiction movie, *The Creature from the Black Lagoon*. When working in the pit we anointed our skin with copious amount of what we referred to as "Goose Grease." This concoction consisted of a quart bottle of mineral oil and a vial of tincture of iodine. We were convinced that it produced a superior tan and minimized sunburn. Once a uniform coating of dust adhered to the goose grease you were protected from a number of skin irritants much in the same fashion as elephants shield themselves with a coating of mud. As luck would have it, the building inspector was not one of them.

Bill shook hands with Mr. James who made a feeble attempted to engage in small talk, but he was choking on the bigger issue that demanded his immediate attention.

"According to my records, we do not have a valid, building permit on file with the county for this project. Before you pour any cement the site must be inspected." The little man was showing Bill the back of the form where the chronological details were listed for following procedures for construction according to the rules. Mr. James continued, "You see Mr. Gribble, I need to check and make sure the proper amount of structural rebar is in place before the mud is poured. It's for the safety of everyone really."

Bill responded, "I made sure all of the construction is up to specs and meets all applicable building codes, I researched the requirements at the library before we started work."

I could see that Mr. James was searching for the words to make his point of contention clearer and not come across as too blunt or arrogant.

"Mr. Gribble, right here on the form it says that I have to check that. See, this is where I put my initials." He was pointing to a little square on the form as if he had discovered where buried treasure was to be found.

Bill reiterated, "I used more reinforcement rebar per square foot than the building code requires. The rebar is cheap and a poor place to try and save money."

"I agree completely Mr. Gribble, but I didn't get to see it. Right here on the form it says that I am required to inspect it before you pour." He was pointing to the blank, little box with his pencil over and over, as if replicating the movement would somehow produce a thundercloud of enlightenment, which would engulf the present dilemma.

The only thunder in sight was brewing on my brother's brow. I had never seen such an expression on another human beings face, let alone on that of my brother. The kindness, empathy, and generosity drained from his features and was displaced by a comet cold, calculating demeanor that reminded me of a cobra ready to strike.

Bill spoke, "Mister, I just told you the rebar is up to code, are you calling me a liar?" Mr. James responded, "No, no! No I wouldn't, I'm not, I mean . . . The form, it says."

Bill walked away from the conversation and into the garage. The befuddled little man looked at me pleading with his eyes for some sort of intervention on my part. I was enjoying the interaction and had not desire to be any more involved than I presently was.

When Bill returned he held a sledgehammer nonchalantly in his right hand. Mr. James instinctively adapted a submissive posture, no doubt his Neanderthal brain kicking into survival mode, hoping to avoid having his skull crushed complements of a club in the hands of a dominant male. Bill held out the sledge to the quivering man and said, "If my word isn't good enough for you go ahead and bust up any wall you like and look at the rebar. Just stay out of my way while you're doing it and make sure you have it completely repaired before tomorrow morning when I pour the deep end."

Mr. James declined the invitation and was explaining the building permit form to Bill's back as he returned to the pit. I assumed that Mr. James would return in short order with the building permit police. We never saw him again and for that matter we were never again descended upon by any representative of our local government that was charged with regulation and oversight of the various activities related to the excavation of the pit and construction of a swimming pool. After this and all the other encounters with agents of the State I have no clue as to why the police didn't show up and fill in the pit, with us in the bottom.

From past experience I was pretty sure that Bill didn't always do things up to code. He had an old Cadillac he was getting ready to put on the market and I was elected to help detail the vehicle. There were some fancy, wheel covers in the garage he asked me to put on the car.

Several attempts to attach them convinced me they would not fit. When I informed Bill he said, "I think I can get them to fit." He got out an electric drill and a hand full of sheet metal screws and proceeded to bolt the wheel covers on. You couldn't tell they didn't belong on those wheels, and probably wouldn't until you tried to get one off to change a flat. Next came the interior. I was instructed to clean the carpets up the best I could. There were cigarette burns in the front and a vast assortment of congealed confections matted in the carpet in the back. Bill provided me with a scrub brush, a bucket of soapy water, and the garden hose, instructing me to scrub it out the best I could then hose it down good.

Once I'd got it as clean as I could, Bill brought out a packet of black clothing dye, mixing it up in the bucket. "Slop some of this around on the carpets and we'll let it soak in over night." It wasn't until years later that I discovered these could be quantified as unethical antics by even the lowest of used car dealers. But it didn't end there. This vehicle had a leak in the cooling system that was not responding to more traditional car medicine that can be acquired over the counter at auto parts stores. Draining most of the water from the system, Bill poured two cups of Quaker Oats into the radiator, topped it off with water, and then warmed up the engine. When the oats started cooking globs of the goop shot out of the mouth of the radiator like phlegm balls from an asbestos worker. He drilled a few pressure release holes in the radiator cap and put it back on. The leak had stopped.

He actually sold that car in that condition. A few weeks later the new owner called and was upset that the vehicle was overheating. Apparently his mechanic said the car had a blown head gasket and someone had put some kind of organic material in the radiator to stop up the leak. Bill told the gentleman, "I feed that stuff to all my kids and cars. I have never had any complaints." Then he hung up the phone.

The next day when the cement trucks arrived again to pour the deep end of the pool Bill and I were giddy, agitated and apprehensive. We paced back and forth watching the level of the mud rise behind the new forms, listening to the timbers behind them creak and complain at the pressure they were enduring. Our ears were vigilant for the sickening snap indicative of a stick of lumber pushed beyond its capacity. As the mud reached the top of the forms neither Bill nor I was actively involved in any detectable respiration. When reality had sunk in that we had accomplished our goal the second time around we began to dance and howl likes the true savages we were.

We spent the rest of the afternoon drinking beer, lounging in lawn chairs by the pool as if it were full of water. In actuality, we were reassuring ourselves that the forms had held and would continue to hold the mountain of mud behind them.

Chapter 18

$\mathcal{I}$ felt compelled to celebrate and proceeded to a self-proclaimed holiday of drunken debauchery. I returned to my brothers, ecstatic about completing our pool project and to commence with the luxurious life of the upper class and wallow like a hippopotamus in our new pool.

"Bill, I have been thinking," I began, "After all the work we have done on the pool what do you think about building some kind of cover over it? Maybe even enclosing it? Probably keep it warmer and cleaner."

"I've been doing some thinking myself," Bill replied, "Talked to my insurance agent about having a pool and he indicated that my home owners insurance would double just to cover the basic liability a guy with a pool would need."

I wasn't sure where the conversation was going but my level of concern was rising. "Couldn't we put up a fence around it and keep people out?" I didn't really consider this a viable option for I knew that if my brother had a pool it would be synonymous with the neighborhood having a pool. He had an open door policy with the community he lived in; his door was always open and the kids who were friends and acquaintances of his children always used it.

"Wouldn't work, insurance is to provide protection in your worse case scenario. It wouldn't matter what kind of security you had around the pool, if someone were to leave a door or gate unlocked and someone were to get in and be injured, you would need insurance to cover it."

"What the hell can we do?" I asked.

"About the only thing I could think of was to fill it back up. I paid some guy with a cat a hundred bucks to come out and fill it up." Bill made the statement in a nonchalant manner as he ate. "Would have been nice in the summer time, but I guess that a pool is, and shall remain, a luxury for rich folks."

I made a feeble attempt to absorb his conclusion in an objective and diplomatic manner, but it felt like a root canal performed in the dark. I retired early that evening, as of yet not having mustered the courage to go out to the pit to verify that the deed had actually been completed.

That night in my dreams I was poolside, my body was dark and glistening with goose grease, surrounded by young women so enamored with my physic and winsome wit, they were oblivious to the heat and the temptation of the cool, clear water. I tore myself away from them and made my way to the diving board. George sat at a control panel looking like a cross between a steam shovel operator and an elevator matron. When I stepped on the bottom rung of the latter it began to move like an escalator. I was telescoped above the treetops with the diving board as I fearlessly walked to the edge of the board and made my plunge to the pool some hundred feet below. During my free fall I executed many dynamic, acrobatic gyrations, eliciting shrieks of approval and admiration from the females below. And why not? It wasn't like I was falling. It was more like flying, soaring with the eagles. I was tantalizing those poor deprived females awaiting my arrival back on earth. I was wondering which one would be lucky enough to be number one. As I neared ground zero I could hear my brother saying, "I paid some guy a hundred bucks to fill it in." I turned midair, saw that the pool was indeed filled in and not with dirt. It was full of huge jagged boulders and a vast array of alcoholic beverage containers. The young maidens in the floral bikinis had transformed into mutant creatures with human legs and the heads and torsos of poodles, each one with what must have been a human appendage in it's jaws. I awoke to the thud of my broken body as my dream decent was abruptly terminated by contact with the debris in the pit.

I had slept with my clothes on, as was my habit, so I arose and wandered about the house and then outside. My brother's car was gone, indicating that he had received a call to work sometime during the night. I drew a deep breath of morning air, it smelled sweet, misty clean and crisp. The dew on the grass felt good on my bare feet and the air seemed a respite to my fitful sleep, cleansing me of the disappointment that had shrouded the previous day. I ambled over to the pit and it was indeed filled to the brim with dirt, the very same dirt my brother and I had toiled three months removing, my coveted summer vacation spent digging a hole. I was thinking that maybe our intrusion into the bowels of the earth was an affront to nature and the only way to return her to a state of homeostasis and make amends for our transgressions was to restore the insult of the injury to its normal state. Like the crazy old man in the Bogart classic, *Treasure of the Sierra Madre*. After digging out all the gold the mountain had to offer, the grizzled, old miner filled the cavern back in with the tailings that had been removed, out of respect and reverence for the mountain that had made him rich.

I pulled a lawn chair up to the partially exposed wall of the pit, sat down and dug into the powered dirt with my bare feet, pondering what I had lost and gained in this endeavor.

Chapter 19

When I was some years older and many a project wiser, I came to the realization that the pit was in many ways a metaphor for life; the whole thing is a process and not a material point of arrival. Bill was a warrior. Once the major battles were won the cleanup operations can be left to subordinates. Once we had accomplished the most formidable challenges of the pit Bill was satisfied that he could have had a pool if that had been his true desire. He was satisfied in knowing that he had beat the pit and could bathe in the cool waters of that realization long after pool water had frozen or fouled. He and I went on to fight many a more battles, thirsting more for comraderary and combat than ultimate conquest.

Unfortunately, George was not able to bring himself to terms with the reality that the pool project had been terminated, nor clearly understand why such a high price had been extracted from him in the process, simply because he was Bill's neighbor. In fact, he never completely recovered from the trauma of his house fire and the ensuing death of his prize poodle. Combine these misfortunes with the enthusiasm with which he took on the task of fabricating pool ladders and other paraphernalia, well it was just enough to push him off a ledge that he was standing precariously close to in the first place. George came to the conclusion that he and his four legged friends would have their own pool. He bought one of those kiddy wading pools and set it up in his front yard. During the next few months there were weekly additions to the pool area, compliments of George's quite remarkable artistic ability with metal fabrication. The first items to roll out were several scale models of reclining, fully functional, lawn chairs, which were later adorned with hand sewn cushions, each monogrammed with a poodle's name: Chi Chi, Cuddles, Mufie and the like. According to George, the different patterns for the material used had been individually selected by the dogs whose names the cushions bore. Next came a pool slide diving board and end tables, all scaled down to doggie size. George dressed his hounds in appropriate, poolside attire and actually taught them to use the slide, jump off the diving board and leisurely recline in the lawn chairs.

Wearing oversized, white, Bermuda shorts, a pith safari hat, and a wild Hawaiian shirt, George spent a considerable portion of his day catering to the needs of his poodles at poolside. Somehow he was even able to extinguish their habit of reliving themselves outside. How the hell he could tell that a dog in a bikini had to piss was way beyond me, not to mention that if you could tell, how would you get one to take care of business on a toilet?

George became a local attraction. People would line up at his fence to watch George and his poodles perform. Turned out to be a windfall of a business opportunity for George. People began to inquire about having miniature and full sized lawn accessories made to order, and George was happy to oblige. He didn't need the money, but he did need to spend less time waiting hand and foot on those damn dogs.

The best way to describe my relationship with my brother was that he was a journeyman home project guy and I was an unquestioning apprentice awaiting the next project to come to fruition. If Bill was contemplating putting on a new roof, I was scurrying around looking for a ladder before he had time to decide if a new roof was indeed a necessary undertaking or currently financially feasible. If the agenda dictated automotive repairs, I would have the vehicle in question on blocks before he could get his coveralls on. At the time I didn't know that I was learning the single most important lesson I ever have in this life, a lesson like so many others, it never came clearly into focus until I tried to illuminate for someone else what I thought it was I had learned.

I was washing dishes with my son. He was of that tender age when a child wants to help but in the process of doing so complicates the task at hand, succeeding in making it twice as difficult and ending up taking twice as long. In casual conversation as I re-washed some of his dishes, I heard myself making the point to my son that in this life the things we accomplish and work at are not nearly as important as whom it is we work at them with. The time and camaraderie we were sharing was infinitely more valuable than the simple task of cleaning a sink full of dirty dishes. As I uttered those words I wasn't sure where they came from, how I had come to that conclusion. The swimming pool extravaganza was but a distant memory, but the bonds of brotherhood Bill and I nurtured and developed toiling side by side had become stronger as the years passed. Now I was doing the same with my son. I don't know if Bill realized what he was providing me at the time, and it doesn't matter much. It's enough knowing that the process strengthened our bonds as brothers. That experience was now paying dividends in my relationship with my son and for that matter, my relationship with myself and the world at large.

My brother is now an old man and I no longer a young one. The lessons I learned in the pit are often revisited, they continue to grow and take on proportions just as my relationship with my brother and this life does. I spoke to him on the phone just the other day. We were talking about some of our adventures and laughing when he said, "We really did live in the best of times, didn't we?" I smiled and nodded my head. We are, and forever shall remain, brothers and comrades, bounds forged in the fires of the pit.

Epilogue

I started work on this story in 2000 when I heard that my brother Bill had been diagnosed with prostrate cancer. There was considerable grief and concern expressed over this revelation by family and friends alike. But there wasn't much distinction between the two for him. It was like he said at our sister's funeral about her husband, "A brother is not always a friend, but a friend is always a brother."

After having had a week or so to think about the situation I got on the phone and called my brother who lived four hundred miles away. We talked about how lucky he had been to retire at fifty instead of sixty five, how lucky he had been to sell his little farm in Portland for three times what he had paid for it ten years ago, how lucky he had been to find a second wife that could actually put up with him.

During this conversation I had one of those moments of crystalline clarity and said, "Christ, I don't feel sorry for you, you sonofabitch. You had twenty years of quality retirement that most men will never see. If I get out of this game with half that much luck I'll be happy as hell."

Bill laughed and agreed saying, "I could jump in the grave right now and have no regrets. I've lived a full life and had more fun than most working stiffs ever dream about."

As his illness progressed his doctor posed the option of chemo and radiation therapies, which could potentially add to his longevity and assuredly, would diminish the quality of his life. After discussing the details Bill summarized what the doctor was offering him, "Let me get this straight doc, you are giving me the choice between having three hundred gourmet banquet meals, or six hundred at the hog trough? I'll take the good ones any day." He wasn't interested in clinging to life at the expense of sacrificing the quality of the existence he was accustomed to.

Another option presented was castration, which would stop the production of testosterone and slow the growth of the prostrate cancer. When offered this unique opportunity Bill politely replied, "You might as well cut my fucking head off. One of the greatest pleasures an old man has is to admire a beautiful, young lady walking down the street and reminisce about when he was a young buck. Do you think I want to see an attractive woman and ask her, 'How are you today mister?' No thanks, I'll hang on to the hardware God gave me."

In May of 2001 my sister passed away. During her funeral services the preacher introduced Bill and said, "And now Velma's brother, Bill, would like to say a few words." The preacher had a hint of condescension in his voice, implying that whatever Bill had to say would be a distraction from the importance of his sermon. He was irritated that a commoner was interrupting.

Bill was in his element when addressing a crowd, claiming that public speaking was the only thing he had ever done in his life that he was any good at. His eulogy was a eloquent as the garment of Gabriel, closing by turning to the casket and saying, "Prepare a place for my dear sister, for where you have gone I to will soon follow." When he left the podium, the preacher reluctantly resumed his sermon, knowing full well he was incapable of recapturing his audience after the oratory he had just witnessed. After the funeral the preacher approached Bill and asked if he might have a copy of the speech and Bill replied, "I just made it up."

In the span of the last five years I have attended the funerals of my sister, two brothers, and a sister in law. Another brother and myself have been diagnosed with cancer and another sister in law will most likely succumb to cancer before the year expires. I'm not complaining, these are just a few facts in my life, and if you are motivated enough to be reading the epilogue of a book, you must be interested to a certain extent in just such details.

Given recent revelations, I have good cause to contemplate the appropriateness and relevancy of eulogies. I would much prefer to hear someone speak about the deceased that actually knew the individual and could address those traits of the person that made them who they were. Most preachers are competent public speakers but it's embarrassing to witness them struggling to pretend they knew the dead person on an intimate and personal level. I am inclined to have them skip my funeral services altogether, spend the money on renting a hall and fill it with people, booze, food and music for a twenty-four hour wake. Please bring this book to my wake, it's your admission ticket. I promise it will be at least as entertaining as the story you just read.

My brother Bill passed away in January of 2002, but not before he had a chance to read a rough draft of this story. Never one to be at a loss for words all he could muster was to say, "Thanks." He didn't need to say anymore, that was enough for both of us.

As my brother has passed on there is one more thing I need to get down to close this project. I indicated in the book that there were only two times during his life that I recalled him expressing to me that he regretted his actions in this life, one was for not spending enough time with his kids, the other was for how he had treated his first wife.

Glad killed herself while I was in the service. I flew back home to be with my grieving family. When I arrived at Bill's house he was in the driveway working on an old car, a therapeutic distraction I'm sure. When I approached him from behind he turned to me slowly with outstretched arms, tears streaming down his face and said, "God help me I didn't know how much I loved her."

Several years down the road Bill and I were working on a project in his garage and the topic of casual romance and true love came up. We both felt that due to inattention and a lack of appreciation each of us had lost the only women we could really love, he his wife; me, I had not the maturity nor experience to understand the vacancy I felt in my soul. When it comes to matters of the heart, time is no healer. Bill expressed what was in our hearts by saying, "Once you really love someone, you can't ever find that kind of love again." Then he looked me in the eye and continued,

"I know you loved Glad the same way I did. I'll take my guilt for the way I neglected her to the grave." We finished the job in silence, a silence that bespoke of the tranquility two hearts share when they contain equal measures of love, remorse, and unabashed humility.

And by the way, both of us were fortunate enough to find love again, wives that make us appreciate what we had lost and gained in the course of our lives, wives that make us better men; wives that made and continue to make us sweat.